Praise for

Wild Penance

"Disturbing discoveries about the secretive Penitentes' past provide the cowgirl sleuth with her strangest challenge to date."
—*Publishers Weekly*

"Nevada Barr fans and mystery aficionados still mourning the late Tony Hillerman will snap this one up as well as other titles in the Mary Higgins Clark Award–winning series. Enthusiastically recommended."
—*Library Journal*

"A riveting story with a wealth of New Mexico color . . . Ault, who writes with precision and occasional lyricism, fills in the gaps in this addictively readable installment in her series."
—*Richmond Times-Dispatch*

"A busy tale packed with whiplash plot twists and taut dialogue . . . Full of suspense."
—*Daily Camera*

"Ault sets a spine-tingling pace that keeps the reader on the edge."
—Mystery Writers of America

"Another fine addition to the WILD mystery series, and fans will welcome this new adventure."
—*The Durango Herald*

"This mystery has it all with tight writing to keep you hooked and enough suspense and humanity to offer an escape into her world."
—*Fort Collins Coloradoan*

"From the first page you are spellbound and captivated . . . *Wild Penance* will keep you on your toes; looking out for the unseen, and always expecting the unknown. A terrific read that will keep you guessing until the end, and then leave you breathless."
—*The Romance Readers Connection*

"Fans are going to love the latest WILD thriller as we are thoroughly drawn into the world of a little known subculture that receives support from the masses."
—*Midwest Book Review*

continued . . .

Wild Sorrow

"A master at describing nature." —*Albuquerque Journal*

"Fans of the late Tony Hillerman will embrace Ault's outstanding third mystery . . . Ault's wildlife expertise and knowledge of Tanoah culture enhance a poignant plot." —*Publishers Weekly* (starred review)

"Cross bestselling author Tony Hillerman with veteran author Sue Grafton and what have you got—the best of both worlds in a hybrid writer named Sandi Ault . . . The result is a set of mysteries that leave fans breathless by the end of the first chapter." —*Sedona Red Rock News*

Wild Inferno

"This edge-of-the-seat sequel to Ault's successful debut, *Wild Indigo*, demonstrates her skill at weaving together plotlines, complex characters, and lots of suspense." —*Library Journal* (starred review)

"Ault smoothly blends a murder mystery plot with Native American lore in this impressive sequel to her debut, *Wild Indigo*." —*Publishers Weekly* (starred review)

"Fast and furious . . . The mystery deepens with every page." —*The Charlotte Observer*

Wild Indigo

"[A] striking debut . . . Scenes of the high, dry, glittering landscape are as clean as sun-bleached bone, and there are thrills galore." —*The New York Times Book Review*

"[A] smashing debut . . . And Ault's intense knowledge of Pueblo culture is [a] bonus." —C. J. Box

Wild
Penance

Sandi Ault

BERKLEY PRIME CRIME, NEW YORK

THE BERKLEY PUBLISHING GROUP
Published by the Penguin Group
Penguin Group (USA) Inc.
375 Hudson Street, New York, New York 10014, USA
Penguin Group (Canada), 90 Eglinton Avenue East, Suite 700, Toronto, Ontario M4P 2Y3, Canada
(a division of Pearson Penguin Canada Inc.)
Penguin Books Ltd., 80 Strand, London WC2R 0RL, England
Penguin Group Ireland, 25 St. Stephen's Green, Dublin 2, Ireland (a division of Penguin Books Ltd.)
Penguin Group (Australia), 250 Camberwell Road, Camberwell, Victoria 3124, Australia
(a division of Pearson Australia Group Pty. Ltd.)
Penguin Books India Pvt. Ltd., 11 Community Centre, Panchsheel Park, New Delhi—110 017, India
Penguin Group (NZ), 67 Apollo Drive, Rosedale, North Shore 0632, New Zealand
(a division of Pearson New Zealand Ltd.)
Penguin Books (South Africa) (Pty.) Ltd., 24 Sturdee Avenue, Rosebank, Johannesburg 2196, South Africa

Penguin Books Ltd., Registered Offices: 80 Strand, London WC2R 0RL, England

This is a work of fiction. Names, characters, places, and incidents either are the product of the author's imagination or are used fictitiously, and any resemblance to actual persons, living or dead, business establishments, events, or locales is entirely coincidental. The publisher does not have any control over and does not assume any responsibility for author or third-party websites or their content.

PRINTING HISTORY
Berkley Prime Crime hardcover edition / February 2010
Berkley Prime Crime trade paperback edition / February 2011

Berkley Prime Crime trade paperback ISBN: 978-0-425- 23884-4

The Library of Congress has catalogued the hardcover edition as follows:

Ault, Sandi.
    Wild penance / Sandi Ault. — 1st ed.
        p. cm.
    ISBN 978-0-425-23232-3 (hardcover)
    1. Wild, Jamaica (Fictitious character)—Fiction. 2. United States. Bureau of Land Management—Fiction. 3. Secret societies—Fiction. 4. Murder—Investigation—Fiction. 5. Colorado—Fiction. I. Title.
    PS3601.U45W565   2010
    813'.6—dc22   2009043999

PRINTED IN THE UNITED STATES OF AMERICA

10   9   8   7   6   5   4   3   2   1

For my husband, Tracy
my soul mate

Acknowledgments

I would like to thank the following individuals for their generous help in my research for this book: Sam des Georges, Multi-Resources Branch Chief for the Bureau of Land Management, Taos Field Office; Dana Weaver, Mary Lou Chernik, and Tamara Stephenson, Field Deputy Medical Investigators for the New Mexico Office of Medical Investigation; Agent Joe Schiel, New Mexico State Police Crime Scene Unit; Terry Coker, Senior Deputy Medical Investigator with the New Mexico Office of Medical Investigation.

Author's Note

This is a work of fiction, and the characters, some of the organizations, many of the places, and most of the events herein are figments of my imagination.

No one outside their dwindling numbers knows much about Los Penitentes, save a few scholars, and a few old-timers who are willing to recount their experiences of a nearly extinct way of life in the remote rural communities of northern New Mexico and southern Colorado. While I have featured Los Penitentes and some of their known practices in this book, I have also taken creative license in order to create a good story. I have featured some of what is known, some of what is written, some of what is rumored, some of what I have been told, a little of what I have seen, and a healthy dose of what I have imagined. As a result, this tale touches upon a real sect and some of their rituals, but does not pretend to be an accurate representation of Los Penitentes or of the Catholic Church. What is true about Los Penitentes is often stranger than fiction, and this yarn is spun from a bit of both. If you do not believe it, it could be true. If you believe it, it could be fiction. Who knows?

One thing that has been well documented is the fact that Los Penitentes practiced ritual crucifixion into the mid-1920s in some remote mountain villages. But that was back when they weren't as good at keeping their secrets.

Preface

As the elders at Tanoah Pueblo say, this story unfolds *time before time*. If we watch the hoop of time spinning, we might perceive that it happened first—before all the other stories in the WILD Mystery Series.

But, as the Tanoah know, all time is now.

Therefore I despise myself and repent in dust and ashes.

—Job 42:6

◂ 1 ▸

Something Falling

It was too quiet, no shrieking. The figure soared downward in silence, the arms stretched out like wings, creating a pale white crucifix form easy to make out even in the frozen gray light of predawn. This jumper did not streamline into a perfect spear for speed like most of them did—rather, this was a swan dive that stretched for seconds before disappearing into the blackness of the chasm.

It was still dark when I'd gotten to the gorge that morning to go for a run on the rim before starting my duty shift. I work at the Bureau of Land Management out of the Taos Field Office as a resource protection agent. My name is Jamaica Wild. Most days, I run at sunset, but on this morning I had awakened early from fitful dreams and couldn't go back to sleep, so I figured I'd get up and get going. I knew every dip and twist of the trail that skirted along the rim of the jagged crack in the earth's crust cradling the Rio Grande—the wild torrent of water that gives life to the high desert. To the east, the sun would soon rise over the Sangre de Cristos, an arm of the Rockies that cupped the Taos Valley and sheltered its fragile beauty. And when the butter-colored light was just beginning to melt down the basalt walls of the gorge, I would be returning to my Jeep at the rest area on the west rim, my lungs full of sage-scented oxygen, my body invigorated, my senses satiated with the beauty around me. It seemed like a perfect plan to begin the day.

I had not gone far down the trail when I looked back toward Taos Mountain and noticed activity on the bridge. In the dim light, I saw a lone vehicle stopped in one of the two lanes, next to a small overlook area where pedestrians could step off the sidewalk onto a bumped-out balcony and gaze down into the rift in the earth at the slim silver river below. Two people scurried around, then centered on the back of the vehicle, where they began unloading something with great effort.

I stopped running and jogged in place, watching.

There had been a rash of base and bungee jumping from the bridge lately—extreme sports whose members thrived not only on the rush from the experience, but evidently on the fact that it was illegal to jump here as well. The scoundrels set up under cover of darkness when there was no traffic on the bridge, then waited for first light to take the plunge.

2

Wild Penance

The Rio Grande Gorge Bridge is the second-highest cantilever bridge in the United States; its depth of 650 feet to the river, remote location, and extremely light traffic made it a dream venue for this kind of thing.

They call it practice for suicide. Rip screaming off the tallest structure around into midair and let gravity take over while a tsunami of adrenaline surges through you, producing such a high that you are almost disappointed when the parachute opens or the elastic bungee cord stretches and slows your fall, then springs you back up by your ankle harness.

At first, this was what I thought I was seeing; but this was not what I saw.

Sometimes your senses perceive something so incredible that your mind intervenes and tries to cancel out the incoming information with logic, reason, or experience. When I saw the figure falling, so began a struggle between eyes and mind, between senses and sense, until the clash ignited a flash-bomb of recognition and a snapshot crystallized in my brain, the details etched so vividly that I will never forget them. Blue-white stars flowered the field of dark sky above me even as a penumbra of purple light began to quiver at the top of the mountain range more than ten miles away across the mesa, behind the unfolding scene. An icy draft whistled over the rim of the canyon and rustled the brush, the air dry and mean. The smell of sage and red dirt mixed with the lingering scent of shampoo in my hair. My feet pounded a tempo on the trail as I jogged in place, as if what I witnessed might merely be a temporary detour in my day's trajectory. There I was: out on the rim, too far away to do anything to change what was happening.

I saw a body on a cross. Falling into the Rio Grande Gorge. And it did not come back up.

◄ 2 ►

Bridge to Nowhere

Over the next two hours, I observed while personnel from almost every agency in the area assembled to the east of the bridge in the dirt parking area normally used by tourists. The first to arrive, a patrolman in a black-and-white from the New Mexico State Police, closed the bridge. Sheriff's deputies set up roadblocks. A crew from the Taos Fire Department assisted, turning around tourists and through traffic and sending everyone eleven miles south to Pilar, where they could cross the river and drive through the village to the highway. A Taos Pueblo police detective joined the task force because the east wall of the Rio Grande Gorge is Taos Pueblo land. County Search and Rescue dispatched a team.

Unfortunately, this was not an unfamiliar scenario for any of the agencies involved, as I was well aware. Beyond its allure for extreme sport jumpers, the Rio Grande Gorge Bridge is a magnet for suicides. One, two, even three times a year, rescue agencies can count on a challenging rescue/retrieval incident here. In fact, in a recent seminar, the state emergency services director referred to the structure as "the Bridge to Nowhere" because dispirited souls came from all over the country to fling themselves over its sides.

Scientists calculated all the known and variable stats and estimated that a two-hundred-pound person would achieve a velocity of approximately 135 miles per hour and make the perilous drop in around six seconds. All this is to say that rescuers never bring a survivor out. Occasionally a jumper will miss the full ride to the bottom and splay herself on one of the basalt shelves along the cliff wall, but this is no less certain a means of demise than the descent to the river. One time, a newlywed couple joined hands just hours after giving their wedding vows and began their honeymoon by climbing onto the rail and diving over the side. The two landed on opposite shores of the rushing river, making double the work for the rescue teams.

Sometimes a jumper secretly makes the plunge and he is not discovered for days, until his bloated corpse surfaces downriver, caught in the eddies. Or a fresh suicide might land in the rapids and get swept along and be discovered soon, but miles from the jump point. I once had an encounter with one of these; but that seemed like a long time ago today, as I waited to give my account of what I had witnessed just hours before.

When the incident initiator and senior crime scene investigator, New Mexico State Police agent Lou Ebert, arrived, we walked onto the bridge together. "Show me where it happened," he said.

I walked toward the center viewing balcony, pointing. "I think it was here."

We stepped up the high curb onto the narrow sidewalk. "Let's stay off the viewing platform. Don't touch anything. Forensics wants to do another sweep of the bridge." He arched his upper body carefully so as not to touch the rail as he looked over the side. "Oh, yeah," he said. "There's your guy."

I moved closer to the rail and looked down. Although the sun now illuminated a wide patch along the upper west rim, the gorge was so narrow and deep here that the remainder of the chasm lay steeped in shadow. From this distance, the scene below appeared in miniature, making it seem all the more unreal. On the bank of the river, a tiny figure lay crucified, his blue-white flesh as pale as the water. Ropes bound his ankles, wrists, and his torso under his arms to a large wooden cross. "Does he have a . . . what is . . . is something on his head?"

Agent Ebert raised his binoculars and peered through them. He handed them to me. "It looks like cloth, maybe a black bag of some kind. It appears to be tied at the neck."

I looked through the field glasses. "A black cloth bag? Oh, no." I focused in tight and swept the corpse from head to toe. "Well, that's definitely a male."

"Yep. I'm guessing that white cloth strung out to the side was probably tied or wrapped around his lower abdomen. It's come completely off, all but that little bit tucked under his left buttock. Probably came undone from the velocity of the fall. We see that with suicides, too. Sometimes their clothes, even their shoes are ripped off. I'm surprised he didn't come off that cross."

"Well, this was no suicide." I handed the binoculars back to Agent Ebert.

"No, definitely not." He focused the glasses again on the figure below us. "This is going to be one hell of a retrieval," he said. "Have you ever been on one of these incidents?"

"Not like this. They don't usually call the BLM for things like this. Besides, I work in the high country. But when we had a river ranger go missing last year, I did work the search and rescue on that one, although we were mostly looking downriver."

"Well, this is a real tricky place. The gorge is too narrow here to get a chopper in. And besides, we don't have a winch on our state police helicopter so there has to be a place to set it down nearby, and there's no place like that for miles. Those cliff walls are so steep, they're almost straight up and down, and the rock face is too slick here to send a foot crew in or even have them rappel. It looks like our best bet is to send the medical investigator and a forensics team on a raft down the river. The water is high enough from snowmelt. They'll probably want to transport the body still tied to that cross if they possibly can."

"Really?"

"You bet. Potential evidence in the knots, for one thing. But also underneath the ropes, under the body next to the wood. Even in the wood."

"It's going to take some real river rats to navigate down through the Taos box with cargo like that. What is it? Five or six hours of white water from here to Pilar?"

"You're right. Plus it's almost two hours from where they put in upriver to here. So that's seven, eight hours just to raft the river, and that's with no time to document and photograph the body and collect evidence at the scene." He shook his head. "About the soonest I could get everybody up to the John Dunn Bridge to put in is maybe two hours. And even if the retrieval went amazingly quick, they could run out of daylight down in that canyon before they got to Pilar. Maybe it's better to have them start out first thing tomorrow morning." Lou Ebert used the mike clipped to the epaulet on his shirt to give the dispatcher detailed orders for the retrieval raft crew.

I looked down again at the body on the cross. The base of the wooden member, below the feet of the deceased, extended into the river. I thought I saw the cross move.

Agent Ebert released the transmit button on his radio mike and turned to me as I continued to study the scene below. "So you saw a light-colored vehicle? Have to be a pretty big one to get a guy on a cross in it. Unless they had him sticking out the back of a pickup bed or something."

I met Lou Ebert's eyes, then pointed across to the rim trail on the west side of the gorge. "I was clear over there past the trailhead, on the rim. It happened pretty fast. And it was still dark. It could have been a truck, maybe a cargo truck. It wasn't a flatbed. The back was covered. Like a camper shell or a van or whatever."

"That cross looks too wide and too long to fit in a van. I'll ask the raft crew to get some measurements on it. That will give us some idea what size vehicle at a minimum. You say you saw two people get out?"

"I didn't actually see them get out. By the time I noticed the vehicle on the bridge, it had already stopped, and there were two people outside of it, moving around."

"Moving around? How?"

"I think one of them might have looked over the rail. I'm not sure. But then they both went to the back and it took them a while to get the . . . the cross with the guy on it out and up to the rail."

"These two people—what were they wearing?"

"Hooded coats. Something with hoods. Everything looked gray. It was dark."

"Were they male? Female?"

"I don't know. I couldn't tell."

"Height? Weight? Build?"

"I don't know. Nothing too extraordinary. I think I would have noticed, even from that distance."

"And you didn't hear anything?"

"No. I didn't even hear the vehicle drive onto the bridge.

I just looked back when I was running and saw it parked there."

"Headed which direction?"

"East. Toward Taos."

"And after they pushed the cross over the rail, then what?"

"I couldn't believe what I was seeing. I don't even remember seeing the vehicle leave the bridge."

He looked at me and narrowed his eyes. "You okay?"

"Yeah, I'm okay." I took another look down into the gorge. "Wait, did you see that? The water is starting to cause the cross to pitch a little."

Agent Ebert looked over the rail again, careful not to touch the metal surface.

The cross lurched, spinning almost a quarter turn counterclockwise, the tip of the base shifting more downriver, from three o'clock to midnight. Again, the water surged against the base of the cross, stealing the tail of white fabric from beneath the body and pulling it into the flow, where it waved on the surface like a white flag of surrender on its way south. Within moments, the wooden form rocked again and then slowly separated from the slender stony banks and began to float downriver, bearing its naked cargo on top, spray rising around it as if it were a raft riding the wake of wild water.

The agent thumbed his radio mike. "Be advised, we have a package on the move. Raft retrieval is now raft search and rescue. Repeat, we are search and rescue again."

I watched the strange craft as it floated farther and farther away, growing more minuscule with each second. "Just when I thought this day couldn't get any stranger," I said.

Agent Ebert brought a hand to his jaw and rubbed it, his fingers stroking the shadow of daily stubble as he studied my face. "Do you have any idea what this whole thing might be about?"

"Why would I know anything about this? I just happened to be running on the rim when it came down."

"When I told you it looked like that was a black bag over his head, you said, 'Oh, no,' like that meant something to you."

I shook my head. "Yeah, that . . . that does. I mean, not to me, but I know who . . . it couldn't be them, but it looks like someone is trying to make this appear as if it was done by Penitentes."

"Penitentes? The guys who whip themselves?"

I sighed. "That's not all they do, but yes, Los Penitentes. They used to do ritual reenactment of the crucifixion, too, around this time of year, although the last confirmed one was decades ago. But some people say they still do it in the dark of night in some of the more remote mountain villages. When they did, the man playing Christ wore a breechcloth and they would put a black bag called a *venga* over his head before tying him to the cross."

Ebert drew in a breath. "Wow. I had heard some stories, but I didn't know all the particulars. I thought they were a secret sect. How do you know so much about them?"

"I've sort of been studying Los Penitentes. I've been drawing some of their shrines—I see a lot of them in the high country where I work. After I had done a number of sketches, I wanted to know more about them. I started doing research and taking notes."

The agent pursed his lips. "So you're a resource protection agent? What got you interested in doing this sketchbook thing about the Penitentes?"

"It started last year when I saw a procession over by the Chama. I was really intrigued. But it's hard to get any information about them, other than what's written, and that's not much."

He nodded. "Well, good luck getting the facts about those guys. I hear they don't talk too much about it."

"That's true, they don't. It's taken me months, but I've finally found a pretty good source. I just met with him last week. It's the first breakthrough I've had in a while."

"Okay, well, from what you know, maybe you can tell me a little something about it—like, why do they do this stuff? Why would anyone flagellate himself or volunteer to get crucified?"

"It's penance. To emulate the suffering they believe Christ endured. Penance is the main sacrament of their faith."

Agent Ebert raised his binoculars and looked down the gorge at the diminutive dark dot that was quickly disappearing into the rapids. "Man, if that's what this is, it's some wild penance."

◄ 3 ►

The Father

When I first talked to him several months ago, his voice on the other end of the phone had been barely more than a whisper. "Father Ignacio Medina," he uttered so softly that it took me a moment to realize what he had said. His rolling Hispanic accent was as smooth and rich as Ibarra chocolate.

"Father Medina? My name is Jamaica Wild. I've been working on a sort of sketchbook about the Penitentes. I've been trying to learn more about them. I was wondering if I could come to see you for some information?"

"Who did you say you are?"

"My name is Jamaica Wild."

"And who do you work for?"

"I work for the Bureau of Land Management, in the Taos

region. But I wanted to talk with you about the sketchbook I'm doing."

"You work for the BLM?" He was still whispering. "What do they have to do with Los Penitentes?"

"No, the BLM doesn't have anything to do with this. I'm doing these drawings on my own. I've done some research, made a few notes, and written a few things about what I've learned and seen. I would like to talk with you about it."

"I am very sorry, I cannot help you. There is really nothing I could tell you." He hung up.

A week later I tried again. And again and again. For months.

Father Ignacio Medina finally agreed to meet me one evening at a coffeehouse in Santa Fe. I was there early, sipping tea, sitting at a *banco*—an adobe shelf along the wall that was covered with cushions—in the back corner of the small room, near a fireplace exuding a comforting dry warmth and the spicy smell of piñon. I had opened my notebook on the table, and I was working with some colored pencils on a sketch of a shrine.

I recognized him by his collar when he came in. He scanned the few occupied tables. I held up a hand and waved. He looked at me and narrowed his eyes, his brow folding into furrows, then made his way through the narrow, irregular spaces between the chairs. "Miss Wild?" he asked.

I stood, extended my hand, and leaned across the table, looking directly into his stare. "Father Medina, I am so honored to meet you. I read your book *The Passion and the*

Light. In fact, I practically know parts of it by heart. Thank you so much for giving me some of your valuable time."

His grip was surprisingly fierce. He studied me carefully. "How could I resist? When I stopped taking your phone calls, you started sending me letters." Then he looked down at the banco. "Do you mind if we change places?" he asked, pointing to the spot where I'd been sitting, watching for him to come in.

In fact, I did mind. I hate sitting with my back to a room.

He stood over me, unbuttoning his coat, waiting for me to move.

"Okay, I guess." I closed my notebook and scooted it around to the other side. I took a seat in the chair opposite him.

He ordered black coffee. His gaze panned the room, came back to me, zoomed in. "I have studied all the things you sent to me. I will admit, I was very impressed. You have done some interesting drawings of some very old and little-known shrines, and you have apparently done a lot of research about them for this sketchbook of yours. It is good." His eyes narrowed. "But when I look at you, I cannot help thinking—you will forgive me, I hope—that you are a very lovely young woman, Miss Wild. Why does a young lady like yourself have such an interest in Los Penitentes?"

"You mean an Anglo?"

He smiled. "Yes, that. And—well, perhaps I was expecting someone . . . older. Perhaps someone from an academic background. You don't look like someone who spends all her spare time doing research, drawing, writing."

"Well, you know what they say about judging a book by its cover."

He laughed. "I know. I know. But when I saw the drawings and read the essay you sent to me, I guess I pictured you . . . well, it is different now that I see you. You seem to look at these things with a wisdom beyond your years." He looked up abruptly and focused his attention on the door of the coffeehouse.

I turned and looked over my shoulder. A man had just come in. He stood at the counter, his back to the room, waiting to give his order. I turned back to Father Medina, who tasted his coffee, looked at the door, then at me, and within a moment, at the door again.

I took a drink from my cup and studied the old priest who sat before me. He was a small man with a beautiful, thick head of blue-black hair streaked near a prominent widow's peak with a wave of pure white. His caramel skin bore deep grooves across the forehead and at the corners of his dark eyes. He continued to look past me at the door.

"Are you expecting someone, Father?"

He smiled. "Perhaps." He pointed toward my notebook. "Is this beautiful book your manuscript?" His hand reached out.

I hesitated.

"May I see it?" His arm remained extended, his palm open.

I tapped my fingers on the book, tamping it down as I tried to diminish its appeal. "Well, it's not really a manuscript. I don't even know if it will become one. It's just all my notes and sketches and . . . "

His fingers wagged impatiently toward it.

I moved my arm over the top of the book, as if to protect it. I felt my pulse quicken as I tried to deflect his request. "I was just hoping to ask you a few questions. I really wasn't planning . . . "

The father's palm remained outstretched, but his face softened from a demand to a plea.

Moments passed, the two of us unmoving, my fingers lingering on the edge of the cover. Finally, I relented and handed him the book. I had never let anyone else look at it. It was a binder filled with pages of original drawings and essays. I had made a tan deerskin cover for it and used tight, perfect loops of chocolate deerskin thong to round-braid seams all around the outer edges. He held the book up carefully in his two hands. "I'm just going to look at it," he said. "I'm not going to hurt it."

I forced a smile.

He set the book down carefully on the table, not opening it. Instead, he looked at me. "Tell me what you do for the BLM."

"I'm a resource protection agent. A range rider. I mostly ride fence lines in the backcountry. In the winter months, I do a lot of odd jobs—handling grazing permits, maintaining gates onto public lands, wildlife rescues, things like that."

"So you're a cowgirl?"

I grinned. "I guess you might say that."

"Are you married?"

"No."

"In love with someone?"

"No."

"Then you live with your family."

"No, I don't have any family."

He was quiet a moment. "You live alone, then?"

"Yes."

Father Ignacio opened the book and began browsing through it. "Look! You have drawn maps and everything," he said approvingly. "It is obvious that you are in love with your subject." He studied one of my drawings. "I like the sketches you've done of the shrines. This one—it's in Agua Azuela, no?"

I nodded yes.

"I remember that one, I know it." He stopped to read a little of what I had written. Then he closed the book and placed it on the table between us. "But you have never answered my question. Why do you have such an interest in Los Hermanos? That is how Los Penitentes refer to themselves—the brothers, or La Hermandad—the brotherhood." His eyes searched my face with intensity.

"I've never really thought about why I'm interested in them. I just am." I looked away from the intimacy of his stare.

"I have a feeling you are afraid to tell me the truth, Miss Wild. What do you think will happen if you do?"

"I don't know how to say it, exactly."

We were both silent for a minute. He sipped his coffee. "Why don't you try?" he suggested, setting his cup down.

"Well . . . " I thought a moment. I looked directly into his eyes. "If I'm drawn to something, it usually has some kind of lesson for me. That's been true since I was a kid."

"And what is the lesson you have gotten from your study of Los Penitentes?"

"I don't know yet."

He studied my face. "And you have had these kinds of experiences since you were a child?"

"Yes."

"Give me an example."

"You're going to think this is crazy, but it started with a possum hand I found when I was a kid. It had been left behind by a predator. It was completely dried and perfect, all the hair on it, even the little fingernails. And the possum's palm was lined, and there were even fingerprints—just like a person's."

His face sobered. He tilted his head to one side, regarding me carefully. He didn't speak.

"I couldn't help myself, I picked it up and took it home. It was—don't be offended by this, Father, please—but it was hideous. And fascinating. I finally sewed that paw on a little deerskin medicine bag I made. I still have it."

Father Ignacio's eyes widened. "So Los Penitentes are like that for you? Just some kind of novelty? Some 'hideous fascination,' as you said?"

"No! Oh, I didn't think you'd understand it."

He held up his open palm. "Well, then, enlighten me."

I drew in a slow breath. "Maybe this won't make any sense to you at all. But I think sometimes you have to embrace the things you are most frightened of. I could tell, even when I was just a child, that the possum hand was some kind of powerful medicine for me. Just the strength of my reaction told me that."

"And what was it that you learned from this 'powerful medicine' in the possum hand?"

I leaned over the table toward him. "I learned not to be afraid of it. I let the possum speak to me and I learned that there is a kind of genius in his nature. I learned that what may look strange or foreign to you at first can prove to be amazing when you get over your fear of it. But you have to get over your fear, or your revulsion, to get to the lesson it is trying to teach you."

"And this is what you have found in Los Penitentes?"

"Yes."

"Tell me about that."

"It started last year when I saw a procession of novices."

"Yes," he urged, leaning closer, his eyes drilling into me.

"They were performing penance. Whipping themselves as they marched. I thought it was terrible. But I couldn't take my eyes off of them."

"Yes, yes, go on!" He gestured with his hand for me to keep it rolling.

"I just wanted to know what made them want to do that. Is that faith?"

He looked directly at me, his eyes wide. "What kind of faith do you practice, Miss Wild?"

"I don't . . . have any faith."

"Ah!" He looked down at his coffee, picked up a spoon, and began to stir in it. There was a long silence punctuated only by the rhythmic, metallic ring of the utensil against his cup. He appeared to be considering what I had told him, but I worried that he might be thinking that I should be committed to a mental facility. I knew my story about the possum hand sounded foolish, even irrational. Finally, the priest spoke: "Miss Wild, you are not just trying to find a way to witness a Penitente crucifixion, are you?"

My mouth fell open. "Do they still do that?"

"Have you ever seen the rituals of Los Penitentes during Holy Week?"

"Well, only the public ones. I'm an outsider. I'm not Catholic. I only know enough Spanish to be dangerous. I'm looking at this from the point of view of a stranger in a strange land."

"Yes. Now you have gotten to the heart of it, have you not? You are an outsider. Your home is somewhere else, no?"

"No. This is my home. Well, I mean, I was raised in Kansas, but my family is all gone. This is the only home I have."

"Just the same, you see, you can never truly understand this faith. You have not grown up eating and sleeping and breathing these traditions, attending these rituals." He looked over my shoulder at the door, then leaned over the table toward me, speaking as if in confidence, of something privileged: "I do not think you will be allowed to observe any of the old rituals. Only a few *moradas*—you know what moradas are?"

"Yes, the places where the brothers meet and worship or practice rituals or whatever . . . "

"That's not what I mean. The word *morada* comes from the Spanish word for 'dwelling,' which comes from the verb *morar*, which means 'to live' or 'to dwell.' It is the home for the spirit, the dwelling place for the soul while it remains on this earth. Los Penitentes consider their moradas to be holy places."

"I know the ones I've seen are usually off the beaten path. Not on a major road, some not even near a road, and never in an obvious place," I said. "You really have to look for them to find them."

"There are only a few moradas left which carry on the old practices, and they have been forced to become more and more covert. It is vital to the spirit of the ceremonies that the penitent ones be anonymous. These rituals are for them and for their community; they are not some circus sideshow for ignorant Anglos converging on the villages, hoping to see a religious spectacle, perhaps even a crucifixion. The attendance of uninitiated onlookers has only added fuel to the sensationalism surrounding the rituals, and that draws more onlookers. It was never meant to be that way." He shook his head in frustration and took a drink of coffee. He checked the door, then looked back at me. "You know that Los Penitentes were once excommunicated by the Church?"

I nodded.

"You will find a tentative peace today between the Church and Los Hermanos de la Luz—that is another name for them, the Brothers of the Light. In some of the larger towns, there might be a procession, a pale imitation of what it once was. The activities will be centered around the church, although a ceremony may be held by the brotherhood in the morada, especially the Tinieblas—the ceremony held in darkness on Good Friday. But it will be nothing like . . . " His voice trailed off. He knitted his brows, making a chevron of grooves across his forehead. He peered at me through squinted lids. "Do you know what made me finally agree to our interview?"

"No. I wondered—I've been trying for months."

"It was one of the pieces you sent me—the one you wrote about that procession you happened to witness near the Chama. When I read it, I was very moved, almost as I would have been if I had been there myself. Where did you learn to write like that?"

I thought a moment. "I don't know. Maybe I inherited it from my mother. She wrote poetry."

He glanced intently at me. "What you wrote about is an ancient tradition—making penance. But there are also the traditions of giving, of service to the community, of charity, of healing. All the traditions of Los Penitentes and their sister order, Las Carmelitas, have been tenderly taught from generation to generation in these tiny villages. And some believe that these lovingly maintained customs come from even before we came here."

"Tell me about that, Father."

He waited, tilted his head to one side to see the door. Then he began speaking almost in song. I was mesmerized by his voice as he told me the story of how Spain had sent Franciscan brothers to colonize the lands that early conquistadors had claimed for the king. Unable to reach all the outlying villages when a priest or brother was needed, they had cultivated a tertiary, or Third Order of lay leaders of the church, who called themselves Los Hermanos de la Luz. The practice of self-flagellation and excessive penance was common in medieval Spain, and some believed that the Franciscans may have introduced these practices here, hence the name Los Penitentes. When the Mexican Revolt cast the Spaniards out, the Franciscans were called home to Spain, leaving Los Hermanos to fend for themselves in religious matters. The unique and exotic practices which developed, including ritual crucifixion, were a result of the remote and isolated nature of the land itself.

"Of course there is yet another theory," he said. "Some say that the practices and the brotherhood came up from Mexico in the late 1700s. Many scholars believe this is the more correct of the two. However, there are certain moradas that maintain they were given their original charter in the 1500s. So it is hard to say which is true."

I propped my elbow on the table and rested my chin in my hand as I listened to him with fascination.

"I have a suggestion for your book."

This roused me. I sat up at once and pulled the notebook to me, turned to a fresh page, and picked up a pencil.

25

"Do you know about El Instituto Religioso de la Santa Hermandad—the Religious Institution of the Holy Brotherhood?"

I wrote as quickly as I could, trying to keep up. "You mean the tract that was supposed to have been published by Padre Martínez sometime around the 1830s? The one defending the Penitentes when the Church was issuing decrees condemning them?"

"The very same."

"I have read about that, but there are no known copies. It might even be just a legend."

"Oh, it is not just a legend, I assure you." He looked beyond me toward the door. He nodded his head at someone there.

I turned and looked behind me at a large man in a long black coat. He nodded at me and the padre, then turned and left the coffeehouse. I twisted around again and looked at Father Ignacio.

He shrugged apologetically. "That is my driver. I have only a few more minutes. Then I must leave."

"So about this tract . . . "

"Do you also know about a man named Pedro Antonio Fresquíz of Las Truchas?"

"Wait—say that again?" I scribbled as Father Medina repeated the name for me.

He pointed to the *i* in Fresquíz. "There is an acute accent there. Look him up. Bring the two things together."

I looked at him, confused.

"Fresquíz and the tract. They will come together. If you search hard enough."

"Where would I find—"

"There is something going on right now. I cannot speak about it. It is not safe. But Los Penitentes are . . . someone is trying to steal their power. I can say no more."

I gave him a puzzled look. "I don't understand."

"There are not so many members these days, fewer and fewer of Los Hermanos de la Luz," he said. "There is also little interest in the true nature of their belief, their role in community life, their bond as brothers, their commitment to service. Instead, they are widely regarded by the general population, and even by some in the Catholic Church, as some sort of cult. Even I am being discouraged by my superiors in the Church from my work in this area. Some of the holy icons have been stolen, others denounced as idols. Moradas have been broken into and vandalized. The sacred oaths of the brotherhood have been betrayed by traitors. And right now, no one trusts anyone." He pointed his finger at me. "No one is going to trust you as you try to find answers to your questions. You must be very careful."

He reached for his coat on the banco beside him and began to get up. But he stopped, sat back, and gave me a curious look, tilting his head slightly to one side, his lips pressed together in a tight, thin line. "I am satisfied that your intent is well-meaning, but I wonder if you are capable of finding the

gentle, loving story of community and service in Los Penitentes." He pondered a moment. "Or if you are merely attracted to their suffering." He waited.

I didn't speak.

"An enlightened person will come to realize that they are
both the same. But you are young, Miss Wild. You are young,
and you did not even grow up here, and also, you say that
you have no faith. What do you know of penance?"

His words demanded a reply, but I had none. I held his
gaze without flinching for what felt like an eternity. Finally
I spoke. "I don't know. Maybe that's the thing I'm supposed
to learn about."

He was quiet a moment, never taking his eyes from my
face. "Yes, perhaps that is so," he said softly. He smiled tenderly at me, then stood and started to put on his coat.

I stood, too. "Father Ignacio—"

He held up his hand to stop me. "If I don't see you again,
señorita, please be careful. There is danger surrounding Los
Penitentes right now. May God be with you."

"But I have so many questions . . . "

He reached out and took my hand and held it. "I think,
Miss Wild, that you are very lonely."

I gasped, his words stinging.

"Do not be so alone. Always remember, my child, *¡Ayuda
a otros y Dios te ayudará!* Help others and God will help
you. It is an old Penitente saying."

◄ 4 ►

Joint Venture

After our walk out onto the bridge, Agent Ebert and I returned to the parking area, where he introduced me to two other members of the crime scene task force. The Taos Pueblo police detective was most concerned about where the body had fallen in order to determine whether he had jurisdiction, which seemed unlikely after some discussion. Deputy Sheriff Jerry Padilla was someone I had worked with before on two separate incidents requiring arrests on BLM land. Padilla listened to Agent Ebert's briefing, then spoke to me. "Jamaica, you probably want to scoot on out of here before the media arrive from Albuquerque. It's a good thing for you it takes so long for them to get here from down south. Come on, I'll walk you back across and you can get your vehicle from the rest area. I'll tell the officer over there to let you drive back through. You'll be the first car on the bridge since we shut her down."

"So the forensics team is done on the bridge, then?" I said.

Padilla's leather holster squeaked as he walked. "Yup."

"How long will it remain closed?"

"Oh, I suspect shortly after you drive through we'll open her up to vehicle traffic only. No pedestrians, though. Not until the incident is terminated and the body has been transported to OMI—the Office of the Medical Investigator down in Albuquerque. We'll keep a uniformed officer here, right through the raft retrieval tomorrow, to keep pedestrians off the bridge until it's all done."

"Thanks for letting me get out of here before the press—"

He cut in: "We determined that we're not going to release your name as a witness until we have more information on this crime. Matter of fact, we're not even going to say we have a witness right now. Until we know more about who did this and why, we are going to keep a tight lock on things, and we want you to do the same. We don't want you to discuss this with anyone who's not involved in the case until we give you the go-ahead to do so. Might be good if you didn't mention it to anyone outside of the task force, if you can swing that."

"My boss knows. I had to tell him why I would be late."

"Well, I'll tell him what I told you, and let's keep this thing under wraps. If the bad guys don't know you saw them do the deed, they won't be out looking for you. And they won't know we're out looking for them."

✖

At the BLM, behind the counter in the main lobby, Rosa Aragon served as receptionist, answering the phones and greeting visitors. Rosa was the river ranger who'd been rescued last fall after a dramatic search of the Rio Grande Gorge that brought the attention of national television to Taos. A chopper sweeping the gorge the morning after she had gone missing finally spotted her brightly colored gear spread out for maximum visibility on a sandbar. This was sixteen hours after her raft had capsized, smashing her against a rock and fracturing her leg in three places. A crew went in at once and got her.

As I had mentioned to Agent Ebert, I was part of that search and rescue mission, because it was one of the BLM's own. But instead of finding Rosa, I discovered the fresh remains of a suicide jumper who had hoped to make the media with his last earthly act. He leaped into the gorge and landed headfirst, smashing his head in two like a burst watermelon. Unfortunately, since it no doubt happened in the wink of an eye, no one was actually observing the bridge at the moment he made the jump (or at least no report was made). His body then washed rapidly downriver, unobserved, and found its way into some reeds just in time for me to come upon him while patrolling the banks of the Rio Grande near the Orilla Verde Recreation Area, as part of the search mission for our river ranger.

Since then, Rosa had been putting in clerical time until

her leg healed. I had been putting in time hoping the haunting nightmares and Technicolor memories of that jumper's broken-up corpse would one day leave me. They hadn't yet. After today, they'd have company.

"Roy in?" I asked Rosa.

"He's in his office. But you missed all the fun. He had this forest ranger guy in here with him this morning. Eeeee! That guy was cute."

"I missed all the fun, huh?"

Rosa winked. "He was really good-looking, I'm telling you."

I headed back to Roy's office and knocked on the door, even though it was open.

The Boss looked up from the list he had been making on a notepad. His thick mass of short, silver-blond hair was mussed from his recently removed hat. "Hey, there. Come on in. Have you had lunch?"

I walked in and slumped into a chair in front of his desk. "Lunch? I haven't even had breakfast."

"You want to go get something to eat?"

"I don't think so. I doubt I could eat right now."

Roy got up and closed the door. He stood beside his desk and looked down at me in the chair. "You want to talk about it?"

"I'm not supposed to talk about it. There's a special task force investigating, and they're not going to release any details, including that there was a witness. So you're not supposed to talk about it either."

"Padilla called me and told me that. I'm not going to say a word, unless you need to debrief with someone."

"I think I'm better off trying to put it out of my mind, Boss."

"Okay, then. Maybe that's a good idea. Let's talk about something else. But before we do, I just want to make sure you know that if you need to take some time off—"

"No, I'm good. I'll be better off if I stay busy, keep my mind occupied."

"All right, then. I got an idea for keeping you occupied, if you're sure you'll be all right."

"I'm all right. Go ahead, shoot."

"Have you ever rode the section up by Cañoncito?"

"Sure. I did a couple months up there from Pilar to Chimayo last fall during the no-burn enforcement. That was a cold tour of duty, let me tell you, without being able to build a fire when I camped."

"That's right, I remember that now. Well, we got reports that there's been some fence lines cut up there, and there are four-wheel tracks leading into the protected wilderness area. The Forest Service says there's also been heavy use on the mud path in through the forest from Cañoncito headed toward Las Trampas, and trucks or whatever have torn the road all to hell. Something's going on in that area. I had Art sweep that section last week, but I think we better go back again and maintain a presence there until we know what's happening."

"That's pretty remote country. Not that I would complain, but are you trying to tuck me back out of sight, by any chance?"

Roy smiled. "Hell, I'd like to keep you out of trouble, Jamaica, but I don't know what that's going to take. Lord knows, I've tried, and nothing has worked up to now."

"You can't blame me for today, Boss. That wasn't anything but me being in the wrong place at the wrong time."

"Nobody's blaming anybody for anything. It's just that there's something about you. You're like a magnet; you draw things to you."

I raised my feet up and propped my boots on the front of his desk. "That's ridiculous. I just think I'm more curious than most. I see things that other people miss."

"Well, go get curious and see if you can find out what's going on in this case." He turned and pointed to a map behind a sheet of Plexiglas on the wall behind his desk. "I want you to take a truck and a horse trailer—not your Jeep—and ride the fence from a point several miles north of Chimayo to Cañoncito on horseback."

"What am I looking for?" I asked.

"Whatever you can find, I guess. Just find out what the hell's going on. Somebody's cutting fences for a reason. And I want you to bust anyone you catch driving in that protected wilderness area. We have every trailhead posted for no vehicles, on- or off-road. Whoever is doing this is just spitting in our faces."

"You know it's Lent; next week's Holy Week. That's right in the heart of Penitente country. Maybe it's all those pilgrims going to the Sanctuario in Chimayo. Or maybe it's thrill seekers looking for a glimpse of some Penitente action."

"I don't think so. The pilgrims go the highway, always have. And the gawkers usually don't show up 'til Good Friday, or the night before. Seems unlikely they'd be looking for much action this early, and even if they were, they'd just take the High Road up through Trampas and Truchas."

"Well, are you thinking poachers or wood cutting or what? You know, even though it's the first week of April, the temperature still drops below freezing at night. This time of year, anyone who could provide enough firewood to get folks through until spring could make a fortune."

"Yeah, well, even though it's still cold at night, it warms up during the day. As a result, we've had enough snowmelt to make all those roads up there muddy and impassable, even with an ATV. I think it'll take a real good rider, so that's why I'm sending you. We're going to work with the Forest Service on this one. I met with one of their rangers today. His name's Kerry Reed. Have you ever met him?"

"I don't believe I've had the pleasure."

"You'll like him. I think you two will make a good team. And since you've already put in nearly half a shift today, I figured you might as well wait and start tomorrow night. I told Reed that, too."

"Okay, Boss," I agreed. I sat up and removed my feet from his desk.

"Oh," he said, reaching into his vest pocket and pulling out a piece of notepaper on which he had scribbled a few lines. "Almost forgot. Here's where he's going to meet you and when. And you two will have to keep any radio traffic to a minimum, not that you can get much signal strength up in that country anyway. But if someone's up to something, they'll monitor our radio traffic, so we need to keep things quiet or we'll never find out what's going on. Now get on home. You've had a tough enough day, no need to hang around here just to pass the time."

On my way out through the front lobby, Rosa stopped me. "I forgot to tell you before. Some guy called for you. He was asking a lot of questions. He asked for your phone number at home. I told him you don't have a phone. He wanted to know when he could call you here. I told him I don't know, you're not usually here. He said it was personal and he didn't want to leave a message. You got a new boyfriend?"

"When was this?"

"About an hour before you came in. Sorry, I forgot. I wanted to tell you about that forest ranger guy, and I didn't think—"

"And he didn't leave a name?"

"No, I asked, but he didn't want to leave a message."

"Did he say he would call back?"

"I don't think so. I don't remember."

"Rosa, you didn't write anything down?"

"What was I supposed to write down? If the guy don't want me to know who he is, then I don't know who he is! I don't know what to write."

◀ 5 ▶

Medicine Woman

I left the BLM at noon, and the rest of the day was wide open. I didn't want to go home, didn't want to have to go back through the command post on the east rim of the gorge, didn't want to have to go back across the bridge.

To pass the time, I decided to go visit my medicine teacher. I drove five miles north across Grand Mesa. At the Tanoah Falls Casino, I turned off the highway and headed in the direction of the mountains along a winding, narrow road through the tiny village of Cascada Azul, almost deserted now with ski season over. Tanoah Pueblo took a backseat in tourism to the larger Taos Pueblo, with its massive adobe architecture. The little walled village of Tanoah had its own ancient earthen apartment-like structures, but was smaller, off the beaten path, and less well preserved.

Anna Santana, an elder of the tribe, lived in a small adobe home outside the walls of the main part of the village. She had taken me under her wing at an art show just a few months before, at Christmastime. I helped her prevent a calamity when her display of handmade jewelry, dreamcatchers, and pottery almost collapsed. On that first day, moments after we met, she had asked me about my mother. When I told her that my mother had left when I was very young, the Pueblo woman had insisted that I call her "Momma Anna." And she invited me to share the Christmas feast with her and her family at Tanoah Pueblo, and later, King's Day and yet another Pueblo feast day. Soon I began coming to her house now and then just to pass time with her as she cooked or made pottery or performed any of the dozens of hardworking endeavors that filled her life. A month or so ago, Momma Anna had announced that she was my medicine teacher, and that she was called to teach me "Indun way." However, I had no sense that any formal training had begun. At least not yet.

When I pulled up in front of her house, I noticed a plume of blue-gray smoke coming from the back, on the side nearest the acequia, the irrigation ditch that carried water from the rio to the tribe's fields. A pack of mutts came to greet me, and I stopped to pet heads and scratch ears. I walked around the house and saw a small brown woman bent over, scraping live coals out onto the ground from the floor of the *horno*—a beehive-shaped outdoor adobe oven used for baking. Momma Anna straightened when she heard my footsteps. She turned, looked me up and down, and then gestured for me to come to her. "You come. We bake pies."

On the table under the *portal* behind her house, four trays of folded and crimped, prune-filled pastry pockets huddled under cotton dish towels. These little triangle-shaped pies were a favorite of the Tanoah, and Momma Anna made some of the best I had tasted. Her dough was always crisp and flaky; the filling, which she made from wild plums that grew along the acequia, was chewy, tart, and sticky, never too sweet. I brought the trays over, and we shoved them into the horno, then closed the door almost completely, leaving just enough of an opening so that the heat inside would not burn the pies.

Anna Santana drew up straight after the door was in place and again looked me up and down. "Today we start," she said. With the shovel she had used to remove the live coals from the horno, she scooped up a burning ember and carried it carefully before her as she made for the back door.

Inside her house, Momma Anna laid the shovel with the glowing coal in its blade on top of the woodstove. She took a pinch of cedar tips from a pottery jar and sprinkled the green buds over the red coal. The cedar began to smudge at once. Momma Anna lifted the shovel handle in one hand, and in the other took up a hand broom fashioned from foot-long stems of ricegrass bound with thread into a short tube shape, the fibers spread on one end for sweeping. She used the broom to fan the smoke over me in a ritual of cleansing and preparation. As she bathed me with the smoke, she mumbled a prayer in Tiwa.

After the prayer, she returned the shovel to the top of the woodstove and left the room without speaking. I stood where I was, inhaling the clean, sharp scent of the purifying smoke. Momma Anna returned with a folded blanket, atop which rested a large elk hide bag. She spread the colorful Pendleton on the floor of her living room in front of the sofa. "Sit down."

I sat cross-legged on the blanket, and so did she, placing the bag beside her. She reached inside and brought out a small drum made in the Pueblo tradition—from a hollowed-out log covered at both ends with stretched and laced rawhide. This drum was no bigger than six inches in diameter, and not as tall. Next, she brought out the beater—a peeled aspen stick, wrapped on one end with a wad of padding covered with deer hide and tied with sinew. Once more, my medicine teacher reached into the bag, and she drew out a small hand-sewn deerskin pouch, tied with a leather thong. When she had arranged these items between us on the blanket, she looked at me and smiled. She picked up the drum and began beating on it in a steady rhythm. After a minute or two of drumming, she set the instrument down and reached for the pouch. "Hold out hand," she said.

I extended my palm and she took it with one hand and, with her other hand, turned the pouch upside down and shook it. I cupped my fingers to catch the smooth stones that fell from the bag. I looked down to see what I had. Seven or eight small flat ovals of river rock rested in my palm.

"Choose," Momma Anna said.

I used my finger to sort through the lot and selected one of the smallest, a smooth black disc. "I like this one best."

She snorted. "Maybe you not like best, next other time. Best teacher not always one you like. That ancestor," she said, pointing to the stone in my hand, "got big lesson for you." She snatched up the other stones and put them back in the pouch, tied it with the thong, and returned it to the elk hide bag. She straightened her back, her legs folded in front of her, and she put out her hand. "Now we see about that lesson. Let me see Old One."

I handed her the stone.

She closed her fingers around it and then held her fist against her chest. She looked at me and took a deep breath, as if she were drawing air through the stone. Time passed, but she did not breathe out. Her eyes remained fixed on my face. Then she let out a blast of air and extended her open palm to me. "Now, you."

I took the stone and did as Momma Anna had done, holding it to my chest and watching her as I did so. I drew in air and held it.

Momma Anna's eyes did not move. They were like the stone—shiny and black and smooth.

I felt my chest tightening, wanting to release the air, but I held on for as long as I could. Finally, I let my breath out.

Momma Anna picked up the beater and began playing her drum again. When she stopped, she said, "Now, we got pies ready."

We removed the trays full of perfectly browned pies from the horno, and the delicious smell of the warm fruit and the crisp pastry reminded me that I hadn't eaten that day. Momma Anna took one of the cotton dish towels she had used to cover the pies before baking and put two of the little tarts inside. She tied the corners of the cloth, creating a hobo pouch. She handed this to me, and when I took it the contents felt warm in my hand. "You need forgiveness," she said.

My mouth came open. "What?"

She frowned. One thing my medicine teacher had taught me was that the Tiwa considered it rude to ask questions. Even one-word questions. She softened her expression. "Ask. You ask forgiveness, everyone you care about."

"But . . . I don't know what I've done. I don't know what to ask forgiveness for."

"You are human being. All people need forgiveness."

"But, I mean—"

"You go now," she said, picking up my free hand and placing it over my cloth bundle and patting it, like one might pat the hand of a child. "Go ask forgiveness. You need that. You take Old One with you."

I had tucked the stone in the pocket of my jeans when we had gotten up from the blanket. Now, I reached my fingers in the pocket and started to take it out.

"No!" Momma Anna said. "Keep him there." She reached

42

out and took me by the shoulder and started shepherding me to the corner of the house so I could go back around front.

"But Momma Anna," I protested, "I'm confused. I don't understand."

She stopped and let out a blast of air. "This your lesson. When you do your lesson, then you understand. Not this time, but next other time when lesson finish. Now go. Do."

◄ 6 ►

The Book

Before going home that evening, I decided to get in the exercise I had missed earlier that day. I drove past the small tent that had been set up for a command center on the east side of the gorge bridge and saw a sheriff's deputy sitting on a folding chair, outside its entrance, reading a magazine. He looked up and waved as I drove past. I proceeded slowly across the bridge, my eyes drawn to the center viewing balcony from which I had seen the man on the cross descend that morning. The bridge was deserted, and the canyon below lay in shadow. Once across, I drove into the west rim rest area and took the roundabout road to the back edge of the circle. I parked my car near the trailhead and got out. I looked back at the five-hundred-foot-long silver steel structure that spanned this fracture in the earth's crust—where a vein of a river had worked its way through sheer rock and carved a deep and jagged crack in the high desert mesa. To the east, the rugged blue Sangre de Cristo Mountains stood guard over the Taos Valley. The sky was cloudless; amber light from the late day sun flooded the miles of lonely sage and piñon flats between here and the mountains.

Because no one was around, I didn't even bother to go in the restroom to change. Instead, I opened the rear hatch of my Jeep and sat on the back deck to remove my boots, then quickly slipped off my jeans and pulled on the running pants that I kept in my backpack. I laced up my running shoes and set out on the trail. I couldn't help myself—I kept looking back at the bridge, as if I needed to be sure that another travesty wasn't about to take place. Almost no traffic. A car passed over from east to west. A few minutes later, a car headed east. The next two times I looked, nothing. I started to relax my vigilance and focus on the run. I breathed deeply, the smell of sage and sun-baked earth rising to my nostrils as I ran the long portion of the loop that crossed open, flat ground. I felt the day's grip on me loosening as I jogged at a steady tempo, the rhythm of my footsteps reminding me of Momma Anna's drumming.

Where the trail turned and circled back, it skimmed along the canyon rim, then dipped below the edge onto a fifty-yard stretch of narrow path bordered by a sharp precipice. I slowed to a brisk walk, intending to savor the shady hues of the rock face on the opposite side of the canyon. But the dark walls of the gorge seemed sinister to me now. I tried to shake the feeling, and I stopped to look down at the Rio Grande rushing beneath me, hoping to experience the feeling of awe and inspiration that usually accompanied this view. But the memory of the cross with its naked passenger being carried off in the rushing water flashed across my memory screen, and I no longer wanted to look at the river. Instead, I suddenly longed to go home to the comfort of my little cabin, and I felt as if I couldn't get there soon enough. I picked up my pace again and headed up the path to the boulders above, then pushed hard as I chugged the last quarter mile of the loop.

As I neared the end of my route, the sinking sun had turned the mountains pink and the light softened to a rosy glow. The temperature was dropping, and I felt the chill air against my arms. I slowed to walk the last hundred yards to cool down. When I came over the rise just before the trailhead, I spotted three guys in the parking lot, two of them going through my Jeep and the third standing nearby, looking in the opposite direction, toward the bridge. I stopped, my mouth falling open like the doors of my violated vehicle. Without thinking, I yelled, "Hey!"

They froze for an instant, all three of them turning to look at me like startled antelope.

And then I charged.

They took off.

My long hair, still damp with sweat, was flying into my face, my open mouth. I pumped my legs harder, ignoring the ache, the fatigue. The lookout darted across the asphalt, up the curb, and around the left side of the restroom building and disappeared behind it, presumably toward a getaway vehicle on the opposite side of the roundabout. But the two who had been bent over searching through my Jeep got a slower start, and as I closed on them, they both broke to the right, toward the gorge, where a row of concrete picnic shelters overlooking the view lined the loop road. The lone man was gone, out of sight now—I'd never get him. But these two were in range, and I knew I could overtake them if I just kept running.

I had surprised them when I gave chase—maybe they hadn't expected that of a woman. As I ran, I chided myself for having yelled at them and blown my opportunity for a stealthy approach. They soon realized they were headed for a dead end and the lead man started to correct course, cutting left and back through the center of the roundabout, making down the right side of the restroom structure.

The second man followed suit, but he was starting to slow, and I pushed myself and maneuvered to close the gap. His thin jacket flapped around the sides of his arms as it blew open. He nearly tripped over the curb that divided the road from the center grounds, then struggled with his footing, recovered, and went on. But it slowed him down. I could almost touch him now; I was just two yards behind him, and I could smell the stink of fear blowing off of him as the cold air hit his sweating body.

As I closed in behind him, I heard a little whine in his breathing, a high-pitched plea from his lungs for rest. He cut to the left, passing behind the restroom building, and I was right on his heels.

Suddenly, a fast-moving black shadow flew from behind the back wall and delivered a breath-propelling blow to my abdomen that sent me reeling backward. The air from my lungs rushed on before me in a spray of fine white mist. *Whhhooooossshhhhh.*

I hit the ground, the impact jarring my spine, my brain disconnecting as suddenly as a downed power line. I couldn't move for a minute; all communication between mind and body had been interrupted. Then I began to reconnect . . . and wish I hadn't. Oh, my back! It hurt the worst—that and my head, which must have hit hard. But I was okay. I sat up. Nothing broken. I was still slightly stunned as the cloud slowly cleared in my head, my senses gradually reengaging. I sat for a few seconds, looking around me, reading out my body's messages. I was all right.

I took my time getting up and heard two car doors slam near the highway, *ka-thunk!* Then the roar of an engine as the car sped off to the west, toward Tres Piedras. I started back to my Jeep. Its doors were still yawing open from the robbery I had interrupted just minutes before. I saw my bag on the ground where the thieves had ditched it. I picked it up and went through it. Everything was still there—my wallet, credit cards, even the small amount of cash inside. I looked in the car. My handgun was still locked in the glove box, undisturbed. The standard car stereo and BLM radio remained intact on the dash. I looked in the floor of the backseat. My shotgun and rifle rested in place. I checked the rear cargo area. My backpack had been rifled through, but nothing was missing. Nothing of value had been taken.

Confused, I stopped looking through the cargo area and straightened, the backpack still dangling from my hand. I scanned in every direction, studying the panorama around me for answers. The pink light had fled across the mesa and left a soft mauve blanket over the desert. A solitary truck rumbled across the gorge bridge, its rear lights creating a neon reflection along the silver railing of the structure that stretched out like a fiber-optic red tail. And way out in the lap of the big mountain that shelters Taos from the blistering cold northern winds that sweep down the spine of the Rockies, tiny lights twinkled on as night overtook day. Suddenly I felt a stab of white-hot burning in my chest as I realized what was gone.

My book! They had stolen my book!

◄ 7 ►

Summoned

When I went to the command center tent to report the theft, the deputy on duty seemed relieved to have a visitor to break the monotony of his evening. But he was not particularly excited about taking a report on the theft of my book, especially when he learned that all the valuables that normally would have been stolen had been left intact. I recalled Jerry Padilla's warning not to talk to anyone except the task force members about the incident that morning, so I didn't mention what the book was about, or that I thought the theft of it could possibly be tied in some way to the crime that had occurred earlier that day. I decided I would wait and let Padilla know that the next time we talked.

I headed west to my cabin, which sat alone in the pines on a remote piece of property that backed to forested foothills and Forest Service land. As I drove up my long dirt drive, my headlights illuminated something white pinned to the door. I killed the lights, then the engine, stopping thirty yards from the house. I reached into the glove box, took out my hand-gun and readied it, then slid silently out the driver's side and eased the car door shut. I panned the property in front of my cabin from east to west. No sign of anyone; however, it was so dark I couldn't see far. I crouched low as I made my way on foot to the end of the drive. I stepped up on the porch, scanning the ground around my place once again, but there was no one in sight. Still holding my pistol up in both hands, I walked to the door. A note written with black marker on a white paper towel had been secured to the wooden door with several pushpins. It was too dark to make out the fuzzy let-ters where the ink had bled into the fibrous paper, so I opened the door of my cabin and flipped on the light. I scanned the one main room before I glanced at the note. It read:

Woman down! Help!
Bennie

I gave a sigh of relief. I knew Bennie. Bennie was a friend. This was the kind of thing Bennie did.

But just the same, perhaps because of the other events of the day, I didn't relax until I crossed through the main room to the pass-through hallway on the other side that led to the bathroom—a shed-style addition that had been added on years after the original one-room cabin had been built. I looked in the narrow closet on one side of the hall as I went through, checked behind the shower curtain in the bathroom. No one there.

I went back outside and pulled my Jeep to the end of the drive, turning it around to face nose-out, ready to go, the way I always parked. I got my shotgun and rifle out of the back and grabbed the little cloth pouch that Momma Anna had given me with the prune pies in it. After I took all this inside, I went back once more for my backpack, boots, and duty clothes, and I took my sidearm with me when I went.

It was a rare night outside of the months of July and August that I didn't want a fire in the woodstove at night. Here in mountainous northern New Mexico, the sunny days of early April held the promise of spring, but the nights clung to the cloak of winter. I opened the doors to the firebox and stirred the ashes around with a little shovel until I saw a few coals from last night's fire pulse red. I left the doors open to let air onto the glowing coals, threw in a handful of twigs for kindling, and laid a couple logs on top of that. Next, I took the cast-iron kettle to the kitchen sink, filled it with water and set it on top of the woodstove, then got the mug I'd washed after my morning coffee and put a little pouch of tea in it for when the water came to a boil.

After washing up and putting on some old sweatpants and a hoodie, I sat down in the chair in front of the woodstove with my tea and the two little pies Momma Anna had given me.

This cabin was my haven, even if it wasn't mine. I rented it from a Denver landscape designer who had inherited the land from his family and had no interest in living or vacationing here—too isolated. There was no water, but I paid someone to haul it to the cistern every other month, and I had learned to be frugal in my use of the precious substance. I had electricity, but there were no phone lines anywhere near me, and the mountains made getting a cell phone signal here impossible. Nor was there any point in trying to watch television, as there weren't enough residents in this remote area to make providing services like that worthwhile. None of this bothered me. I had learned to love the quiet, and I liked my own company.

I sat in my chair, sore where I had hit the ground and from whatever had hit me. The events of the day replayed in my mind, beginning with the vision of the man on the cross—upside down—soaring silently into the gorge. I shuddered at the memory, and my mind wandered on to Momma Anna's strange assignment and the stone she called the "Old One." I got up and went to get the tiny black river rock out of the pocket of my jeans. I brought it back to my chair and rubbed the smooth surface between my thumb and index finger as I remembered the startled faces of the three men I caught going through my Jeep. All three looked Hispanic, in their forties, plainly dressed in jackets and jeans. What on earth did they want with my book?

I ate my pies and I drank my tea. And as the quiet of the night and the fatigue of the day settled on me, I grieved the loss of my book. It was the only copy I had, all those hours given to it gone now, and for nothing.

Father Ignacio had been right. I was lonely. Right then, I yearned for the book like a lost love. I wanted to pick it up, to feel the smooth, cool deerskin cover. I tried to remember how many shrines I had mapped, which ones I had sketched. I went through the book in my mind, page by page, trying to see what I had written.

The names the father had given me were in the stolen book. One of them was the tract by Padre Martínez, I remembered that. But for the life of me, I could not remember the other name. I tried to remember it as I sat there, staring at nothing, twisting at the ends of my hair with my finger, unable to think of anything else for the moment. Or perhaps not wanting to think of anything else, grateful for the distraction.

Finally I got up and took my mug and the cloth towel to the sink and set them on the counter beside it. On the table was the paper towel I had taken off of the door. I held it up and read again the curious summons from Bennie. What did "Woman down" mean? I would have to find out tomorrow.

◄ 8 ►

Bennie

I woke the next morning with a plan. I was going to start over on my book, do it all again. And this time, make copies of everything.

I brewed some coffee while I took a shower, then sat at my table and ate a bowl of cereal while I made a list of things to do that day before starting my night ride duty. I packed my backpack with items I would need. The first thing on my to-do list was to go see Bennie.

The red dirt parking lot in front of the Golden Gecko was deeply rutted from the snowmelt. As I rode the dips, I jounced and jostled in my seat. A row of five pickups lined the front part of the building near the door. The pink and blue neon Open sign buzzed in the one small window, and the plain plastered face of the adobe building basked in the bright morning sunlight. The only other sign was a big carved wooden gecko mounted on a post by the road. It had once been painted all over with gold enamel, but the paint had peeled and flaked off in patches, making the place's namesake look more like a spotted salamander.

When I opened the car door, I felt the sting of clear, cold air on my face, and the bright sun hurt my eyes. I squinted and got out, narrowly missing a puddle of red clay and icy water. The smell of grilled chorizo, onions, and peppers wafted from the groaning grease fan on the roof. I walked toward the entry and heard the faint sound of a jukebox.

When I pulled open the heavy door, the sound grew louder and I made out the harmonies of Los Lonely Boys serenading through the speakers. Inside, the Gecko was like a dark cave. I stopped to let my eyes adjust until I could see more than the neon beer signs over the bar. The aroma of warm tortillas and breakfast burritos mixed with the sour smell of last night's stale beer in the closed room.

On the left was the black, yawning mouth of the empty, unlit stage. In front of it, in disorderly rows, stood tiny tables with chairs upturned on them. Built in the late 1950s, the Golden Gecko was a famous nightclub in its heyday. Film crews maintained an almost constant presence in northern New Mexico then, unable to supply enough westerns to meet the seemingly insatiable demand. The Gecko, conveniently located on a two-lane blacktop near several scenic film locations, served as a watering hole and recreational outlet for the casts and crews and attracted brand-name celebrities as both entertainment and clientele. But in the sixties, the glamour of westerns began to wane, and with it, the Golden Gecko. Since then, the place had been alternately closed and opened for long periods of time, resurrecting and then dying in a variety of incarnations: a strip club, a dinner theater, even an exercise and dance studio. The Gecko was now open in a dual role: as a restaurant through the week and as a club featuring rock and country bands on the weekend.

A group of men, mostly Anglos, were sitting at the tables in the right half of the room, talking loudly among themselves, guffawing over something one of them had said. They turned to look at me when I came in, and a little wave of sniggering and elbowing erupted as I felt their eyes scanning my figure. There is something about dark places that makes some men forget that they have daughters or sisters or mothers. Or manners.

I walked across to the counter. I could feel grit under my boots from all the mud the breakfast crowd had tracked in. White diner plates stained orange from red chili shared the tables with wadded-up napkins and plastic soda cups. The men were now silent, all eyes on me. I nodded as I came close. One of them nodded back.

There was no one behind the bar. I heard dishes clatter in the kitchen, so I stepped around the end of the counter and went on back. A man leaned over the grill, spritzing it with a spray bottle then swabbing it with a rag, sending up a hissing cloud of chlorine-scented steam each time the spray hit the hot metal plate. He turned and picked up a stack of dirty plates from the island counter in the center of the kitchen and headed across the room to the dishwasher.

He hadn't seen me, so I moved a step farther into the kitchen. When he turned around to get more dishes, he gave a start, stopping in his tracks, his eyes opening wide with surprise. *"¡Ay, señorita!"* In a thick Hispanic accent, he said, "I didn't see you come in. You surprised me."

"Sorry. I was just looking for Bennie."

"Bennie went to the trailer in the back to get something." He picked up the next stack of plates, turned away, and started rinsing and stacking them in the rack of the dishwasher.

I stood for a moment wondering what to do next—wait here or go out front and sit with the sharks. The man stole a worried glance over his shoulder at me and seemed embarrassed when I returned the look. There was something unnerving about his surreptitious peeking.

He was a large man with a barrel-shaped torso. He looked like he had done time in the ring: his nose was wide and flattened, and his lower lip was bisected by a badly healed scar. His forehead also bore a scar over one brow and to the side of one eye. He looked over his shoulder again, and when he saw that I was still there, he turned to address me directly, wiping his hands on his apron. "Señorita, what are you doing here?"

"I told you. I need to talk to Bennie."

"You should wait out there." He gave me a stern look as he pointed back through the doorway into the main room.

As if to help me make up my mind, I heard chairs scraping

on the floor and tables jostling as the crowd out front broke up and left. I turned and walked through the kitchen doorway back into the dark club. The jukebox was silent now, all the customers gone. I headed around the counter and was going toward a table to sit down when, from the kitchen, I heard the sound of a door opening and then slamming shut again.

A small figure shuffled steadily along behind the bar and then around the counter. "Who's that?" she called, holding her hand like a visor above her eyes, as if to shield them from the almost nonexistent light.

"Hi, Bennie."

"Jamaica! Is that you?" She hurried to hug me. She was tiny, not five feet tall, yet strong and wiry. She felt like a child in my embrace.

"Lord, kiddo, I'm so glad you came. I really need your help. My office is a mess; let's talk out here. Do you want something to eat? Let me get you a breakfast burrito." She started to go back behind the counter. "Did you meet Manny?"

"No, I'm okay. I already had breakfast."

"Manny's our new dishwasher." She came back and pulled out the chair opposite me at the table. "I don't know what I would have done if he hadn't shown up, especially for this weekend. He just wandered in here last night, asking for me by name, didn't seem to know exactly what he was looking for—I don't think he's too bright. But I told him about the big event this weekend and how bad I needed a dishwasher.

I offered him a job, and he took it, right on the spot. He just started this morning. Sit down." She waved a hand over the table. She yelled toward the kitchen, "Manny, we got dirty dishes out here."

I took my coat off, then my hat, ran my fingers through my flattened bangs, placed my stuff on a chair, and sat down in the one beside it.

"I was just thinking about you the other day. It seems like it's been forever since you came by. Then, this thing happened. Kiddo, I really need your help."

"What's going on? What's this 'Woman down' thing?"

"I'm desperate. I really need you to do something for me. I need someone who is in good shape."

"In good shape?"

"It's for a good cause. It's for the wildlife rehab center."

As we were talking, Manny shuffled out and started clearing the tables. He picked up several of the dishes in his hands and started back toward the kitchen.

"Manny, honey, bring a tub," Bennie said. "You can get them all in one trip that way." She turned back to me. "Now, where was I?"

"What's for a good cause?"

"Oh, right. We need to raise money. Fast. We've just had so many critters to take care of, our expenses have doubled over the past two years. We need to build on; we can't keep working out of that tiny little building."

"What's this got to do with me?"

"We're doing a fund-raiser. It's all set, we're ready to go, and then one of the girls that was part of it has sprained her ankle. I need you to take her place."

"Take her place at what? What does it entail?"

Manny reappeared with a large gray plastic tub and a wet rag. He loaded all the dishes and plastic cups from one table into the tub, then washed the tabletop with the rag.

"It's a fashion show," Bennie said. "We have a dozen girls, and we're bringing in a great band, Ailsa Ten and the Decade—they're from Colorado, one of the best bands in the Southwest. And we have the director of the Taos Community Theater choreographing the show."

"A fashion show? Me?"

"I wouldn't ask, kiddo, but I'm desperate. We were good to go until we lost one of our girls. We have to have someone take her place."

I gave a little snort. "I wouldn't know the first thing about how to do that. Unless you let me model outdoor gear."

"Well, that's the thing." Bennie pursed her lips and dipped her chin. "It's a lingerie fashion show."

"A what?"

Having cleared the rest of the tables, Manny moved the tub to the counter and started washing the stainless steel countertop.

"Look, nobody around here is going to pay good money to see girls wearing high fashion. This is New Mexico, for goodness' sake! We know we'll pack the house with a show that has good-looking women modeling lingerie. It's a sure bet we'll make a lot of money for the rehab center."

I put my hands on the table and started to get up. "Sorry, Bennie. I just got put on a team assignment with the Forest Service. I'm doing night rides, starting tonight."

"Are you working Saturday night?"

I stood up and reached for my hat. "No. But I'm not the modeling kind. I don't want to strut around in lingerie in front of a bunch of slobbering men. Sorry."

Bennie stood up, too. "Look, Jamaica, I'm desperate. Please? I'm not asking for me; it's for the wildlife center."

I put my hat on, then lifted my coat. "I'll make a donation. I left my bag in the car, but I'll go get it and write you a check."

Bennie put a hand on my arm. "Look, kiddo, remember that time you had me come out and trap that family of skunks that got under your cabin so you wouldn't have to kill them? I hauled those stinkers all the way to Tres Piedras to release them in that watershed area for you. Anyone else would have poisoned them or trapped and killed them."

I held my coat in midair. "I remember. And I'm grateful. I told you, I'll make a donation."

Bennie still held her hand on my arm. "And I also helped you with that bear when Game and Fish was going to have it shot," she said.

I let out a sigh. Bennie had retired from the New Mexico Department of Game and Fish two years ago. But in the time before that, she and I had worked closely to preserve wildlife habitat on BLM land. We had shared a handful of wildlife rescues—either injured animals or orphaned young. Our most daring endeavor was when we managed to trap a bear who had been shot in the leg and transport it in a cage in the back of a pickup truck to the wildlife rehabilitation center in Española. This was a clandestine endeavor, as the director of Game and Fish had declared the bear unsalvageable and ordered it shot. I was the one who persuaded Bennie to risk losing her job to help save the animal. Bennie now served at the wildlife center on the board of directors as well as working nearly full-time as a volunteer. Running the Golden Gecko was an investment for her, but her heart still belonged to wildlife.

"You'll only need to rehearse once, just a quick run-through on Saturday morning," she said, knowing she had called in a debt I would have to pay.

I gave a little grunt of surrender. "I can't believe you're asking me to prance around in a nightie in front of a crowd."

She winked. "I couldn't believe it when you asked me to haul a bear down the highway from north of Taos all the way to Española in a pickup truck. That's a hard thing to do without attracting attention, you know."

◄ 9 ►

Agua Azuela

My next stop was Agua Azuela, a scattering of old adobes tucked into a crevice carved between two mountains by a bubbling stream, which the Hispanic residents referred to as the *río*. In the village center, an ancient-looking church, poor and sad, struggled out of the lower slope of the mountain. Farther up in the hills, newer homes built by Anglos perched on lofty precipices with panoramic views. Their owners did not have to concern themselves with protection from Comanche and Apache raiders, as the original inhabitants of Agua Azuela did. The early settlers here needed to be within quick running distance of the well-fortified churchyard wall in case of attack, and so this was the sole basis for the original design of the community. There were no streets other than the one-lane dirt road that ran through the narrow canyon right up to the church. Rutted dirt drives fed off the main road back into the folds of terrain where the houses nestled. An old wooden bridge spanning the rio rumbled whenever one of the residents drove over it. An abundance of large gray-white cottonwoods and red willows lined the blue-green water for which Agua Azuela was named.

I aimed my Jeep toward the home of a friend of mine. Regan Daniels lived right on the rio in a beautiful adobe with a wall of south-facing windows. I left my Jeep at the bottom of her drive and walked up the hill to a corral-style gate. Her silver Toyota was in the open-front garage there. Neatly stacked cords of firewood stretched from the corral to the house, and an old nag stood catatonic in a patch of brush beyond a fence. I walked up a path to the kitchen entrance, grabbed the leather loop on the bottom of the old iron bell that hung beside the door, and gave it a hard shake. The sharp clanging pierced the quiet day. I shuffled my feet, looked in through the sidelight at the elegant terra-cotta tile on Regan's *cocina* floor, the intricate carving on her handmade cabinets. No answer. I walked around the house and looked farther up the path toward the barn. Its doors were closed. Still higher up, beyond the barn, at the casita Regan rented to bed-and-breakfast guests, I saw a mud-covered green Land Rover with California plates. I knocked loudly on the French doors at the back of Regan's house. No answer still. I could see the cool, dark living room within. No one in sight.

Knowing Regan was a little hard of hearing, I wanted to open a door and call to her, but somehow I knew that would not be well received. I sensed that she hoped no one would notice this infirmity. In her youth, Regan had been a dancer and even performed her way around the world doing USO tours. She had done a smattering of bit parts on television and ended up a long career as a dancer in summer stock musicals. She had retired here because she was born and raised in northern New Mexico, and she appeared to have plenty of money, from what I could see. Her beautiful home was by far the largest and most distinctive in the old part of Agua Azuela, and perhaps even among most of the newer homes in the surrounding mountains. She had told me that her house overlooking the rio was once a morada, where the Penitentes held rituals in the old days.

This was, in fact, how I came to meet Regan. Her land abutted BLM acreage, and I had occasion to patrol this area once last fall when I discovered a nearly abandoned old Penitente cemetery, or *campo santo*, as they are called—which means "field of saints." The graves were scattered along a flat shelf of open ground about a hundred yards below the canyon rim, just above Regan's land. The view of this unique landform was blocked from below by boulders and stands of scrub piñon and juniper.

When I first happened onto the cemetery, I recognized Penitente features in the headstones and other markers. And one of the graves had an exceptional marker: a massive, weathered wooden cross, crude and simple, its base piled with great stones. The upright stand of the cross had split; shards had broken away in such a way that it was partly hollowed out just above the base. Above the transverse beam, a relief of glyphs had been carved in the surface of the wood, but these had eroded so much that they were impossible to make out. A stipe—such as that on which the crucified's feet would either rest or to which they would be nailed—was affixed to the cross; however, it had gone askew and was positioned almost vertically. In the center of this cross, a broken crucifix, the large ceremonial kind—perhaps ten inches in height, ornately cast in metal and with trefoil ends—had been screwed to the cross, the two pieces at angles to emphasize the break between them. On a flat stone in front of the rood, a small bunch of wildflowers, recently placed and barely wilted, marked the shrine.

I took a small notebook from my pocket and made a quick sketch and a few written comments, jotting a note to come back and do a more detailed drawing later. I was studying the shrine, thinking how lucky I was to have found it, when I heard a deep, husky voice calling, "Hey! You there!" I stood up and looked around. Coming up the slope from below was a tall, lean, white-haired woman, obviously quite agile. She was wearing a long oatmeal cotton sweater. Her khaki pants were tucked haphazardly into big, sloppy work boots caked with dried mud, which looked as if they had been hastily pulled on and not tied. The tongues of these monsters flapped against her pant legs when she walked. I waited, and as she came near, I could see her tan, deeply lined face and dark eyes, which were looking at me the way a raven might regard a hawk who had just invaded her nest.

"You're not supposed to be on this land."

"I'm with the BLM, ma'am." I opened my badge holder and showed her my RPA shield. "I'm a resource protection agent." I pulled my folded quad—the detailed map of the terrain for that quadrant—out of my back pocket and held it up. "I'm pretty sure this old cemetery is on BLM land. We can look for the survey marker, and I'll show you, if you'd like."

"Oh." She began shaking her head up and down as if in agreement. "Yes, I think you're right, don't bother. This *campo santo* used to belong to the village, not to anyone in particular. That was before the BLM came in here. But things have changed. Nobody looks after it now. I own the land below here. I try to keep trespassers off my land, you see. Not too many people know about this place, but if I see anyone up here, I try to run them off. You never know what someone will do."

"Well, I'm pretty sure you're not going to be able to keep everyone from coming up here, no matter what you do. There's a shrine up here, and it's being tended."

"Oh, that? Yes, you're probably right." She had a deep, contralto voice, a smoker's voice, but age had given it a tremor more characteristic of a tightly wound tenor. She extended her hand. She must have been nearly six feet tall. Even though she was standing below me on the slope, our eyes were at the same level. "I'm Regan Daniels. I guess I'm sort of territorial about this place. I've never seen you here before—are you new with the BLM?"

I shook her hand, noting her pleasantly firm grip. "No, ma'am, I'm not. But this is my first time in this section. My name is Jamaica Wild."

"Jamaica Wild. My, that's a pretty name. Unusual, isn't it?" She turned her head to one side and peered intently at me out of one eye, like a crow. She had strong features—high cheekbones, almond-shaped eyes, a long, elegant nose, and a full mouth—the kind of face a model could take to the bank while young. I could still see that youthful beauty behind all the decorations that maturity had bestowed. "Will you be assigned here permanently?"

"I don't believe so, Ms. Daniels. I usually work the high country, mostly range-riding the fence lines in remote areas. But when the weather starts to get cold, I do other assignments. I'm just familiarizing myself with the BLM land in this area right now."

"Oh, I see." Her questions answered, she looked now as if she were in a hurry to end the conversation. She made as if to leave, then stopped and looked back at me. "Would you like to come down to the house? I was just about to make some tea."

In Regan's cocina, she brewed some poleo, a native wild mint that grows near water. I wandered through the large, open rooms of her beautiful house, through the dining room and the enormous living room, looking at all the pictures on the walls—many of them featuring a young Regan with well-known television stars and even a former president, once a movie star himself. Others were of Regan in front of the world's landmarks. The glazed tile floor in the living room was a deep, lustrous blue. Three modern, oversized, white leather sofas seemed to float like barges on this vast expanse of glistening ultramarine, with artfully tossed fur throws and big woven pillows riding on them like passengers. The coffee table in the middle was a horizontal slice through the trunk of a giant cedar—pink, white, and deep red—that had been glazed with a heavy coat of polyurethane. On this table rested a stack of large art books. The sun streamed in the windows, and the exquisite antique porcelain and cast-iron woodstove threw off a pleasant warmth. I tried one of the plush barges and sank deeply into the cushions. I felt like I was being cradled in a soft deerskin glove.

"How did you know that was a shrine?" Regan asked, that fast, uncontrolled vibrato causing her voice to oscillate. She handed me a cup of the fragrant tea.

"I've started a sketchbook about the brotherhood." I took a sip. The sharp, intense mint flavor of the poleo cleared my head. "I've been mapping and sketching shrines all around this area, trying to find out more about them, and about the Penitentes, but the locals don't much want to talk to a white girl like me."

Regan perched on the edge of one of the sofas, but she didn't allow herself to sink in—or to sit still. She fidgeted nervously with the arrangement of the art books. "You're doing a book about the brotherhood? I'm sure that must be very difficult. They're very enigmatic, those Penitentes. They don't want anyone knowing what they're up to, although there aren't many of the crazy old fools left anymore to keep their secrets." She twisted her tea mug around and around in her hands.

"I don't need to know their secrets. I'd just like to know more general stuff, really. I think it's okay for them to have some mystery and intrigue. That's what makes them interesting."

Regan did not respond, but instead stared out the windows at the rio. We sat in silence for a minute or more. She seemed absorbed in her own thoughts. Then a quite unexpected event occurred—one that instantly endeared this nervous, high-strung, somewhat peculiar woman to me. Over this, our first of many cups of poleo, Regan became the first local elder to break the silence and talk to me.

"I want you to know that I don't hold to any of their beliefs," she said, raising the flat of her palm up to me as though she were swearing in at a trial, "but I could tell you a few general things. If it would help with your book, that is."

She began by telling me about the processions of Easter week. "Around here, everything stops for La Semana Santa, Holy Week. In many of the small villages, you will see several processions of the Penitentes to and from their moradas. I promise you, it is not for the fainthearted. You see, they flagellate themselves with yucca whips. One of them uses a sharp flint, called a *pedernal*, to cut the brothers' backs so they will bleed and not swell." She mimed the cutting action. "It makes deep, mutilating gashes. Then the ones doing penance scourge these wounds with their own whips. Sometimes they even lash themselves with ropes tied with tiny thorns or nails called *la disciplina*. Or they press cacti into their bleeding backs and bind it to them with ropes. I've seen them lash fence wire together with rope and whip themselves, and even ask others to whip them with this." She shook her head back and forth and grimaced with displeasure. "They march out of the morada in a procession, whipping themselves. They go back to the morada for nursing and cleansing with rosemary water. Again, they march and whip themselves. Over and over and over. A Penitente will sometimes walk on his bare knees for hundreds of yards in beds of razor-sharp cacti. Others half carry, half drag huge crosses that are half again their weight and height up the side of the mountain to the Calvario—the place where they reenact the crucifixion. In the old days, if one of them died in these rituals, his death was like a sacred event," she said, raising both palms toward the heavens in a pantomime of praise. "If he survived, his sins were forgiven, and he was absolved from worldly sin, at least until the next season of Lent. They are still extremely superstitious about all this. One day of suffering is supposed to pay for a year of sin.

"Oh, my, I can still remember it," she said, her deep voice cracking with an occasional low-pitched squeak. "On Good Friday, when they would make procession from the morada to the church, we would get blood spattered all over us as

they passed by whipping themselves! You see, this was supposed to make them pure, even purify the community, or bar-
gain souls out of purgatory—making these brutal penances."

I called on Regan many times after that. Each time, I brought
her a little gift—tamales, fresh bread from the pueblo, candles.
It was clear that she looked forward to our visits as much as
I did, and we developed a kind of routine. She would always
brew the poleo while we made small talk. Then I would take
out my book and a pen, and she would have a story ready.
Over time, she relaxed more and more in my presence, if one
could ever call Regan relaxed. And her fondness for our time
together was made evident as she began to prepare for my
visits by making notes of her own, so she would not forget
to tell me something she felt was important—either some of
the local history or more of her own personal experiences.

Once she told about a time when she was a child, and
she and a friend had gone up into the mountains to an old
morada. "We couldn't have been any more than eight or nine
years old. We hid behind large boulders, watching as the Penitentes prepared for a crucifixion. This man had a black bag
tied over his head with a rope, and he was made to drag this
enormous cross up the hillside. And then they tied his arms
and chest and feet to it and raised him up! If they had found
us watching," she said, her big dark eyes almost popping out
above her high, pronounced cheekbones, "they would have
stoned us to death!"

She paused for a moment, then went on: "They left him

there—they would leave them there sometimes for the whole day, even overnight, you see—exposed to the weather, almost naked. It's very often freezing that time of the year! And they bind their limbs tight, to cut off the circulation, as part of the emulation of Christ's suffering. They bind their chests tight."

I was taking notes as fast as I could write, trying to capture every word Regan said. When she hadn't spoken for a minute or so, I stopped writing and looked up.

"You know," she said softly, "if a wife found her husband's shoes on the doorstep after a night of ceremony, she would simply know that he had been chosen, and he had not survived the ritual. No one was permitted to speak of this, and no one did. Whoever was selected to endure the trial of crucifixion was supposedly blessed"—Regan raised her eyebrows—"whether he lived through it or not."

Regan seemed lost in her thoughts for a moment as she shook her head repeatedly in disbelief. "It was barbaric, like they were trapped in the dark ages. Some fool started this ridiculous behavior—what was it? Five hundred years ago? And they were still doing it, without question, even thirty years ago. But at least not too many do these things anymore," she insisted, still shaking her head. "It was the old ones—they believed in this terrible penitence. They thought the way to salvation was to experience Christ's agony, his pain. As if they could. They believed that nonsense about paying for their own sins and those of others with their anguish." Her voice got louder as she went on, "You know, the Church forbade this, even the law forbade this. But they didn't listen. Instead, they moved their rituals to secret places and held them after dark. They even had the sympathy of some of the local priests."

"But if someone died," I asked, "how could they cover that up?"

"What little government there was here turned heads and allowed all this. Deaths were not investigated, some not even reported!" She set her tea mug down hard onto the cedar table, and the poleo sloshed out of the cup and onto the beautiful pink and white, making a pale green pool. She didn't seem to notice the spill. "You see, many times, the authorities were Penitentes themselves." She paused. "But that was in the old days. Now, thank God, we have returned to the Catholic Church, and almost nobody does those things anymore. New Mexico needs to move out of the dark ages."

She stopped talking and was quiet for a few moments. Then she began the conversation at a new place. "You know, Jamaica, you must come to mass here in Agua Azuela sometime. I think you would surely enjoy it. We have one monthly mass, usually on the second Sunday of the month. We have to share Father Ximon with Embudo, Dixon, and Pilar, but he does still make it here once a month."

She had repeated the same invitation every month, and I always answered that I would try to come to a mass sometime. But for months, I had never gotten around to it.

Now, I had come to tell Regan about the theft of my book, to enlist her help in starting again, but there was no sign of her.

And I felt the least I could do was to try to make it to mass, as she had so often requested. I owed her that much for all the help she had given me.

As I was walking back to my Jeep, I saw something on the ground beside the path near the corral. I went toward it and found a rosary that looked to be quite old. It was made of intricately carved wooden beads with a large, ornate, carved wooden crucifix. The drops of blood on Christ's hands and feet and where the crown of thorns touched his brow were the only places where color had been applied—a red stain of some kind. A larger patch of the same color symbolized where his side had been pierced. I turned the cross over and saw the name *A. Vigil* crudely carved by hand into the back. The writing had almost been rubbed smooth from repeated handling.

As I examined this find, I heard footsteps coming down the path from the direction of the barn and casita uphill from where I stood. An attractive man came toward me. He was tall and dark haired, wearing a black sweater and jeans. "Hello, there," he called in a deep, pleasant voice. He smiled as he approached, his white teeth gleaming.

I smiled back.

"Are you here to see Ms. Daniels?"

"Yes. I'm a friend of Regan's; I hoped I would find her home, but I guess I missed her."

"She went into town on some errands. I'm a temporary resident—I'm renting her casita for the month."

"But I saw her car—"

"One of her neighbors drove. I guess they take turns driving when they go for groceries together. What's that you have there?"

I held up the rosary. "I just found this on the path, right here next to the corral."

The man smiled at me again and held out a hand. "Mind if I take a look?"

"No, not at all. It's quite old, I think." I handed it to him.

"Oh, I recognize this," he said. "Regan takes it to church with her every time she goes. They only have mass here . . . "

"I know, once a month. She's told me."

"That's right. But a few villagers gather at the church every morning and a lay member leads a worship service. Regan goes to that most days. I would be happy to give this back to her when she gets back from town. That is, if that would be all right with you." He smiled and looked at me with handsome dark eyes.

"Sure. That works for me. I'll just be going now. I'm headed into Santa Fe."

"It was nice talking to you," he said, his eyes still holding mine, his lips still forming a pleasant smile.

"Nice talking to you, too," I said. "Have a nice day." I turned and started down the drive toward my Jeep. As I came back past the corral, the old mare flinched suddenly as if I'd startled her out of her catatonic state. She shook her head in a slow pendulum motion, from side to side, tossing her strawlike, scruffy mane. I think that was the first time I ever saw the horse move at all. I remembered Regan telling me that twice she had paid a neighbor to dig a grave for that horse in the fall before the ground froze, thinking the nag would not make it through the winter, and twice she had paid the same neighbor to fill the hole again in the spring.

◀ 10 ▶

The Tail

In Santa Fe, I stopped at a gas station to use the pay phone. "Father Ignacio Medina, please," I requested.

There was a long silence. I was about to repeat what I had just said when the woman at the St. Catherine Indian School—the same one who always told me that the father couldn't take my calls—finally responded in typical fashion. "Father Medina is not available right now. May I take a message?"

"Yes, this is Jamaica Wild. You know, I'm the one who used to call almost every week?"

"Yes, Miss Wild, I remember that. Would you like me to leave a number?"

"I just want to ask the padre one quick question. It won't take more than thirty seconds. If he's there, can you tell him that?" I wanted to get the name the father had given me, the one I'd written in my book and couldn't remember now.

Another long pause. "I am sorry, Miss Wild. I would be happy to take down your number and if I see him, I will give him the message."

"I can't leave a number. I don't have a phone. I'm just in town for an hour or so and I really need to talk to him. Isn't there somewhere I could reach him?"

"Wait just one minute, please." I could tell she'd covered up the mouthpiece of the receiver; I heard her muffled voice as she spoke with someone else, but I couldn't make out what she was saying. She came back on the line. "I am sorry. Father Medina is not available at this time. I will tell him that you called." There was a quick click as she hung up the phone.

Since I couldn't reach Father Ignacio, I went to the library to look for the tract by Padre Martínez. I found several references to it in other works, but no copies in the system, as I had feared. I asked the librarian for direction.

After making a few search attempts on her computer database, she said, "Let me make a call. I know someone who works at the archives for the archdiocese. I'll find out if he knows anyplace you can look."

I browsed impatiently through the section on New Mexico history and found two books I wanted to take home to study.

The librarian signaled for me to come back to the desk. "My friend didn't have any idea where to find a copy. I'm sorry."

"But he didn't dispute its existence?"

"No, he didn't. I know that some say that tract is just a legend. But I think it is likely that all the copies of it have been lost over time. You see, Padre Martínez and a friend operated the first printing press in New Mexico. The first book published in this state was a *cuaderno*, a schoolbook that Martínez wrote for the school he ran in Taos next to the church. He probably published other booklets as well. He was known for his political and religious writings at the time. But the tract you are looking for is not something I have ever seen. And if my friend at the archdiocese hasn't seen it either, I doubt if there are any copies around anymore."

Frustrated, I shoved the books I wanted across the counter and put my library card on top. She took the card and swiped it in the reader, then said, "Just a minute. There's a problem with your card."

"What do you mean, a problem?" Before I could get it out, she disappeared into one of the offices behind the counter and was on the phone again. I searched my memory for any stray books I might have forgotten to return, any unpaid fines I might have on my account. *Nada*.

A few minutes later, she reappeared. "I don't know what the problem was; I couldn't find any reason for a hold on your card. I cleared it." She zipped the scanner over my books and pushed them across the counter at me. "There you go!"

I threw the books onto the passenger seat of my Jeep and backed out of my parking space, looking over my shoulder. Down at the end of the lane, perhaps five or six car-lengths back, a late-model Lexus sedan idled, not a typical vehicle for these parts. The car was one of those noncolors somewhere between metallic fish scale and wet sandstone. Through its smoked windshield, I could just make out the silhouette of the driver, his elbow bent as he pressed a cell phone to his ear.

"Everyone has to be on the phone all the time these days," I muttered, as I put my Jeep in drive and proceeded toward the exit. Living and working in remote and mountainous terrain as I did, a cell phone wouldn't even work most of the time. The world was changing in ways that I didn't understand.

The drive from Santa Fe to Taos journeys through dramatically varied terrain. At one end, the Santa Fe Mountains rise up to the northeast and the City Different nestles in a seven-thousand-foot-high navel. From there, foothills roll away to the west as piñon- and juniper-covered slopes crowned with adobe palaces give way to red earth, purple mesas, and arid moonscapes marked by strange rock outcroppings formed centuries ago by spurts of planetary heartburn. Here, the highway travels through Tesuque, Nambé, and Pojoaque pueblos, and the descent into the Rio Grande Valley starts to level off. Wherever reservations meet the road, Indian gambling casinos sprout from the desert landscape—ranging from utilitarian temporary constructions to a mammoth casino-centered golf resort. And away to the west, high atop a precipice at the edge of the Jemez Mountains, Los Alamos stands like an android sentry, visible from as far as a hundred miles away in the clean, clear air of the cerulean New Mexico sky.

As I drove past the turnoff to Los Alamos, I glanced in the rearview mirror and realized that the car about a quarter of a mile behind me had been there for some time. I couldn't make out what kind it was because the bright sun reflected off its hood like a mirror, but its shape was new looking, low profile, a light color, I thought.

I sped into Española, slowed enough to get through it without legal intervention, and then put the pedal down again across the flat land between Española and Velarde. I watched as the car behind me sped and slowed, too, always keeping the same distance between us.

In Velarde, where the road climbed a shelf overlooking the cultivated orchards of the bottomland and the river itself, the route began to twine and curl as it wound along parallel to the Rio Grande. The sky narrowed between towering bluffs armored with chiseled sheets of stone. In the twisting turns, I lost sight of the car behind me.

The canyon widened at Embudo and through the village of Rinconada. Chile *ristras* dangled from the low shed roof of a roadside fruit stand. Hand-painted signs along the road offered up a diverse menu of cultural charm: a taxidermist, home art galleries, a massage therapist, a winery, and bed-and-breakfasts. I kept checking the mirror and the shiny shadow car was always behind me in the distance, disappearing as I went around the curves and bends, reappearing on the straight stretches.

At Pilar, the Rio Grande and the road straight through to Taos kissed and parted, and a little county road followed the river, while the highway climbed hard and fast through the mountains. I pulled over at this junction and backed my Jeep in behind a little hut that served as a rafting company in the summer, making sure the nose of my car was all the way behind the structure, out of sight. I pulled out my field glasses and got ready.

In less than a minute, the tail sped past but the car was going too fast for me to read the plate. It was a Lexus, the same model and color as the one I'd seen in the library parking lot in Santa Fe.

◄ 11 ►

Night Ride

It was almost dark when I started riding just north of Chimayo. Redhead, the paint mare I had chosen, was my favorite from the BLM stables. She had done trail riding all her life and was strong and sure-footed. Like most mares, she had a belligerent streak, but we usually got along.

Roy had been right: the backcountry was treacherous. Melting mountain snows had left the slopes muddy and the roads deeply rutted on each side, with perilous high rocks in the middle destined to wipe out even a high-riding vehicle's oil pan. During the night, these ruts and puddles froze, making the raised earth ridges on either side of them as hard as concrete. We didn't use horses that much anymore, not since four-wheel drive became the main means of transportation in the Southwest. But, unless one had the time to do it on foot, a horse was the only way to follow this fence line right now.

Riding was one of the reasons I took this job in the first place, one of the things about my work that nourished me. In the saddle, I was someone else—half horse and half human. On a horse, there were no clocks, no stoplights, none of the rigid constraints and limitations of civilization. Instead, I felt a sense of freedom, of rugged challenge, of rightness with the world.

My normal routine would have been to establish a base camp before dark fell and make planned forays from that point, doing the bulk of my range riding during daylight hours. In the remote country where I normally worked, I had few human interactions, and my greatest concern was survival in bad weather. In the areas I patrolled most, I buried caches of supplies and survival gear so that I could travel light. I chose the most beautiful spots for my camps because there was no reason to camp elsewhere. But for this assignment, I would try to cover the fence line first—all the way from one end to the other—so I knew the terrain. After that, I could determine where to place a base camp for the following night, in a spot where I felt it was most important to maintain an active presence. Tonight, I planned to ride just over five miles to meet the forest ranger at our appointed rendezvous site near Cañada de la Entranas, more than halfway to Cañoncito.

There were things only a night rider could discover and report. At least half of the illegal woodcutting went on after dark, for example. A crew of men would muscle four-wheel-drive trucks into a remote area where they wouldn't be seen or heard at night. Using a generator to power work lights, they would put their chain saws to work and quickly denude a swath of pristine forest, piling their trucks full of cut logs and vamoosing out by daylight, before being discovered. And much of the vandalism and destruction of rock art, ruins, and even fences on public lands took place in the dark, fueled by cases of beer and a lack of respect for the earth's beauty. Poachers came to take up their positions at watering holes at night so they would be ready to bag illegal prey at first light.

Redhead and I set out in the cold, and soon the sky became a dome of ebony pierced by the cold points of blue-white stars. A low bank of snow clouds in the east obscured the stars in that direction, while a weak quarter moon hid behind another patch of clouds directly above, leaving this isolated landscape as dark as pitch. The biting chill in the air promised to deepen as the night went on, and the dense, pungent smell of mountain sage hung like incense. There was no real trail along the fence, and occasionally a thick stand of brush or an outcropping of rock would force a wide detour from the fence line. The terrain was rugged and sloping. Surging upward to the east were the high peaks of the Sangre de Cristo mountain range. The only evidence of civilization was the ever-present barbed wire barrier that separated Carson National Forest from the BLM land I now patrolled.

The quiet was broken only by Redhead's steady plodding and blustering, as warm breath fogged from her nostrils and quickly vanished into the frigid, dry air. Wherever a rock outcropping sheltered the snow from the day's sunlight, stands of drought-stunted piñon huddled together like wolves at a watering hole ready to drink the melt. Thin tendrils of white mountain sage reached out to touch Redhead's legs, seeking to pollinate and thrive for another season.

My nose hurt from the cold. It was slow, tedious work, picking our way along in the dark, looking out for rocks and other hazards. My eyes had barely adjusted to the darkness. I could only make out what was immediately before me.

Redhead was unhappy with the routine, too. She balked going down hills and tried to race going up them. She stopped abruptly several times for no apparent reason. And one of those times, like a mule, she stubbornly refused to take another step. I pushed my heels lightly into her side. "Come on, Redhead."

She snorted, shook her head.

I dug a little harder with my heels and bounced my seat once on the saddle. "Getup!"

She pawed at the ground.

I kicked a little harder, not wanting to hurt her, but determined to give her the message that I was in control. "Come on, Redhead!" I said.

She'd grown deaf. And apparently immobile.

Damn, it was cold! "Okay, all right. Fine. We'll rest a little." I slid off the saddle.

Redhead blew steam out of her nostrils, flicked her ears.

She turned to look back at me, then, catching my mood, quickly faced forward again.

"You ought to be ashamed of yourself," I told her as I worked the strap of my canteen out from under where my rifle was holstered beside the saddle. My butt felt like it had been pounded flat and put in a freezer. I walked around a little, leaving Redhead's reins wrapped around the saddle horn. She followed me like a dog.

"Oh, you can move now, can you?" I challenged, spinning around to confront her.

She turned her head away but her eyes watched me. I pulled off my glove and held my hand out low, palm up. She pressed her warm muzzle into it and felt with her lips for a treat. "Oh, all right." I reached into my coat pocket and pulled out a carrot, broke it in half, and offered it to her. She took it, and as she chewed it, I stroked her cheek, then her neck. She pushed at me with her nose, almost knocking me over, her way of showing affection.

My joints were stiff, my muscles nearly asleep from the cold. I drank a little water, my lips freeze-burning as they touched the steel mouth of my canteen.

After a few minutes, the chill was unbearable. "Do you think we might get on with it now, Your Highness?" I tied my canteen back on the saddle strap, then tightened her girth strap.

Redhead nosed the ground, threw her head back, and whinnied.

I climbed aboard. "Well, let's go then." She broke into an easy trot.

As morning drew near, I had to cross a narrow, steep-sided stream. I eased Redhead down the bank into a cold cloud of mist and through the ice along the edge, and then the fetlock-deep water. As we crossed, the fog grew thicker and rose to encompass and obscure the horse's legs, as if her massive torso were floating on a thick pool of steam. I felt her feet striking ground but I could see nothing beneath the tops of my boots. I saw the opposite bank rising sharply ahead of us and thought we had made it across without incident. But as we started back up the slope on the other side, a figure suddenly loomed up like a ghost out of the mist right in front of us, a dark cape or blanket obscuring both face and form. A man's voice cried out in a horrible scream, "Aaaaaaghhh!" Redhead reared and bolted before I knew what was happening, and she threw me flailing into the fog as she charged up the slope. I landed hard, a stone smacking so violently against my right buttock that I could hear the jarring impact ringing in my ears along with the thud of Redhead's hooves and the sound of someone scrambling up the slope in the opposite direction on foot and then running away. I was stunned for a moment, and when I tried to get up, I felt like I might faint. I sat groaning and rolled my weight off of my right side. The smarting emanated from a strong, tight epicenter out in recurring, circular, throbbing waves—growing more diffuse as they got farther away from the point of impact. I gave myself a minute or two before I tried to get up again, muttering under my breath, "Great, Jamaica. That's twice you've landed on your backside in just two days!"

I listened for any sign of the specter. He was long gone by now. I limped around on the icy bank of the stream a bit, testing my weight on my right side. It hurt when I walked, but I was pretty sure it would be better if I kept moving. Redhead whistled from above me and shook her head as if to say, "Let's go!"

"You did this!" I griped at her. "Don't tell me to hurry up!" I groped around among the thin willow reeds looking for a limb to use for a cane. The bank was too steep for me to climb without support.

I whistled. "Come here, Redhead."

She pawed at the ground and snorted. She didn't like the slope any better than I did.

I whistled again. She looked at me. I made a gesture, waving her toward me. "Come on, Redhead! Come here!" I was calling her like a dog trainer, in that fake-happy voice, trying to make my tone pleasant while my buttock ached unbearably.

Redhead wasn't buying it. She lowered her head and looked at me. She reached down and pulled with her lips at the vegetation on the ground, feigning interest.

There was a stand of cottonwoods downstream a bit, so I staggered along the frozen water's edge, wincing as my butt throbbed with each step. I almost stumbled over some whitened, weathered limbs lying at the edge of the water. I picked one of the limbs up and tried it—it would do in a pinch.

I noticed a ring of stones demarking a campfire site. I pulled a small flashlight out of my coat pocket and examined the area. The mysterious stranger had evidently camped under these cottonwoods; the ashes looked fresh but no longer warm, no more than a day old. There was no sign of litter or debris, and it was a poor choice for a camp as there was no dry, flat ground for a sleeping bag. The site of the fire was the only dry spot. A downed tree trunk probably served as a seat near the fire, but other than that, the steep ascent up the bank and the close proximity of the water to that slope ruled out camping. So, why would anyone build a fire where they couldn't camp? Especially back here where the nearest dirt track was still miles off, and the only way in was to hike or ride.

Sweeping the area with my penlight, I spotted a canvas backpack. I picked it up and straightened, looking around, wishing I could see farther in the dark. My rifle was in the scabbard on Redhead's saddle. I had no idea where the pack's owner had gone, nor if he might have doubled back and was now watching me. I pressed the button, switching off the flashlight, and stood quietly for almost a minute, listening and looking for any sign of the illegal camper. I put an arm through one of the backpack straps and, using the limb for support, scrambled up the slope to my horse.

An hour later, as I listed to my left in the saddle, I tried not to grimace when I rode up to the Forest Service truck at the rendezvous point. The ranger was leaning against the hood of the truck watching me approach. His narrow hips were pressed against the front quarter panel and one long leg was crossed at the ankle over the other. He wore a uniform coat, his hands thrust casually in the pockets. Beneath his ranger hat I saw a shadow of stubble on his handsome face. Rosa had been right!

I leaned over Redhead's neck and whispered in her ear as I drew her to a halt. "You be sweet and hold real still, okay, girl?" I had lashed my cottonwood "cane" behind my saddle, and I untied this and used the staff to support myself as I gingerly stepped off the left stirrup and onto the soft ground. I could not suppress the contortion of my face as I felt the anguish that came with standing upright.

The forester came toward me in long strides. He wore a worried expression. "What happened?" he asked, arms reaching to help, moving as if to gather me up.

"Crossing that little stream back in the valley, my horse threw me," I said, embarrassed to admit it.

He took charge, extending his right arm around my waist and holding my left forearm with the other. We walked toward his truck, almost as if we were promenading in a square dance, two by two, except that I limped on the off-beat. Redhead followed us, a few paces behind. At the truck, he opened the door and then watched as I awkwardly tried to turn around. He startled me when he reached out with both hands and lifted me by the waist. Our eyes met as he gently eased me into the seat. "I'm sorry," he said, his face full of concern. "I probably shouldn't have . . . " His eyes were a warm green-flecked brown color, with small crinkly lines at the corners.

"It's okay, "I said. "But my horse—"

"I'll get her in the trailer with mine. You just make yourself comfortable."

I felt my poor backside throbbing and I was cold and tired. It had been a wretched night. I was too numb and sore to protest, so I just watched with pleasant surprise as he took a blanket from behind the seat and began tucking it in around me. Redhead looked at me over the ranger's back as he bent over. She was flicking her ears, which usually meant she was excited. That made me grin.

The man had a healthy look about him. His face was roughened a little by wind and sun, and his prominent brow was dressed with thick eyebrows that almost met over the bridge of his slender nose. His eyes were deep-set beneath that brow, and his long, thin face was set off by a strong jaw. There was a small white scar on his chin, and another narrow one under the outer corner of his right eye, adding some masculine character to what otherwise might have been called a pretty face. He was too good-looking for me not to notice, no matter how much my bottom hurt.

"You sure there's nothing I can do?" he asked. "Maybe you'd let me take you someplace warm where we could get some breakfast while we exchange reports."

"Okay," I said, "I could use a decent meal and something hot to drink."

"Let me just see to your horse," he said, "and we'll get on the road." He grabbed Redhead's reins.

She followed him like a slave.

I sent her a telepathic postcard: *Be nice.*

She nickered softly.

I could hear the ranger talking to her in a low, quiet voice. "Yeah, you're cold and tired, too, aren't you, girl? Yes, you are. We'll get you some hay up at the ranger station, how would that be?"

We had to crawl back to the Forest Service road in his truck, easing over one bump at a time, and the riding was rougher than in the saddle. Redhead and the ranger's horse had to be working hard not to get slammed around in the trailer behind the truck. I kept looking back to make sure they were all right.

"Your horse is going to be just fine," the ranger said. "Peter—he's a guy that works up at the ranger station—he's excited about having horses there this week. They normally don't have horses in their stables there except in the summer. So both these guys will get lots of attention." He had brought a big red travel mug full of coffee, and he wiped the cap off with his glove and handed it to me. I sipped a little of it, but after the second time I sloshed it all over myself, I gave up and just held it to warm my hands. I was wrapped up to my chin in the blanket and I felt like my nose was about to thaw out, but my feet still ached from the cold.

"So you're Jamaica Wild." He looked at me and smiled.

"And you're Kerry Reed." When I returned the smile, my face felt like it would crack, it was so dry from the cold.

"Where'd you get that handle of yours?" He reached across me to take a pair of sunglasses from the glove compartment.

I could smell his scent as he leaned near, his head over my lap, his smooth, tan neck right below my left shoulder, a perfect line where his hair had been recently trimmed. I could almost feel the warmth of his skin, right through the blanket.

He straightened up in the seat, put the glasses on, and turned to look at me, waiting for an answer.

I stared at him blankly for a moment. "Oh, my name!" I recovered. "Well, same as most people, I guess. My father gave me the second one, and my mother gave me the first." I looked out the window, hoping to change the subject. Everyone asked me about my name. I got tired of trying to come up with a glib rejoinder.

"So, was your mother from Jamaica, or were you born there, or what?"

"No, I was born in Kansas, but I don't think my mother liked it there very much. Maybe Jamaica sounded better to her somehow." I fidgeted in the seat. I always felt uncomfortable when the subject of my mother came up.

He seemed to sense my mood and let it go. After a few minutes, he tried a different approach: "Did you see anything out there last night?"

"Only one thing, I don't know what it means. It's the reason Redhead threw me. Some guy had built a campfire in the draw of the stream—an impossible place to camp. Who builds a campfire where there's no dry ground to sleep? Anyway, I would guess that he'd been dozing, maybe sitting on a downed tree. He was wrapped up in a blanket and it was dark—I didn't get a look at him. We must have startled him and almost ran him over because I didn't see him there. He screamed, Redhead bucked, and I landed on my behind. The guy ran off. I tried to track him after I got back up but the ground up top was frozen, no tracks. He didn't have any gear there except a flimsy canvas backpack. I didn't get to look through it yet. The ashes from his fire looked to be a day old. Besides having an illegal campfire, something must have been up for him to run off like that."

"Huh," he uttered. It was the kind of sound you make when you notice something curious and you can't quite figure it out.

"What?"

"Oh, probably nothing." He shifted into low. "Someone has definitely been going back in there for some reason. Last night, I saw Santiago Suazo's pickup pulled over on the four-wheel track north of there in the national forest. The truck was down that track about two clicks. The road is impassable, so he must have gone in farther on foot. There was no one around, and I didn't see anything in his truck I could hold against him, but of course I couldn't get inside it to look around. It looked like there were several sets of ruts there that were fresh. Maybe someone with a good four-wheel drive met up with him, and they managed to get down that road. When I went back around dawn to check on it, Suazo's truck was gone, and then it was time for me to come meet you. I don't know what he's up to this time. He can't lift much firewood when the roads aren't passable, but he could have been scoping out a site to cut from later, or he could even have been poaching. He's been known to take elk out of season. You know who I'm talking about, don't you?"

"Oh, yeah. Everybody knows who Santiago Suazo is. He'll sell you illegally cut firewood in the afternoon, then steal it from you that night and sell it to your neighbor the next day. One of ours busted him two years ago with three eagles that had been shot with a high-powered rifle, and he got off because the agent hadn't followed procedure to the letter; the judge wouldn't even allow the photographs of the birds to be used as evidence. Suazo has done probation for petty theft, a little lockup time for an assault with a deadly weapon conviction, but he's gotten off on two different charges of possession of unlicensed firearms and one minor drug charge. He's got a second or third cousin who's a lawyer. Nobody has managed to nail him for illegal woodcutting yet, but almost every time we discover an area that's been clear-cut, he's been seen around. We get reports, the sheriff gets complaints, but we can't prove anything. One of these times Suazo is going to steal somebody's firewood and they'll shoot him. We won't hear about it, but they'll find that pickup of his at the bottom of some arroyo the next spring."

He looked at me and chuckled. "You got it."

By this time, we had reached the Forest Service station. Kerry pulled the truck into the dirt lot and backed the trailer to the path in front of the stables.

I began trying to untangle myself from my blanket cocoon, balancing the full mug of coffee carefully in one hand. "I'll get Redhead—"

"No." He reached out a hand and pulled the blanket back over my shoulder, tucking me in. "You stay here and get warm. I'll take care of your horse. I think she likes me better than you, anyway." He winked and smiled.

"Well, that's probably true. But she needs to be brushed and her hooves . . . "

"Look—here comes Peter. He would probably love to do it."

"Well, okay. Here." I reached into my coat pocket. "Give her this." I handed him the other half of the carrot. "And could you get my rifle and that backpack that's tied to my saddlebag?"

"Yes, ma'am," he said, tipping his hat playfully. "Anything else?"

"Yeah, how long do I have to wait for this breakfast?"

"We'll just drop your royal steed at this here palace, Your Highness, Peter will help me unhitch the trailer, and then we'll be on our way." He smiled again, then got out of the truck and left it running so I would have heat.

I watched Peter lead Redhead to the stables and felt a pang of guilt for not taking care of her myself. I turned on the radio and let the morning sun warm my face through the windshield. I could barely hear the broadcast above the low rumble of the truck's idling engine, so I reached to turn the volume up. "And in local news," an announcer said, "a search and rescue team has recovered the body that had been carried downriver after it was spotted beneath the Rio Grande Gorge Bridge two days ago. New Mexico State Police agent Lou Ebert said the investigative team is not releasing any details in the case, other than to say that the body has not been identified. When contacted, the Office of the Medical Investigator in Albuquerque declined to comment."

Suddenly, I felt too hot. The windshield had amplified the sun's rays like a magnifying glass and I felt like I was roasting. My mouth tasted sour from the few sips of coffee I had taken and it made me feel a little queasy. I opened the door of the truck and worked my way out from under the blanket. But I had forgotten about the mug of coffee, which fell to the asphalt and bounced, coming apart, the red cap spinning away, the liquid from inside flying up as one glistening brown steaming organism in slow motion, and then disconnecting into hundreds of drops and falling down to the cold asphalt, where it immediately began to freeze.

I squatted to retrieve the cup and its lid and felt a pang as the muscles in my backside stretched. Although it hurt, it felt good to have my weight off the bruise and to stretch the muscles. And the cold air made my tummy relax. I sat on my haunches and took several deep breaths, feeling better with each one.

After I'd taken one last deep breath, I noticed a pair of brown smoke-jumper boots on my periphery. I had no idea how long Kerry Reed had been standing there. "You okay?" he asked, his hat shading my face from the now-blinding sun.

I straightened up, guardedly. "Yeah, I'm good. I'm sorry about the coffee. All of I sudden, I just felt hot."

"You going to be all right?"

"Yeah. Yeah, I'm good." I turned and started to get back in the truck.

"Here, let me help." He took my arm and held it for support. "Do you need to go home?"

"No, I'm all right."

In the truck, he looked at me before putting the truck in gear. "If you're not feeling well, I can take you back to the BLM, and if you want, we can go get your truck and trailer at the drop point later. I got your rifle. Your horse is all taken care of."

"Did you get that backpack?"

He reached behind the seat, pulled up the canvas bag, and handed it to me. "It's right here."

As we drove, I stuck my head out the window and into the wind. I could feel the numbing cold move from my face through my chest and into my middle. After a few minutes, I was too chilled. I rolled up the window.

We drove in silence for a few minutes. Then I zipped open the top on the backpack and rummaged through its contents. "There's no wallet or I.D. in here, no personal items at all. No way to tell who that guy was. The only things in here are a few camera accessories."

"What kind?"

I held up the items one at a time. "This looks like some

kind of lens filter. This must be a lens cleaning kit. There are two of these—extra batteries. I think that's everything." I swept the bottom of the bag with my hand. "No, wait. What's this?" I held up a small flat square.

Kerry took his eyes from the road for a moment and glanced at the item in my hand. "That's a memory card."

"I wonder what's on it."

"We can find out. I bet I've got something that you can use to read it."

I put everything back in the pack and zipped it up again.

"How are you feeling now?" Reed asked, looking at me.

"I'm good. But I think I need to eat something."

"So, breakfast?" He looked at me with a hopeful grin.

"Yeah. Breakfast would be nice."

◄ 12 ►

Gift of Life

"So you're from Kansas," Kerry said, pouring honey into the last sopapilla. He'd eaten a three-egg omelet with green chili, hash browns, bacon, and a basket of the fry bread while we exchanged reports and laid out our plans for the team effort in our section.

I'd had a healthy breakfast myself—a veggie omelet, wheat toast with orange marmalade, and cranberry juice. "Yep. Land of Oz. Where are you from?"

"Northern California."

"Well, that explains how you became a forest ranger."

"Yeah, I guess so. My first love was a redwood. No woman's ever been able to take her place." He winked.

"So you're not married?"

He shook his head no.

"And is that where you started as a forest ranger, in California?"

"Actually, no. After I got out of the army, I went to work as a smoke jumper for the Forest Service, in Redding." He pointed at the hash browns on my plate that I hadn't eaten. "Are you going to eat the rest of that?"

I shoved the plate across the table at him. "Wow. That's a dangerous job."

"I moved on from that to a helicrew. I had good training for that in the army. Wildland firefighting only goes on for part of the year, so it was a good job while I went to school and got a degree in forestry." He took a forkful of the spuds.

"How did you end up here?"

"There are about ten million too many people in California for me. I wanted to be someplace where I could be around beauty. Wild beauty. I really wanted to go to Alaska, but there weren't any openings there when I applied. I also kind of liked Utah."

"So how long have you been in the Taos region?"

"Four years. I started out in Peñasco. I'm about to get a new permanent assignment, though. How about you?"

"I've been working out of the Taos Field Office the whole time. Six years."

"And how does a Kansas girl get to be a resource protection agent?" He gave me that grin of his. It was like a baby's—irresistible. He grinned, I grinned. Automatic.

"I wanted to find a job where I could ride a horse, be outside. Kind of like you."

"Cowgirl, huh?" He still held the forkful of potatoes in the air. "Better learn how to stay in the saddle."

"Yeah," I laughed. "You must have decided you liked it here. You didn't leave for Alaska or Utah in all this time."

"This is a good place. Not too crowded. I love to watch the sun rise and set over the mountains. Do you ever take that in?"

I nodded. I couldn't believe this guy.

"I love the light here. A lot of times, I'll take a run at sunset. The light is unbelievable."

"I run, too, usually on the rim of the gorge. I try to run at sunset in the winter. You can see the light play out all across the mesa and down the Taos Valley and back up to the tops of the mountains."

His eyes looked right into mine. Neither of us looked away. "Really?"

"Yes."

Kerry Reed put his fork down and pushed the plate to the side, the hash browns still uneaten. He drew one hand up and rubbed his eyebrow as if he were puzzling over something, his eyes still locked with mine. "I knew I liked you the moment I saw you coming up over the rise on that big paint. I said to myself, 'Kerry, now here's a woman as good as a redwood.'" He broke into a big smile.

"Oh, I'll bet you compare all the girls to virgin lumber."

"No, ma'am. Never have a one before."

"Well, that's high praise coming from someone like you."

"You bet it is. So, before I step out of line, is there a Mr. Wild?"

"No."

"Not even a wannabe?"

"No."

"Hard to believe. Woman like you, I would have guessed there was a waiting list."

"Well, there's not."

We were both quiet now, still looking at one another.

"So, what did you do in the army?"

"Army Rangers. Got to see a little bit of the world. Mostly the Middle East, a few months in Haiti. Finished up at Fort Benning, and used my GI Bill to get my degree so I could work for the Forest Service. That's all I ever wanted to do. The army was just a means to that end."

"You couldn't have just gone straight to school?"

"No, there was no way. My mom was a solo parent; my old man ran out on her when we were young. I have two younger brothers. She needed my help while they were in high school; I couldn't just go to school. By the time I got out of the service, my brothers were both out on their own. It worked out all right."

"Well, that was awfully good of you," I said, meaning it.

"I owed her. She did without so we could have what we needed. Somebody needed to help her, and I wasn't going to run out on her, too. I figured I'd be a nice guy. The way I look at it, she gave me the most precious gift I've ever been given—my life. And she gave me love. No matter what, I always knew that she loved me. She still does. There's something to be said for loyalty, for sticking by the people you love, don't you think?"

Now I wanted to leave. I just wanted to be at home, in my cabin, in my bed, under my down comforter. "I'm sure that's how it's supposed to be," I said. I shoved my arm into one coat sleeve and turned in my seat to get the other side. "Well, are you ready to go? I need to be going."

"Sure." He gave me a curious look.

"I'm sorry, I'm just tired."

"Of course," he said. "No problem."

Instead of going home to get some rest before going out again that night, I drove all the way to Tanoah Pueblo after that. I found Momma Anna hanging wash on a thin rope strung from the apple tree in her front yard to the corner of her brush and log *portal* on the front of her adobe house. She stopped what she was doing when she saw my Jeep pull up in front. The resident dogs barked and yipped a few times out of obligation, but then quickly returned to the spot where they had been napping together near the base of the tree.

I approached my medicine teacher, bowed my head slightly as a sign of respect.

Without a word, she picked up her basket of laundry and

handed it to me so she wouldn't have to bend over each time she got another item from the basket to hang on the line. I followed her along as she pinned dish towels and washcloths to the rope.

"Momma Anna, I am not sure that I understand the lesson you gave me."

"Not I give. Old One give."

"Okay, but I still am not sure I understand."

She stopped hanging wash and looked at me.

"Am I supposed to be practicing forgiveness? Forgiving others? Or asking others to forgive me?"

She made a *tst-tst* sound. "Lesson clear. *You* the one need forgiveness." She pointed her finger at my chest. "Now, go. No more fool around. You see this wash?" She pointed at the basket in my arms. "I hang all the wash, then I go in house. Not hang some thing, go in house, leave some thing still in basket wet." She grabbed the laundry basket out of my hands. "Now go do lesson, come back when you have empty basket."

Before going home, I drove across the gorge bridge and down the canyon rim road a few miles to the south. I parked on top. Still a little sore, I walked gingerly out to the edge. I could see almost to Los Alamos, as the bright morning sun made long, lilac shadows of the faraway peaks to the southeast. Below me, only an inch wide, and green as clover, the Rio Grande—like any errant child—deepened the furrow on the face of its Mother. An immature bald eagle floated effortlessly on a thermal loft in the canyon below me, its head and tail feathers just beginning to turn white. I made it to be about three years old, finally out on its own, without parents to help it survive.

I let the wind blow through me until I was hollowed out. Then I went home and tried to sleep.

◄ 13 ►

Only the Lonely

That evening, I picked up Redhead from the stables at the ranger station and rode up the fence line. I made base camp in an area almost exactly between Cañoncito and the site of my rendezvous with Kerry Reed that morning near Cañada de la Entranas. I was just a few miles from a tiny mountain village called Boscaje. From my camp on a high slope, I could look down the mountain to the southwest and see part of the four-wheel track that intruders into the wilderness area had been using, and even a little of the Forest Service road farther off to the northwest, which seemed to be another primary point of access. If someone drove down either of those, I would know it.

Just before dark, I mounted Redhead again and set out to sweep a circle with a mile or two radius from my base.

Because my backside was still a little sore, I didn't plan to do much more riding than I had to. Forest Service land lay immediately to the east, and on my sweep, I checked the fence bordering their jurisdiction and ours. The fenced boundary stretched a line north and south of where I sat. Looking north, I lost sight of the barbwire within a few hundred yards in the trees. Looking south, toward Cañada de la Entranas, I followed the straight line of fence posts with my eyes until it became a point and then disappeared in the distance.

I don't know why, but I rode south along the fence line, contrary to my original plan to sweep a small circle around camp. It was getting cold, and the light was fading, but I just kept riding along the wire at a slow but steady pace. I leaned on my left hip to protect my bruised buttock, watching the posts a few dozen yards ahead, riding mindlessly, no particular method in what I was doing, no fully formed thoughts in my head.

When I had gone about two miles, I saw tracks cut into the slope where a vehicle had left the four-wheel-drive road and taken to the backcountry. The vandal had cut through the fence and pulled it down, then carved a swath through the brush and scrub piñon with a vehicle. The tracks indicated that someone had headed up and around the higher grade, in the general direction of Boscaje. I followed the ruts onto the Forest Service land and a hundred yards or so back in. For twenty or thirty more yards, the tracks ran above, but roughly parallel to, the four-wheel-drive road. Small saplings had been broken and crushed by the intruder's tires, and there were signs of some sliding and swerving around larger scrub. The hard freeze of the last two nights was probably the only reason this vehicle had not been mired.

I stopped and took a pull on my canteen. I patted Redhead. "Good girl," I cooed into her ear, leaning over her neck. "Good girl."

She did a little volt, stepping high to the side. She wanted to go, I could feel that. She was excited, ready to get on down the trail.

I looked back down the incline at the four-wheel-drive road, and it reminded me of riding in Kerry's truck that morning. A look ahead in the direction the tracks were leading gave me a strange feeling of internal sparks, the same way I feel when I'm tracking and close to my quarry. The trees grew denser ahead, and I knew it would have been impossible for someone to drive a vehicle much farther in. The ruts cut away from the road, higher up the mountain, and directly into what would soon become an area of impenetrable forest.

It was past twilight now, and the moon, nearly half full, was high in the sky so I knew I'd have moonlight to see by. I started to give Redhead a little dig with my heels, but she was already moving. As we rode forward into the trees, I thought I heard coyotes howling far off in the distance.

I did not ride far into the heavy growth before I saw the place where the vehicle had stopped, tried to back up and go forward again a few times, and then had finally turned around. I pulled out my flashlight and examined the turn-around site, trying to discern the reason for this intruder's foray into the woods. A long, narrow trail of low-lying vegetation had been ripped and crushed, as if someone had pulled something heavy along the ground. I followed the path this made, but it was getting too dark for me to see, even with the flashlight. The thick timber growth forced me to ride bent over, ducking the low-hanging limbs and branches. I was watching the ground for tracks, not looking where I was going, when Redhead cut too close to a tree and banged my knee into its trunk.

"Ouch!"

She nickered.

The leather saddle squeaked as she walked, rolling like a small craft over the sea-swell shifting of her wide back. I focused on the ground again, my flashlight illuminating only one small area at a time. I was forced to lean well over Redhead's withers. *Smack!* She ran my knee into another tree trunk.

"Damn it, Redhead. That was deliberate!" I pulled her to a stop, massaging my throbbing knee. "I know I'm not paying attention to you right now, but you know how to walk a trail with a rider, so cut it out."

She blustered and pawed at the ground.

I looked ahead. The vegetation was only getting denser. I pulled on the reins, exerting light pressure on Redhead's bit, signaling her to back up to a place where I could better turn her around and head back out of the thicket. I heard the howling sound again. I loosened the reins. *That's not coy-*

otes! My skin began to tingle, and I felt as if a cold hand had just brushed the back of my neck. Redhead was alert, too, her ears scanning for the source of the wailing. In unison, we turned our faces to the northeast.

I tied Redhead's reins to a branch and went ahead on foot, only using my flashlight when I had to. As I grew closer to the noise, it sounded more like human voices. At first I thought they were moaning or crying, but the nearer I got, the more it sounded like fervent singing. Ahead, the foliage was thinning out some, and beyond that was a grove of high meadow grass. I felt sorry that I had left Redhead behind—she would have liked to graze on this.

I started to cross the field when I caught the glint of moonlight on steel ahead. In the dark, I could see the shape of a long, low structure against the tree line on the other side of the meadow. Standing in front of the building were two men with rifles slung on straps over their shoulders. From inside its walls, the voices of men rose in an anguished concert of Spanish song.

They were singing *alabados*—Penitente hymns in Spanish, songs of praise. This was a morada! I was so excited by this discovery that, for a moment, I failed to grasp the irony of so peaceful and private a group as Los Hermanos de la Luz posting armed guards at the entrance to their sanctuary. When I sobered to this thought, I retreated back into the cover of the trees and watched. What would cause them to post armed guards? I had read about *los hermanos vigilantes*—

the vigilant brothers who kept watch against intruders. But I had never known of them being armed with guns. In fact, normally during Lent, the Penitentes were strictly forbidden from handling guns, hunting, and even doing some kinds of work or using certain tools. And was there a morada that was still in use on Forest Service land, or had I wandered off course and not realized it?

I watched for twenty minutes or so, but nothing much transpired. The door to the morada never opened. The singing stopped, and in a few minutes it started again. The two men outside spoke to one another a few times, although I could not hear what they were saying. I was ready to leave when I heard the faint sound of women singing. I held my breath so I could hear them. Their high, beautiful voices came nearer, transforming the meadow into a glorious amphitheater with stars for an audience.

They came toward the morada in a long procession of two rows. Before them came three young Verónicas wearing long white dresses and bearing tall staffs with crosses atop them. These adolescent virgins, whose hair had never been cut before this Lent, sacrificed their hair for the *santeros* and *santeras*—the carvers and painters of the large, three-dimensional icons of saints called *bultos*—to use for the hair on these statues. Behind these young women, Las Carmelitas—about twenty women of the morada's community—marched in long black dresses with black shawls covering their heads and shoulders. The first two carried a shiny fabric banner with a figure painted on it—most certainly that of the Virgin Mary. Behind the banner bearers, each woman carried a basket or bowl or a pot. The guards rose and came to attention.

The song the Carmelitas were singing was a call-and-response. One row sang the first line, their voices lifting as they asked a question: *¿Quién te llena de alegría?* (Who fills you with joy?)

The other row answered: *¡María!* (Mary!)

When their song was finished, the guards opened the door to the morada and the sisters passed inside. The night grew dark and quiet. Within a few minutes, the *hermanos vigilantes* were seated again and talking quietly with one another.

I made my way to Redhead, then back to the BLM perimeter, and we followed the fence line again toward my camp.

In camp, I built a fire, then removed Redhead's saddle and gave her some feed. As she ate, I brushed her down, cooing to her. "You're a feisty girl, aren't you? I'm pretty sure you already know this, but if you don't, you're going to have to learn how wide you are and not run my knees into any more tree trunks. Okay?" She shook her head up and down as if to agree. I picked out her hooves, combed her forelock and her mane. She gleamed in the firelight. I reached into the saddlebag and got an apple and gave it to her. She fluttered her big lips around it in my hand, showing gratitude and affection. Then she carefully took it from my palm and chomped it down.

I unrolled the horse blanket that I always used for a seat and spread it onto the ground. By the light of the fire and my headlamp, I rummaged through my backpack for my map, and then, using the flashlight, too, I located a thin strip of land along the unpaved Forest Service road that held the tiny village of Boscaje. It must have been the Boscaje morada that I had chanced upon. In many of the older villages, the morada was set apart from the town, often at a higher elevation. And a place of sanctuary still higher was set apart for the ritual of crucifixion. Processions during Holy Week would take place from the village church to the morada and to the top of the mountain and back.

I pulled a lined, spiral-bound notebook from my pack and opened it to write. My right hand was poised above the paper. I remembered the sound of the alabados rippling across the meadow grass in the cold air, the voices pleading and crying as they sang. I had intended to write a description of what I had just seen and heard, but I couldn't find a way to begin. And then suddenly I questioned whether I wanted to begin at all. I had tried to talk myself into starting over on my book, but my enthusiasm for the idea had begun to wane already.

Why had I wanted to write about the Penitentes? Father Medina was right—I wasn't from this area, I hadn't been raised in this faith, I didn't even have any faith.

And even more importantly, what was going on with Los Hermanos? Father Ignacio had tried to warn me that there was trouble brewing with the Penitentes, and it had even made him vigilant at our meeting. A man on a cross was thrown over the gorge bridge! And, on the very same day, my book was stolen. Nothing else, just my book—which happened to be about the Penitentes. And the morada at Boscaje had armed guards at the door. What was I doing in the middle of all this?

A sound in the brush above my camp startled me. Redhead jerked her head up, ears forward, alert. I crawled fullspeed to her saddle and removed my rifle from the holster. I levered a round into the chamber, knelt upright with one foot placed firmly in front of me, shouldered the rifle, and watched for any sign of movement. Not so much as a twig snapped.

"Federal agent! I'm armed. Show yourself," I yelled, still peering intently into the dark thicket.

I heard the sound of hooves bolting away up the slope at top speed—elk, from the sound of it.

I went back to my seat on the horse blanket. But I brought my rifle with me and set it on the ground within reach. I picked up the notebook and pen again. My train of thought broken, I had no answers to the questions I had been asking myself earlier.

Now I moved to make a list of people for Momma Anna's strange assignment to ask forgiveness of everyone I cared about. I wrote four names: Roy, Momma Anna, Bennie, Regan. I tapped some more with the pen, realizing that I did not have many people in my life that I truly cared about. I wondered if I would be on their lists if any of them had been given the same task to perform. Roy, maybe, I guessed. So perhaps even fewer people cared for me than I had listed here. And then I remembered Father Ignacio holding my hand and looking into my eyes, saying: *I think, Miss Wild, that you are very lonely.*

I got up from the horse blanket, shook it out, and rolled it up. I kicked the embers of my fire apart, outward toward the ring of stones, and then used the side of my boot to push dirt over the top of the stones. I emptied part of one of my canteens over it all to extinguish all the live fire. "Come on, Redhead," I said, as I picked up her saddle. "We're going back on patrol."

I wasn't the one who spotted Santiago Suazo in our section. I had spent the night pretty close to my base camp, making only short forays. In the morning, I had broken camp, and was riding Redhead down to the Forest Service road, when I saw Kerry Reed's truck speeding up to where I had parked the truck and horse trailer. He got to me before I could load Redhead in.

"Suazo just eluded me again!" He whomped the back door of the trailer with the side of his fist in frustration. "I spotted his truck down by some off-road tracks. He saw me coming and blazed off down the four-wheel-drive road. I had to backtrack quite a ways before I found a safe place to turn around, and by the time I did, he was long gone. He had to have lost his oil pan, the way he was driving."

"Yeah, well, you know Suazo. He probably keeps baling wire and duct tape on hand for wiring up mufflers and taping up holes in things to get him down to the next village where his cousin or someone has a welder." I thought for a moment. "Just curious—was Suazo on your side of the fence or mine?"

"Yours." He shook his head, still chagrined, his lips pressed into a tight little frown.

"That's funny. I rode over that piece early last night. I can't imagine what he's doing in there. He can't be getting wood out; there's only scrub on this side of the fence line. And we would have heard him if he was cutting."

"I don't know what he's doing either, but it can't be anything good."

"So you think it was Suazo who cut down that section of fence?"

"I don't know, but if he didn't, he knows who did. You remember, his truck was pulled over a good ways west of there the other night, like he knew better than to try to drive on any farther or he would have gotten stuck. But he wasn't with his truck, and that fence wasn't down the night before that when I checked it. It's a safe bet that Suazo was back in there on foot or some other way then, since he wasn't in his truck."

"Why don't we go pay him a friendly visit?"

"You mean go to his house?"

"Why not? We'll make it official. We're conducting an investigation into vandalism and destruction of federal lands. And we're off for the weekend now. If we don't go intimidate him, he'll just come back tonight and get away with whatever it is he's doing while no one is here. I'll make a courtesy call to the sheriff's department to let them know before we go."

"We can go, but he's not going to tell us anything. And he's not easily intimidated; laws don't mean a thing to that guy. He always finds a way to weasel out of whatever he gets himself into. I don't think it's going to deter him one bit to see us at his place."

"I want to find out what he's doing up by the Boscaje morada," I said. "I think he was headed up there."

"I'm guessing there's no chance that he could be a member there."

"No, trust me, Santiago Suazo doesn't have a penitent bone in his body. But we might find out something by seeing him on his own turf, whether he's willing to talk or not. And I do think it would rattle him."

"Okay, then, I'm game if you are."

"I have an appointment I have to keep first," I said. "Let's meet about noon at the BLM."

I called the sheriff's office to make what is known as a "courtesy call" from one agent or officer to another. Technically, I had no authority outside of BLM land, and even there, only for the purposes of resource protection. But, as a courtesy, I was commonly permitted to question anyone with respect to issues related to my jurisdiction, provided that I informed the local law enforcement agency of my intent to do so. I asked for Deputy Padilla, hoping to find out if they had made an identification of the body on the cross and if there had been any developments in the case. But Jerry Padilla was not in, and I had to leave my courtesy advisement that Kerry and I would be going by Suazo's house with the dispatcher.

◂ 14 ▸

Number Six

When I pulled up at the Golden Gecko, the parking lot was full. The front door had been propped open with a large rock. Bennie was outside trying to coordinate as a half-dozen women loaded clothes racks and garment bags into the club.

"Hey, kiddo," she said when she saw me get out of my car, "could I talk to you for just a second?"

"Sure, what's up?"

Bennie scratched her head. "I just want to say thanks. For doing this, I mean."

"Yeah, you'll never be able to play the wounded bear card again after this, I'm warning you."

She laughed. "It was the only way I could get you to do it. You know I'm right."

"True. Listen, Bennie, I . . . "

"What?"

Inside the Gecko, the band began checking their instruments through the sound system, and the noise blasted out the open front door of the club, the bass booming, a saxophone honking, cymbals crashing—nothing coordinated—each of them producing clamor at once. I had to raise my voice to be heard over the cacophony. "I . . . if I've ever hurt you or offended you, I want to ask for your forgiveness."

Bennie squinted at me, as if she was trying to see me better. She had to shout over the din. "What on earth are you talking about?"

"I'm talking about forgiveness," I shouted back.

Bennie shook her head and put a finger in her ear and twisted it. "Look, kiddo, it sounds like they're ready to start. You better go get into your outfit."

The lights on the stage changed from red to blue to yellow, and spots came on and went off as the technician tested his lighting sets. A dozen young women bustled around with cosmetic bags and hatboxes. A woman named Wynetta was in charge, and she wielded a clipboard to prove it. She wore enormous, red-rimmed glasses with a beaded chain on them. "Who are you?" She looked at me, then at the clipboard in her hand, as if the answer might be there.

"I'm Jamaica. Bennie asked me to fill in for the girl who—"

"I see," she said, pulling her glasses down slightly with one hand and scanning me up and down over the tops of them. "Were you going to get your hair done this afternoon before the show tonight?"

"My hair?"

She shook her head back and forth. "Well, you can't go on like that. Do you have an appointment to get it styled today?"

"No. This is how I wear my hair."

She raised her chin up now and looked down through the big lenses at me, her lips pushed out in a disapproving pucker. "Well, this is not how we wear our hair in this fashion show. We'll have a wig backstage for you tonight. Did you bring some heels?"

I gave a little snort. "I don't wear heels."

She widened her eyes. "You don't wear heels?"

"No."

Just then, Bennie—who had been watching from the sidelines—interceded. "Jamaica has probably got some cute cowgirl boots. That would be more her style. You have some cowgirl boots, don't you, kiddo?"

"You want me to wear western boots with a nightgown or pajamas?"

Wynetta laughed out loud. "Pajamas? You'll find the ensemble you're wearing over on that rack." She pointed a pen. "You're number six."

There were only a few garment bags left. I found the one with a tag with the number six on it and took it off the rack.

"Come on, Jamaica," Bennie said. "I'll show you which dressing room you're in."

In the dressing room, a whole lot more undressing was going on than what the name indicated. There were twelve models in the show, and half were assigned to each of the club's two large backstage rooms. I worked my way down the aisle, meeting a few of the other gals as I went, and found myself a spot at the long counter in front of the aging mirror. I laid the garment bag on the counter and unzipped it. Inside, I found a black leather bustier that laced up over a wide opening in the front and a tiny V-shaped item made of black see-through lace with some strategically placed bits of the same leather as the bustier was made from. "Bennie!" I yelled.

She came running. "Now, Jamaica, it's only for this one day. Just rehearsal now and for an hour or so tonight."

"You expect me to wear this?" I held up the thong. There wasn't enough fabric in the thing to blanket a butterfly.

"Just put it on. Let's see how you look."

"I thought I would be wearing a nightgown. Or shorty pajamas. I didn't agree to trounce around with my behind exposed in a roomful of people!"

Right then, the band struck up a rocking rhythm out front, and Ailsa Ten's distinctive bass drove the beat. The music was so loud that the mirror on the wall vibrated. The girls in the dressing room began to swing their hips and snap their fingers. Knowing there was no way we could continue our conversation over the band's high-decibel din, Bennie looked at me with a pleading expression and mouthed the words *Remember the bear*.

I wasn't the only one with a backside in plain sight. During a lull in the music, Wynetta instructed us all to line up by number and I counted five of us with derrieres on display. Of course, the other seven made up for what wasn't exposed in the back by having more flesh uncovered in front. The other girls wore elaborate jewelry, strappy stiletto heels, scarves, tiaras, and other accessories, as if they were all dressed for the prom. I noticed the tan line where I wore my watch, how naked my bare feet looked without polish on the toenails like the other girls had.

Ernie, the sound and lights technician, came by and made notes on his own clipboard, determining what color lighting to use based on the color of our lingerie. When he got to me, he said, "Okay, number six. You're blonde wearing black." He looked me over. "Is that a tattoo?"

"What?"

"On your . . . uh . . . you know, back . . . there."

Wynetta hurried over and gave a big gasp. "Is that a bruise?"

I tried to look over my shoulder but couldn't see what all the fuss was about. "Probably," I said. "Is it on the right side?"

Ernie didn't speak, but with wide eyes, he nodded yes.

"My horse threw me—"

"This just won't do!" Wynetta threw up her hands. "You'll have to put some makeup on that tonight to cover that up."

"I'd rather put some clothes on it to cover it up," I said.

Wynetta gave me a seething look. "These lingerie ensembles," she said, pronouncing each word with a brief pause afterward for emphasis, "were provided by a prominent designer from his Dallas showroom. We do not have time to get another outfit for you before the show tonight." She looked down at my bare feet. "You'll be wearing boots, right?"

"Sure."

"Do you have makeup?"

"A little."

"Never mind. We'll find some. And we'll see if we can get you a rope or something to carry at the hip."

We ran through the program twice, Wynetta referring to each of us by number instead of by name. She coached us to place one foot exactly in front of the other when we walked, and to take long strides, thereby emphasizing the swinging of our hips. This was actually much harder than I ever could have imagined, and I had to concentrate intently to time my steps so that I made it to the points on the stage on cue.

"Number Six with the bruise!" she shouted as I tried my first stroll across the stage. "Do you think you could try walking on the balls of your feet, just so we can imagine what it would look like if you weren't barefoot like a peasant?"

One at a time, we entered stage left, walked to down-stage center, posed, turned around and paused for the back view, then turned front again and waited for a cue in the music. Then we walked to center stage, posed again front, turned and posed back, and then front again. After all that, we sauntered across to stage right and exited into the wings. Six of us then crossed behind the curtain to stage left again and waited. When Number Twelve had completed her solo routine, we all entered together, half from each side, doing a brief ensemble routine, during which Ailsa Ten and the Decade performed a smoking version of Bob Marley's "One Love."

After a time—perhaps because of the infectious beat of the music, but surely also because every other girl in the show was equally exposed and the only man in the club was Ernie—I forgot about my bare backside and focused instead on not tripping, not starting too soon or taking too long, and on doing my best to get through it.

"Number Six with the bruise," Wynetta scolded me on my second time out, "stick out your chest and suck in your stomach!" The band stopped playing.

"I can't move if I do that," I countered.

In unison, all the other models' heads turned and looked at me, as if I had just admitted I was a demon.

"This bustier thing is so tight, it's got my breasts pushed up to my chin," I griped.

The room was quiet. Wynetta pulled her glasses down and looked at me over the rims.

I stuck out my chest, feeling like the laces on the front of my top might burst.

Wynetta yelled, "Ernie, will you open the front door again and leave it that way? All this lingerie is going to smell like grease if we don't get some air in this place!" Then she looked at Ailsa Ten. "Well, go on!"

The band started playing.

When the rehearsal was finished, I was glad to get back into my jeans. I was on my way to the open door at the front of the club when Ernie stopped me. "You can leave through that door now, but use the stage door when you come in tonight."

"There's a stage door?"

Wynetta saw us talking and hurried over.

"Yeah, around back," Ernie said. "It's unlocked."

Wynetta grabbed me by the shoulders and drew back her head, examining my face. "Your complexion is fair, I'd say ivory tan. We'll go a shade lighter for your bottom, a number three pancake to cover that bruise. That is all." She released me. "And don't forget your number," she called behind her as she started to walk away.

"Six with a bruise," I muttered under my breath. I turned and went out the open door.

But she must have thought I said something else. "You go on sixth!" She yelled it after me, loud enough that anyone in the parking lot could have heard, even maybe the people in the cars passing by on the highway.

"I got it." I turned to give her a thumbs-up.

"You forgot it?" she bellowed. "How can you forget so quickly? You go on sixth!"

I held up six fingers and tried to smile through gritted teeth. *This woman was driving me nuts!* I spun around and smacked my left shoulder into something large and yielding. I gasped, startled, and looked up into the sunken eyes and battle-scarred face of Manny, the dishwasher. His two big hands grabbed me by the upper arms as we collided, and he held on to me for what felt like several moments, then set me back from him as one might a disobedient child. I was so shocked by the unexpected run-in that my heart was pounding, and I noticed I wasn't breathing.

"You better watch where you're going, señorita," he said. "Somebody could get hurt real bad." He released my arms and maneuvered around me. I watched as he went into the club and crossed the room toward the counter in the back, heading for the kitchen.

◄ 15 ►

Mrs. Suazo

The Suazo residence might have been a nice place at one time, but it cried out with the pain of neglect as we drove up the dirt drive. The adobe face on the house was cracked and water had seeped in, causing some of the bricks to melt. In previous summers, vines had grown up the wall on the north side, and now their skeletons looked like bony fingers clutching at the structure as if to pull it back into the earth. A pack of lean and sickly dogs ran up to boast territorial rights to the property, their barks turning to pleas for attention and squeals of complaint about their sordid lives as we walked among them toward the door of the house.

A large picture window had fogged up between its panes of glass—the compressed gas barrier that had promised good insulation now almost totally obscuring any view. Over the window hung a faded sheet, and the fabric moved at one side and then swung back into place. A place beside the front step had been repeatedly used to empty the cat litter, and the acrid ammonia smell of cat urine was the only welcome besides that of the dogs.

Kerry opened a listing aluminum storm door with no glass in the bottom and banged on the peeling wood door. He removed his hat and began shuffling his hands around the outside of the brim, turning the hat just slightly with each new hand grip. I looked at him in profile and felt a warm flood of attraction. The door opened.

A rake-thin, middle-aged Anglo woman peered timidly around the edge. Her coarse gray-brown hair tried to escape from a sad bun at the back of her neck. Her face was blotchy and red against the pale white of her neck and shoulders. The one eye we could see was swollen and moist, as if she had been crying.

"Mrs. Suazo?" I asked.

"He ain't home," she said, matter-of-factly, anticipating my next question.

"Do you know where we might find your husband?" Kerry said in a gentle voice.

"He's probably somewhere drunk." She clutched a tissue to her nose as her eyes watered over with tears.

"Where does he do his drinking, ma'am?" Kerry pressed.

"If it's not with someone else's wife, it's usually at that biker joint down in Española." Her voice cracked with anger and frustration as she cried. "I just don't care anymore, and

I'm not protecting him." The door fell open a little wider now, and we could see that one eye was bruised and blue, the side of her face swollen. She might have been pretty at one time, but the years since her youth had not been kind or easy ones. There was a delicacy to her features, as if she once had been becomingly childlike, perhaps even baby faced. I could imagine that her slight frame had seemed willowy or sprightly then, instead of empty and used up, as it did now.

"What has happened here, Mrs. Suazo?" I asked.

"He's gone clear around the bend this time, and I can't even tell you what it is. It ain't this"—she pointed to her black eye—"he's done this plenty of times, usually when he's drunk, which is most of the time. This time it's different. There's something going on." She used the tissue to blow her nose, making loud honking sounds.

Kerry and I exchanged glances while she did this, and then waited until she was finished.

"What makes you say there's something going on, Mrs. Suazo?" I asked.

She looked past us into the yard, as if she were speaking to the trees. "He says he's really struck it rich, that this time, he's really hit pay dirt. He has, too. I looked in his pocket when he was asleep. He had him two rolls of twenties in there—each one was as big around as my arm!" She held up a thin, bony wrist. "I don't know where he got that, and I have a feeling I don't want to know. I should have never come out here with him! I shouldn't never have left my family! I have had nothing but trouble since the day I met him, and it just keeps getting worse. My family ain't even speaking to me now, on account of he's ripped them off, too, just like everyone from here to Santa Fe. I don't have a friend in this world thanks to him. I can't even go home!" She began sobbing now in earnest.

I looked at Kerry. It was awkward here—her tucked half behind the door, us standing on the *portal*. Uninvited, and without any jurisdiction, we were tentatively holding the ground between inside and out by virtue of the aluminum storm door resting against Kerry's left shoulder.

"Mrs. Suazo," I tendered, "could we come in for a minute?"

"There ain't no need of you to come in here, and I'm ashamed of the way we live anyway. I already done told you everything. I don't know where he got the money. That there is the most money I ever saw him carry, and I know he didn't get it from selling no wood. I should have never left east Texas. I had a good job at the oil refinery there. I can't even find work here, except as a maid during the ski season, and that's been terrible this year on account of the snow not coming until late. And then, he leaves me here without no car about half the time. I can't keep a job like that. Even when I do make money, he takes it all and drinks it all up. I just don't have nothing. He makes sure I don't have nothing. That way, I can't leave."

"Is there someone we can call, or would you like us to take you someplace? There's a shelter in Taos," I said, my voice as tender as I could make it.

"No. I don't want to be with nobody, I don't want to talk to nobody, and I don't want no help from nobody. I'm sorry to complain like I did."

I pulled out a business card and handed it to her. "If you change your mind, just call me."

She took the card gingerly and pulled it in to her chest.

Kerry looked at me. He raised his eyebrows and held them there for a moment, his forehead wrinkling, his face asking me *What now?* He turned to the woman. "Mrs. Suazo, is there somewhere we might find your husband? Besides that bar in Española? Maybe someplace he hangs out here in Taos?"

"He ain't here. That's all I know. And when he has money, he ain't hardly never here. And when he don't have money, he ain't worth being around, because his mood's so foul." A little anger was creeping into her voice, and she was sounding less pathetic now, and more resigned.

"Mrs. Suazo." Kerry spoke very gently. "Is there anything we can do for you?"

"I'd tell you to run over him," she said, her voice growing increasingly bitter, "but he ain't got no life insurance, and I'd just have to pay for someone to bury him." She snickered at her own black humor. "No, I reckon I've got myself into a real mess, and can't no one help me but myself. Thank you, though. Thanks a lot." She pushed the door shut softly, and I had a feeling that more doors than that one had just closed for Mrs. Santiago Suazo.

◄ 16 ►

A Man of Many Talents

"Mind if we stop by my place real quick—just so I can pick up something?" Kerry asked. "It's right up ahead, won't take us out of our way." We had taken his truck when we left the BLM to pay our little social call at the Suazo residence.

"Sure, I guess."

"Thanks. I'm going into Santa Fe this afternoon, and there's something I need to get first. I'll make it fast."

"When do you sleep anyway?" I asked, feeling tired.

"Working nights like this? Usually right after a shift. But I have an errand to run. I'll grab some shut-eye when I get back. I'm off all weekend. I can make it up by sleeping late tomorrow morning."

"I'm off this weekend, too." I yawned. "Sort of."

"What do you mean, 'sort of'?" He looked across the cab at me.

I blushed. "I have stuff I have to do. I won't get much chance to rest up."

"Well, that's too bad. I was going to say—when you said you were off, too—maybe we could go to a movie or something." He focused on the road now.

"I'd like that. Can I have a rain check?"

He glanced at me and smiled. "You bet. Just say when."

We rode in silence for a few minutes. I was thinking about poor Mrs. Suazo and how hopeless she had seemed.

"You're upset about Mrs. Suazo, aren't you?" Kerry kept his eyes on the road ahead.

"Yeah. She seemed pretty beat down."

"Seeing her like that makes me wish I could run into Santiago Suazo on my time off," he said. "I'd like to show him what it feels like to have somebody pound on your face. Not that it would really solve anything."

"I know. You're probably right. But it feels kind of good just to think about doing it, huh?"

"Yeah," he chuckled. Then he nudged me on the shoulder with the back of his hand. "You know, you have a little ornery streak in you, don't you?" He was giving me that devilish grin again, and I had no tools to resist it. My boundaries seemed to malfunction with this guy. All my fences turned to open gates, my battlements became highly decorative entry ramps, my moats became swimming pools with neon signs hanging above them reading: *Come on in, the water's fine!*

Wild Penance

When we pulled in front of a row of apartments near the Forest Service office, Kerry offered, "Want to come in? I'll just be a minute."

"Well, I . . . "

"Come on. I promise I won't try to get you to cha-cha."

I don't know whether or not I felt relieved about that.

When he opened the door, I smelled incense or copal. In contrast to the bright midday sun outdoors, the efficiency apartment contained a soft shadow—gray-green, hushed, halcyon. I paused on the threshold. Kerry urged me in. It was clean, spare, everything carefully considered, everything in harmony. The pine bed was made up with plain white sheets and a Hudson Bay trade blanket. A gun cabinet housed four polished rifles, their stocks gleaming, the barrels burnished black. A well-used blue enamel camp-style coffeepot waited on the stove like an old friend, but the counter and table were clean and uncluttered. Along one wall, books lined a built-in shelf. Wild treasures—stones, feathers, small animal skulls like perfect white sculptures—were the only decorative accents. Except for the pictures.

Arrestingly beautiful, large, framed photographs hung like windows looking out into beautiful landscapes. There were shots of desert canyons, their rock strata a lasagna of mauves and umbers—statuesque pink and gray demoiselles erupting from them like exotic mushrooms. A view of a thin white toenail moon in an otherwise azure sky, with the Rio Grande Gorge moving like a highway from the bottom of the photo to the blue and pink mountains in the distance. Anasazi ruins in the side of a cliff. A long view featuring the red dirt of the Carson road, with green scrub growing up the center line and rising in clumps on either side, the track wide at the bottom of the frame, but dramatically narrowing to a point in the distance beneath an indigo sky full of white clouds. And there was one of a local mountain range, Tres Orejas—Spanish for "three ears." The trio of rounded peaks stood in perfect black silhouette against a red-orange sunset, the valley floor in dusky darkness.

"These are incredible! Who did these? Eliot Porter?"

"No. Guess again."

"David Muench?"

"Nope."

I turned to look at him. He was smiling at me, his face full of amusement. "You took these?"

"Guilty as charged." He was beaming.

"Oh, Kerry! They're so . . . I don't have a word!"

"You like them?"

"No, no, no. If I said I liked them, that would be a lie. No, I love these. They make me feel almost exactly like I do when . . . when I see these places."

"And how is that?"

I put one hand on my abdomen. "I don't know if you will understand this," I said, "but they are so beautiful, they grab me here." I patted my tummy. "They almost make my stomach hurt."

He laughed. "You and your stomach!" Then he reached

out an arm and gave me a squeeze, just for a moment. His arm dropped to his side. "Have you had anything to eat today?"

"Not yet."

"Come on," he said, knocking my hat askew with the palm of his hand. "I've got some things in the fridge. Why don't we make that stomach of yours some lunch?"

We boiled eggs to make egg salad sandwiches. I diced dill pickles while Kerry washed lettuce and toasted whole-grain bread. As we were peeling the cooked eggs, a bit of shell flicked from my fingers and landed on Kerry's cheek. "Hey!" He laughed. "So, that's how it's going to be, huh?" He used his thumb and index finger to flip a piece of shell at me, but I dodged, and it missed.

I picked up a small square of diced pickle. "You're not very good at this, are you?" I lobbed it at him. It struck his upper arm and stuck on his shirt.

We both laughed. "Oh, so you don't think I can hit a target?" Kerry threw a leaf of lettuce, striking me in the neck.

I looked around for something new to toss and spied the small rubber spatula waiting beside the mayonnaise jar and the bowl of already peeled eggs. *No,* I thought to myself. *That would be bad.* Then I grabbed the spreader, scooped up a gob of the white stuff, and catapulted it. It made a *splat* sound as it struck Kerry's forehead. I shrieked with laughter, pointing my finger at his newly decorated face.

Kerry's hand flew out fast and grabbed me by one wrist. With his other hand, he reached into the jar and scooped up two fingers full of mayonnaise. Even though I wriggled to get free, his grip was firm around my forearm and I couldn't get away. Despite my dodging and ducking, he succeeded in cornering me against the cabinet, his body pressing against mine and bending me backward over the sink, both of us laughing so hard we were gasping for air, and me shouting "No!" between peals of laughter. As his loaded fingers moved in on my face, I shook my head back and forth, but he still managed to paint my nose and right cheek with the cold goop and get a lot of it in my hair. I squirmed out of his grip, grabbed a paper towel, and made for the bathroom to clean off my face, still laughing out loud.

"Jamaica, you're a dangerous woman in the kitchen," he called after me.

"That's not the only place I'm dangerous," I said.

◄ 17 ►

Show Off

I was so tired when I went home that afternoon that I fell into a deep sleep and didn't hear my alarm until it had been sounding for more than half an hour.

Consequently, I was late getting to the Gecko that evening, and the parking lot was completely full when I arrived, only fifteen minutes before the show was scheduled to start. I had to park down the road a hundred yards and jog up to the stage door with my cowboy boots and a little bag of cosmetics.

I was hurrying to put on mascara when Bennie dashed in holding a foam head block with a black-haired wig on it. "Here's your cover, kiddo," she said. "Quick, let's put it on."

"But it's black!"

"Wynetta said that was all she had." She helped me pull

my own hair up into a flat bun and put on the wig. I looked in the mirror and didn't even recognize myself. It occurred to me that wearing this wig might be a good idea. It would serve as a disguise.

Bennie seemed to read my thoughts. "You don't need to worry about someone recognizing you, kiddo, they won't be looking at your face anyway. Now hurry up and get out there. Wynetta is about to bust a gasket about you being so late."

I darted out of the dressing room, tugging at the bustier to keep things from falling out. The other girls were all lined up by number, and I tried to slide into my spot without Wynetta noticing, but she turned and fixed her eyes on me like a snake.

"You're late!" she snapped. She pinched her lips together and scanned me from top to toe. "I suppose those boots will do," she said. "How did the number three pancake work out? Turn around, let me see."

I grimaced. "I forgot!"

Wynetta had already seized me by the shoulder and spun me around. "You cannot go out there like that!" Her voice was as sharp as a siren. "Someone go get Ernie!" She squeezed her eyes shut as she shook her head rapidly back and forth and drew in a long breath. "You," she said, pointing at the dressing room door, "go get some number three pancake on that cowgirl ass!"

Within a matter of seconds, I was standing on one leg, my other hiked up on a bar stool with a blown-out seat, pointing my behind toward the dimly lit mirror, trying to see around a wavy spot and some spattered paint blobs on the mirror's surface. I heard Bennie at the mic, thanking everyone for coming and for supporting the wildlife rehab center. A man's voice shouted, "Get the girls out here! Let's see the show!"

I picked up the tin of pancake makeup and tried to open it, but I couldn't get the top to twist off.

Out front, Bennie introduced Wynetta, and the band did a short blast of music as an intro.

I used the T-shirt I had worn to the club to get a better grip on the makeup tin, and squeezed and twisted until I got the cap off.

Wynetta worked the crowd like a pro, promising them a good time for a good cause, and telling the audience they were in for a real treat. She touted the lingerie designer and then finished with, "And let's hear it for our all-girl band, Ailsa Ten and the Decade!" The audience applauded, the band started playing, and I heard the cue for Number One to start her strut down the improvised runway that was the Golden Gecko's stage.

Looking over my shoulder, I swiped my fingers across the pancake makeup in the tin, then tried to camouflage the bruise on my right cheek, all the while cursing the day I met Bennie and hoping to hell that damn bear was off somewhere in the wild having a good old time while I paid the price. I blotted at the makeup to try to get it to blend in with the skin nearby.

The band kept up its driving rhythm, and I recognized Number Two's cue.

I had gotten some of the makeup on the top part of the thong. I looked around for some water, but there was none.

I heard the cue for Number Three. I could hear the audience whooping and roaring, even over the band.

I grabbed a paper towel, spit on it, and dabbed at the thong.

Number Four.

A few more dabs. I had gotten most of it off; that would have to be good enough.

Number Five.

Ripping off another paper towel, I hurried to clean the excess makeup off my hands. The audience was now creating a near-constant roar.

I heard the cue that would have been mine as I raced to take my place at the front of the line.

Wynetta seized me by the shoulder before I could get there and whispered harshly in my ear. "We had to switch you with Number Seven. Now get ready."

I took a deep breath and waited for the cue. When it came, I stepped out onto the stage, remembering to place one boot directly in front of the other, trying to take as long a stride as I could. The stage was flooded with bright light, and I couldn't see much beyond that, but I could certainly hear the audience clapping and cheering. I walked in time to the beat that the band laid down, and when I got to center stage, I paused and posed, the front two rows now visible beyond the lights, the seats filled with wide-eyed men looking as wired as if they'd just taken amphetamines. I was so nervous that my pulse was racing. I turned around as in the rehearsal, ready to pause and pose, the men going wild and whistling, the beat from the band driving, when suddenly there was a loud crack, then a thud, from backstage, and the spots above the stage went out, leaving only footlights shining up at my near-naked backside.

A woman screamed from the wings, stage right. The band stopped playing. I heard muffled shuffling, then a chorus of screams. A voice from backstage cried, "Oh, my God!"

I stood mired at front and center in my black leather and lace. The audience went silent, the faces I could make out like a school of carp, mouths open. The curtain abruptly dropped, the weights in the hem of the old velvet making a dull *whomp* against the apron of the stage.

Ernie rushed past me, behind the curtain. "Oh, God, oh, God! We have a situation back here!"

◄ 18 ►

A Talk with the Law

Deputy Sheriff Jerry Padilla looked at me with a lecherous grin. "Did Roy know you were doing this thing tonight?" A toothpick bobbed in the corner of his mouth as he spoke.

I shook my head.

"You're gonna have to let him know, or somebody else will. Your name will be in my report. Word will get around, especially about something like this."

"Yeah, I know."

We were sitting at one of the small round bar tables in front of the stage at the Gecko. The audience members and everyone in the show had been questioned and then sent home. Padilla and another deputy had taken statements from Wynetta and the rest of the models, leaving me until last.

Bennie had announced that the club would be closed indefinitely and left the keys to the front door dead bolt on the bar. "Holler at me when you get ready to leave, kiddo," she had said, her voice thin and strained, on the verge of tears. Then she had taken a bottle of Dewar's into her office.

"Can you think of any reason why someone would've wanted to kill Nora?" Padilla asked.

"Jerry, I don't even know Nora. I just met her today. I knew her as Number Seven. I was Number Six. I don't do this all the time, you know. They just needed someone to fill in because one girl sprained her ankle. Is Nora going to be okay?"

"Don't know, Jamaica. The EMT said they'd need to do an MRI. They rushed her to the head trauma unit in Albuquerque. Whoever did this meant to put her lights out for good. She had a real bad blow to the head, and she was unconscious for a little while after it happened. I'm no doctor, but I know that's not good."

"Have you figured out exactly what happened?"

"Well, you know most of it. A steel bar mounted with four of those big stage lights dropped on her as she was exiting the stage. I went up in the rafters and looked around. Two cast-iron pipe clamps that should have held that mounting bar in place with no problems had been tampered with. It looks like someone took a pipe wrench up there and loosened them, had the whole thing ready to go with a quick twist of the fingers. After he dropped the bar, the bad guy must have scooted out the stage door when the lights went out, or maybe during all the commotion after it happened."

"It would have been easy for someone to slip out. It was pandemonium backstage."

"So, let's see . . . you were out on the stage when this happened," he said, tapping his notebook with the end of his pen.

"Yes. There was a big crash, like something heavy had fallen or had been knocked over, then a lot of shuffling. I didn't know what it was until after Ernie dropped the curtain and I could get backstage."

"This Ernie—where was he while you were onstage?"

"He has a sound and light console on one side of the stage."

"Who else did you see backstage?"

"Just Wynetta and all the other models . . . oh, and Bennie brought me the wig."

"Wig?"

"Yes. A black wig."

"Now, why would a woman with beautiful blonde hair like yours want to wear a wig?"

"Wynetta had her own ideas about my hair. I think it's a little too wild for her taste. Anyway, she wanted me to wear the wig. I guess a black-haired one was all she had."

He shuffled back through a few previous pages in his notebook. "Okay, let's see, how many people knew you would be switching places with Nora in the show?"

"Nobody. I mean, it happened at the last minute. I had a . . . I had a costume emergency. I was supposed to go sixth.

Wynetta is the one who pushed Num—I mean, Nora out in my place and told me to go seventh."

"So, Wynetta is the only one who knew about the switch? Nobody else?"

"No. It happened right at the last minute."

"Yeah, that's what . . . let's see . . . " Thumbing through the notebook again, "That's what Ernie said. I guess it took him by surprise." He found the page he was looking for, flipped the previous ones under, and looked over what he had written. "Okay, well, Nora can't talk, and nobody we talked to knows of anything much going on with her." He put his finger next to something he had jotted on the page. "Wait a minute. Nora has long blonde hair."

"Yes."

"She's about your height, too—what are you, five-five?"

"I'm five-six. Yeah, I guess she's about my height. Why? Do you think . . . you think someone . . . "

"Let's look at this another way, Jamaica," Jerry said, shifting his weight in his chair. "Do you know of any reason why anyone would want to kill you?"

My mouth fell open. I looked at him.

He widened his eyes, as if to emphasize the question.

"Not unless someone knows I was a witness—"

He cut me off. "No one knows but the investigators on the task force, and we've all been working together for years. I trust every one of them. You haven't talked to anyone about it, have you?"

"No, not a soul."

"Have you had any problems on the job, any significant incidents?"

I put my elbow on the table and dropped my forehead into my hand. I was starting to develop a screaming headache. "Not at work, no. But there is one thing, although I don't see how it could have anything to do with this."

"Why don't you let me decide about that?"

"My book—I've been working on a sketchbook. It was stolen. On the same day as the . . . the thing at the gorge."

"I saw a report that you had a book stolen. I thought it was just some book you bought, or maybe one from the library. It sounded like vandals broke into your car and didn't find what they were looking for."

"No, that's not how it was. Three men broke into my Jeep when I was out running that evening on the West Rim Trail. I came back as they were going through my things. They stole the book—the sketchbook with all the drawings and things I'd written."

Padilla turned to a fresh page and poised his pen above it. "Let's see. So three guys broke into your car while you were on the trail out there. And did you say they stole your bag, too? Was the book in your bag?"

"No, they went through my bag, but they just dropped it on the ground outside my car. Everything was still in it."

"They left the bag? They didn't take any money?"

"No. No credit cards, nothing."

"How about your gun? You carry a sidearm, right?"

"Yes. My pistol was locked in my glove compartment, but they didn't take it either. It would have been just as easy to break into that glove box as it was to use a slim jim on my car door to get it open. And my rifle and shotgun were on the floor in the backseat, untouched. They went through everything, but the only thing they took was my book."

"What would they want with this book you were writing?"

"That's the thing. I didn't think I should mention this when I reported the book stolen because you told me not to talk to anyone about what I had seen that morning."

"That's right."

"The book was about the Penitentes."

He whistled. "You're writing a book about the Penitentes? You sure like to stir it up, don't you? Have you ever heard of the *reata*?" He was referring to a brutal torture reputed to be the punishment for telling the secrets of the religion. A man is supposedly tied about the waist with two sets of ropes—while his accusers pull one set toward his head, the other toward his feet, and then drag him naked up the side of a mountain, through beds of cacti and over rocky terrain until he is bloody and unconscious, or worse.

"There's nothing in my book that isn't common knowledge, Jerry. I don't know any of their secrets. I've just written about what I've seen. And I was mapping the shrines, the moradas, sketching them. I tried to talk to some of the locals about the shrines, but most of them wouldn't even talk with me."

"Well, you've got more guts than most, Jamaica. Maybe

someone took your book to find out if you did know their secrets. Did you ever think about that?"

I was struck dumb for a moment. "No. That hadn't occurred to me."

"Okay, so this book of yours—who knew you were writing it?"

"No one, really. Except a priest in Santa Fe, and a woman in Agua Azuela, both of whom were helping me, so I think we can rule them out."

"All right, so let's backtrack here just a little. Tonight, in the show, who knew you were originally supposed to go on sixth?"

"Well, all the models. And Wynetta, of course. Ernie. And Bennie."

Padilla consulted his notebook again. "What about this guy Manny Trujillo? Do you know him?"

"Who? Manny? No. Bennie told me he was the new dishwasher. I've seen him here twice. But I don't really know him."

"Oh, really? Well, Deputy Hernandez found Manny Trujillo hanging around out in the parking lot after everyone else had left. When Hernandez questioned him, Trujillo said he was waiting to see if you were all right."

"Me? I don't even know him! We've never even been introduced. I just came in looking for Bennie earlier this week, and he was in the kitchen. And then . . . " I paused.

"And then?" Jerry prompted.

"And then I bumped into Manny when I was leaving after

rehearsal this morning. I had just stepped out the door. I'm sure he heard Wynetta yell at me that I would go on sixth. Of course half the county probably heard it—Wynetta yelled it two or three times at the top of her lungs."

Jerry got up and picked up the keys off the bar. He went to the front door, unlocked it, and swung it open. "Hey, Tony! Did you let that Trujillo guy go home?" There was a pause. "I think we better go get him. I'm almost done here."

He came back, sat down, looked at me as if he were asking a favor. "Can you think of any reason why this guy Trujillo would have it in for you?"

"No, Jerry. I told you. I don't even know him."

"Well, I think we'll go get Manny Trujillo and talk to him a little more. Why don't you get back with me if you think of anything else that might help, okay?" He was folding his notebook cover over and putting it in his pocket as he said this. He pressed both palms flat on the table and pushed against it as he started to get up, then stopped in midstoop and sat back down. He leaned forward. Two vertical folds formed like small flesh columns above the bridge of his nose, and his eyes narrowed. He lowered his voice almost to a whisper. "By the way, Christine Salazar needs to do a witness interview with you. She was the field deputy medical investigator on the search and recovery crew in the gorge. Get to her as quick as you can, okay?"

"I'll call her on Monday. Have you had any developments in the case?"

"We don't have much to go on. Lou Ebert and the state

police are working the cargo van angle. Checking at rental places in a four-state area. Checking registration records for owned ones."

"Do you know who the man on the cross was?"

"Negative on the I.D. But I guess the OMI has determined it wasn't the fall from the bridge or the trauma from the crucifixion that was the cause of death."

My mouth came open. "What was it?"

"Better you don't know any more than you do right now," Padilla said. "You be careful, Jamaica. With all that's been going on, if I was you, I'd lay real low."

◄ 19 ►

Mass

The next morning, I arrived at the church in Agua Azuela after the monthly mass given by the priest had already begun. I entered as quietly as I could and slipped into a seat in the back pew. I knew my friend Regan would be there; I wanted to tell her that my book had been stolen. After all the information she had shared and stories she had told me, I knew she would be almost as devastated about the loss as I was.

This small adobe chapel had been built nearly five hundred years ago, under the oversight of a Franciscan priest direct from Spain. Its one narrow room held nine short pews, all on one side, and the high ceiling was supported with large vigas. A little wiring had been added to string a few lights from these vigas, but other than that one concession to modernity, it remained the same rustic adobe fortress as when it was first built. A member of the village had come early that morning to light a fire in the woodstove, but the three-foot-thick walls clung to the cold and refused to be persuaded to warmth. Two small stained and leaded glass windows were mounted high in one of the long walls, but these let in little light. Here in the deep crevice of the canyon, the sun was still behind the mountains, even at ten o'clock, and it felt more like twilight than the early part of the day. A small table behind the altar housed a group of carved santos, looking like caricatures with their crudely hewn, disproportionate features and bold, brilliant paint. Before them, candles burned in glass containers. On the back wall, a polychrome *retablo*—a small painted altar screen—depicted the patron saint of this chapel. A wooden statue of the Madonna, with real human hair and a carved, aquiline nose, wore a white polyester wedding dress like the kind made for a child to use for playing dress-up. This, together with a thin, shapeless veil, hung limply about Mary's stiff form. Above the altar hung a large, graphic crucifix, the pinkish white paint of the figure's skin flaking and peeling, the drops of blood where the crown of thorns touched the brow a faded shade of reddish purple. This bulto of Christ, built with hinged arms and legs so it could be hung on the cross or used in other ways, had real hair and human teeth, giving it a gruesome appearance. The image of the man on the cross falling from the bridge flashed before my eyes, and I had to look away from the altar to make it stop.

It was a curious mass. There was no piano or organ

here, and the villagers sang the only hymn dispassionately in Spanish. While the priest was reciting the litany—also in Spanish—the local dogs began a haunting chorus of howling in the hills that surrounded the church. The worshippers seemed not to notice, but I was borne away on this sound and lost track of the service entirely. It was not until the parishioners began filing forward from the pews to take communion that I came back to the cold, sorrowful church. It felt like a house where someone was dying.

I went outside to wait, since I was not partaking in the communion. One by one, the villagers came from the church after receiving the sacrament. None of them spoke to me. Some waited for a friend or relative before leaving; some gathered with their neighbors to visit. Others lined up to use the outhouse at the rear of the churchyard, and a few scurried away to Sunday activities elsewhere. When Regan appeared at the door of the chapel, she was holding the priest by the forearm, speaking animatedly with him.

I felt fingernails clutch the back of my arm. I turned around to see a small bent figure in a thick lavender wool shawl and tan sackcloth dress. Her hair was pure white, and her bushy white eyebrows framed a deeply etched face. Two black eyes peered from under her brow at me. She squinted, as if to bring me into focus, then opened thin lips to reveal a random arrangement of seven or eight brown teeth, most of them in the top half of her mouth.

"Come have tea," she demanded. Her harsh voice made me think of a bat's cries, as if she were sending her voice out—not to be heard by me but rather to get a reading by bouncing it off me. Her grip on my arm tightened, her nails biting into my flesh.

"I have already made arrangements to visit a friend," I said, wresting my biceps from her tenacious hold. I looked more carefully at this intrepid stranger. She was misshapen. Her back was twisted and a large hump at the base of her neck above her left shoulder had the effect of weighing the top of her torso down and pushing it forward, while the lower half seemed to be turned to the right. Even though it was very cold, she had bare legs beneath her dress, and her calves looked hard and knotted, like two twisted ropes. She wore a tired pair of too-large men's brown wing tips without laces, the toes of which turned up like an elf's.

"Do you know where I live?" She pawed at me with her left hand as if to grab me again.

"No," I said, bewildered—almost repulsed. I did not recollect seeing this woman in the small church—from my seat in the rear pew, I would have noticed her sitting in front of me. Nor did I recall seeing her file out the only door after communion.

"Do you know the casita with the blue door?" she persisted.

Three out of five houses in New Mexico had a blue door—the locals believed this kept evil from their homes. They called the distinctive, sun-washed turquoise color Virgin Mary blue.

"Which one?" I asked.

"Go up the arroyo to the north," she said. "There is a little hut behind some white willows. Turn to the west just past the hut and follow the acequia up into the hills. When you see a boulder with a hand on it, go north on the goat path. You will have to climb. I live on the slope that faces the sun. I will be waiting on the *portal*."

From behind me, Regan's voice intervened. "Jamaica, what a surprise! I'm so glad you came. I'd like you to meet Father Ximon Rivera."

I looked around to see the padre and my friend walking toward me from the church, but instead of responding, I turned back to finish my conversation with the old woman. She was gone. A handful of villagers lingered in the dirt yard inside the wall, calling *adiós* to one another, promising to meet one another in Dixon for mass tomorrow, for it was Lent, and many of them tried to take communion every day.

"Jamaica," Regan prodded, sounding embarrassed.

"I'm sorry," I said, and I turned and looked at Regan apologetically, then met the priest's puzzled gaze. "I'm Jamaica Wild. Please forgive me. I didn't mean to be rude. I was just talking to someone, and now she's disappeared."

Regan said, "Jamaica, I am so delighted you came for mass. I'm having a brunch at my place. Why don't you come? You and Father Ximon can get acquainted where it's warm."

As she and the priest walked away, I turned once more to where the *mujer* had been standing. I panned around the churchyard, but she wasn't there—only a few people remained inside the churchyard wall. I walked around the side of the church—nothing but a narrow patch of weeds between the building and the wall. I passed through the gates to the area in front of the wall where the road through the village ended in a wide dirt lot. The few cars that had been parked there were now gone. I saw three people walking down the road together, a lone man was walking up a lane to a house in the trees, and I saw Regan and the father leading a group across the bridge over the rio on the way to Regan's house. I looked all around for the old hag who had wanted me to come for tea. She had simply vanished.

◄ 20 ►

Ill-Advised

Regan held up a nearly empty wineglass. This was her court and she looked like a queen as she perched on the throne of her white leather sofa, her guests hanging on her every word. She had been telling amusing anecdotes about the colorful people in the village. Regan's experience in show business had made her a wonderful storyteller, and she clearly loved all the attention this was bringing. "So this poor couple from Kansas City who were staying in the brown trailer wake up and find a white bull in the orchard below the house. They ask everyone whose bull it is, but no one will claim it. The acequias that run through their orchard are lined with watercress and wild asparagus, even in the winter, and the bull is eating all their salad vegetables. And the couple's two big dogs are going crazy with this intruder. Well, of course there is no one to call—there is no 'Animal Control' like in the city. Every time the couple tries to go down in their orchard, the bull charges them. This goes on for a few weeks, and finally one day, little Gilberto—Augustus's son—takes a willow switch and herds the bull out of the orchard. The gringa from Kansas City confronts the boy. 'If that is your bull, why did your father tell me otherwise?' And Gilberto says, 'He probably knew you would ask him to move the bull, and everyone—even the bull—knows your orchard has the best grazing in the winter. Papa didn't want to claim an empty bull when a full one would be there in his place in a matter of weeks.' "

Everyone laughed. This was the same Regan who had schooled me about Los Penitentes—totally in her element when telling a tale, her finger right on the pulse of the people. After a few warm-up yarns about the locals, she began to relate amusing tidbits about the guests present. One couple had brought some of their delicious chèvre to have with the wine, and Regan told about when they had tried to make extra income giving goat-walking adventures to rich Santa Fe women. "These two would pack their goats down with gourmet food, linens, tableware, and even little cushions to sit on. Then they would lead a bunch of wealthy women on a hike up to twelve thousand feet, serve them lunch from the goat packs, and listen to those ladies whine about broken nails and blistered feet all the way back down the mountain." Regan laughed, and so did her guests. Then she turned to me and tilted her head, trying to decide what she would tell the others. "And Jamaica has taken on her own unique New Mexico adventure. This young woman is working on a book of drawings and stories about the Penitentes."

The guests gasped in unison.

Father Ximon looked amused. "The Penitentes? Then you should get together with Ignacio Medina," he sniggered. He looked at Regan as if they were sharing a private joke.

Regan rose gracefully from the sofa and said, "Well, I'm a terrible hostess—look at these wineglasses, they're all empty! Please excuse me, everyone. I'm off to the cocina for more wine. I'll be right back to fill your glasses."

To Father Ximon, I said, "I have talked to Father Ignacio."

"Well, then, you probably know all there is to know about the subject." He chuckled, but his sarcasm cut like acid. His blue eyes looked hard, like marbles.

"I don't get it," I said. "What's so funny?"

Before the padre could answer, the French doors at the back of Regan's house opened and the good-looking renter from Regan's casita with whom I had talked earlier that week came in. Regan peeked around the kitchen door to see who had just arrived, then hurried across the room to take his arm. "Oh! Look here, everybody, this is my guest in the casita, Andy Vincent. Andy's from Los Angeles."

Andy swept the room with a glance, his eyes widening when he got to me. The gesture was so subtle, I almost wasn't sure whether he had done it or I had imagined it. In the midst of this group, this well-dressed, fifty-something man seemed an outsider—more polished, his look a little contrived. His black hair was feathered with a few perfectly matched wisps of gray, his shoulders broad from faithful sessions at the gym, and beneath the drape of his clothes he looked lean and hard, like a runner.

Regan introduced each of us, beginning with the priest. As she presented her guests, she spoke loud and fast, as if she were nervous that she might forget a name. Andy Vincent appeared not to notice this and was charming and well mannered.

Until now, all eyes and ears had been on Regan. But as she made the introductions, she seemed to grow smaller and fade into the background. And this commanding newcomer—full of exotic intrigue—took center stage.

When they came to me, Andy Vincent engaged my eyes. "Miss Wild and I have already met one another, but we did not have the privilege of an introduction then. It's very nice to meet you, Miss Wild," he said.

"It's Jamaica. Nice to meet you, too, Andy."

When the introductions were finished, Regan went back to the cocina for the wine. I got up as discreetly as I could and went to join her.

Regan set the bottle she was about to uncork on the counter. "Jamaica, I'm sorry I put you on the spot out there. I didn't know it was going to go that way when I mentioned your book." She placed her palm on my back, patted me several times, and then began rubbing between my shoulder blades as if to comfort me. I could feel her hand quivering.

"I want to talk to you about my book in a minute, but

first—since we're alone—let me say something real quick that I need to say."

She stopped rubbing and looked at me.

"Regan, if I have ever done anything to hurt or offend you, I want to ask your forgiveness."

My hostess surprised me when her eyes grew moist with tears. Her lower lip trembled, and she reached out with her hand and squeezed my arm. "My dear, that is so touching. I am honored that you cared enough about me to say something like that. Of course, no forgiveness is necessary, but that is a lovely custom. Especially for Lent."

Before I could raise the matter of my book again, we were interrupted. "I thought I heard something about there being wine at this affair," Andy said, leaning against the door frame at the entry to the cocina. The light behind him gave an auralike glow to his large, lean frame, his face in shadow. He tucked his thumbs into his pants pockets so that his fingers hung in front of them, and I could see two thin gold bands, one each on the fourth and fifth fingers of his right hand. I caught a faint whiff of citrusy aftershave. His hair gleamed. I stared at him, intrigued. "Regan, you're in here keeping Jamaica all to yourself. That's not fair." He looked at Regan, but he came toward me. He picked up the corkscrew and wine bottle from the counter and deftly removed the cork. "Where's your glass?" he said to me.

"I'm having tea."

"Tea? You don't care for the wine?"

"I don't drink."

"Jamaica loves the local poleo," Regan said. "I always make that for her when she comes." She took the opened bottle of wine from her renter. "I better take this out there before all my guests get parched and go home," she said and scurried away.

"I hear you're doing some kind of book about the Penitentes," Andy said.

"I *was* doing a sketchbook. My book was stolen."

"Stolen? How? When?" His face showed genuine concern.

"Last week. Three guys. They went through my Jeep. I—"

He interrupted again: "But why would they steal your book?"

"I don't know. All I know is they took it."

"Well, that's about the lousiest thing I ever heard of. You kept a copy somewhere, I'm sure?"

"No, I didn't keep a copy. It was all pretty much hand-drawn and handwritten, some of it typed using an old type-writer. I lead a pretty low-tech life."

"Wow, that's too bad, I'm so sorry." He put the cork he'd been holding on the counter.

"What brings you here to New Mexico?" I asked, eager to change the subject.

"I'm an art dealer. I'm here on a buying trip."

"Well, there's plenty of art around here. Every other house in New Mexico is a gallery."

"That's what I hear."

"Are you looking for any kind of art in particular?"

"No, nothing in particular. I buy what I like. Perhaps you

can recommend an artist, or even show me your favorite gallery?" His eyes met mine.

I pulled my gaze away from Andy Vincent. I had felt ill at ease the whole time I'd been at this brunch, and I was also feeling the exhaustion of too much anxiety and too little sleep. After what had happened to Nora the night before, I had gone to bed with my pistol under my pillow and my shotgun on the floor beside me. I had been unable to rest, mulling over every moment I could remember from the past week, trying to make sense of the series of strange events. I wouldn't even have come to mass today, but I had wanted to tell Regan about the book. I guess I also had hoped that the mass might distract me, maybe even inspire me to write again. Instead, with that garish life-size crucifix hanging above the altar, it had left me feeling even more off balance.

"All this talk about your book has upset you." Andy's voice called me back to the present.

"I've just had a hard week."

"Well, then maybe you need to have a little fun this afternoon!" He smiled.

"I think I'm even too tired to have fun," I said. I started to move around him and go toward the door.

"Wait." He took my elbow gently and stopped me, leaning in front of me so he could see my face. "We could get out of here—just take a drive or something. Something easy, laidback." His eyes revealed a hint of desperation.

I hated to rebuff him, but my head was starting to pound. "No, thanks. I think I need to go home and get some rest," I said, and I turned and went back to the party. He followed me.

"Andy, did you and Jamaica get acquainted?" Regan asked, coming toward us.

"I think Jamaica is too tired," Andy said. "Even my considerable charms did not get her to talk much with me." He smiled, but he looked chagrined.

"I really am tired," I said, "and I don't mean to be rude, but I think I ought to go. Thank you for inviting me, Regan." I squeezed her arm. "Mass was an extraordinary experience." I shifted my look to Andy Vincent. "Perhaps we'll see one another again before you go," I said.

"Maybe we can have dinner sometime? I am staying through the end of the month, and possibly a day or so after that." He looked from me to Regan. "We could all have dinner."

"I'm sorry, I can't. Not dinner. Not for a while. I'm working nights. It was nice meeting you, Andy."

Regan took me by the arm and walked me toward the French doors that led out onto the patio. "You do look tired, Jamaica. Is anything wrong?" Her face showed concern.

I took my jacket from the iron sculpture that served as a coatrack. "We'll have to talk another time. I had something I wanted to tell you." I reached for the door handle. "Did you get the rosary—"

"Rosary?" Regan paused a moment, then nodded her head. "Oh, yes, yes, I did. I do wish you would be nicer to

Andy. He doesn't know anyone here, and . . . Well, my dear, I must get back to my other guests. Get some rest, and we'll talk some more next time you come."

When I stepped outside, Father Ximon was standing on the patio alone, looking out over the rio. I pulled on my jacket and began buttoning it against the cold.

"Have you ever seen the eagles fish in the rio here?" he asked.

"Yes. It's thrilling, isn't it?" The crisp air felt good on my head.

"Yes . . . yes, it's thrilling." He crossed his arms over his chest. "I think your book is ill-advised, Ms. Wild."

"Why?"

"What exactly is your interest in the Penitentes?"

Now I was starting to get angry. "I'm not sure that it's any of your business, Father."

He drew up at this, then gave me a sardonic smile. "Well, I doubt seriously that you have a full understanding of the nature of your subject. I think the fact that you have aligned yourself with Father Medina indicates your ignorance of a salient fact. You see, the Penitentes are considered a hetero-doxy by the Catholic Church." He emphasized the word *het-erodoxy* with a grim tone. "Father Medina seems to have a morbid fascination with that barbarous sect, some say to the detriment of his service to the Church."

I took a deep breath of the bracing air. "I don't recall 'aligning' myself with Father Ignacio. I consulted him because he is a scholar who happens to have expertise in this area. Besides, have you read his work? He's not advocating their religion, he's simply recording for posterity."

"The Penitentes are not just a part of history, Ms. Wild. They still exist. To give them attention is to fuel their continuation. It arouses interest. It defies the Church. It is a kind of advocacy!" As he said this, his voice had become harsh and gruff. "Ignacio Medina's desire to be a renowned scholar in this regard appears to have led him to break faith with the Church."

"Why do you say that?"

He smiled as if he had just announced a small victory. "You don't know?"

"Know what?"

"Let's just say that Father Medina may be in jeopardy of losing his position as a teacher at the St. Catherine Indian School due to his extracurricular activities. And you, Miss Wild—you should be careful, too. Here in New Mexico, the Church is everything. The Church is everywhere. You don't want to end up on the wrong side of things, I assure you. That, too, would be ill-advised."

◄ 21 ►

Unforgivable

Once again, instead of going home to sleep, I drove to Tanoah Pueblo and sought out the company of Anna Santana. When I knocked on her door, I worried that she would be upset that I had come back before completing the lesson. But she surprised me with a warm smile. She invited me in and we went to her kitchen where I helped her to sort through a large bundle of stiff, reed-thin red willow branches, selecting one at a time and trimming off any roots and side feeders, then slowly working the straight stalks around the inner edges of a large galvanized washtub full of hot water. It took patience to do this, as we had to wait until the first section of each willow branch softened before we could push more of the length into the circular tub—not unlike putting uncooked spaghetti into a small pot, only one stick at a time. "I make basket, these," she said with a smile. "Grandma Bird, you know my mother, she best one make basket, Tanoah Pueblo. But she only make basket next other time. Now she is done. So, I am basket maker now."

While she finished working the last few willow branches into the hot water to soak and soften so they would be pliable enough to weave into baskets, I made us each a cup of hot tea. When our tea was ready, Momma Anna washed her hands and once again went to get a folded blanket. She spread it on the living room floor, and we sat together on the brightly colored wool and drank our tea.

"I am not finished with my lesson with the Old One yet," I confessed.

"I know," she said.

"Momma Anna, I have asked a couple people for forgiveness now. Both times, I felt . . . I don't know . . . ashamed, I guess. Like I had done something terrible and I really needed forgiveness. But I don't know what I've done that would make me feel that way."

The old Pueblo woman pressed her lips together until they almost disappeared. She seemed to be thinking about what to say to me.

I knew to remain quiet and allow the silence to blossom between us. Sharing silence is a form of both intimacy and respect to the Tanoah, and they often measure someone they meet by how much silence the newcomer can tolerate.

"You ask Old One," Momma Anna said.

I thought for a moment about this. Then, suddenly, I had another idea. "Momma Anna, if I have done anything to hurt or offend you, I ask your forgiveness."

The elder smiled at me, and light from the window twinkled on the surface of one of her eyes. "I forgive you," she said. "Maybe you need forgive you."

I was so tired when I got to my cabin that I wedged a chair under the doorknob of my front door and hurried to change into sweats. I went directly to bed for a nap, placing my pistol under my pillow once more and the shotgun on the floor—just under the edge of the bed where I could reach it. It had been a long week full of strange events, odd hours, and little sleep. I held the Old One up between my fingers to look at it while I lay on my pillow. "What are you trying to teach me?" I said aloud, turning it this way and that, as if the answer might be on the stone itself. I tucked it in the pocket of my sweatpants and closed my eyes.

I must have dozed off instantly. When I woke, I felt groggy and hungover, and I had drooled on my pillow. I propped myself up against the aspen log headboard, still drowsy and unable to prod myself fully awake. The sun was low outside and my cabin was in the shadow of the mountain now—I could see the fading sky out the window near my bed. The gray semidarkness inside the house made everything seem fuzzy and out of focus. Within seconds, just as if a trapdoor

had opened beneath me, I dropped deep into a memory—
one that had held itself in perfect waiting for a time like this,
when I let down my guard:

*I am twelve. It is early spring in western Kansas; the days
are growing longer and the weather warmer. A boy named
Skip has been flirting with me all week at school.*

"Want to see our new foal?" he asks on the bus home.

"I have chores to do. My dad is expecting me."

*"You can hop off the bus with me, I'll show you the
foal, and then I can drive you home on my four-wheeler. I
bet we can get you home before the bus gets to your road."*

*We have fun talking and teasing while we look at the
new foal. Somehow, an hour passes before we realize it. I
panic. "I have to get home. My dad will be worried."*

*We hurry to get me home, taking a cross-country path
on his four-wheeler. When we drive up to my house, I tell
Skip to let me off at the road. I pretend to be lighthearted,
smiling and waving as he drives away, but I dread seeing
my father. I know I am in trouble.*

*He isn't in the house or in the barn. I think maybe I
am home free, that he is working in the fields and doesn't
know I have come home late. I change out of my school
dress and into my chore clothes. I walk out to the field he
has been clearing in the back forty. I see the tractor and
the big green brush-hogger behind it turned on its side.
I start running. I run as fast as I can, and as I draw near,
I see boots and denim-clad legs sticking out from under*

the back of the tractor. "Daddy!" *I scream.* "Daddy!" *The rotary mower has careened into the side of the tractor, and I have to run to the other side to see underneath. I slide into place beside his head and find that his body is pinned between the machines. He needs help.*

I look around, frantic, trying to decide what to do. And then I see it. Three feet away, like a fat blue snake, an arm lies in the dirt, a dark stain in the earth where the blood has drained from it.

I hear the engine of the tractor, still running. The motor is making a knocking sound. A pounding sound. Someone is pounding . . .

"Jamaica! Jamaica! Jamaica, are you all right?" Roy's voice called from the other side of the door, his fist thumping demandingly on the thick wood slab. I hoisted myself out of bed feeling like I weighed a thousand pounds. I staggered to the door, removed the chair, and swung the door open.

"Jamaica! For Christ's sake, I've been banging on this door and yelling for you for five minutes! I thought we were going to have to get a medic out here. Boy, you look like you've been drug through a knothole. Are you all right?"

"Yeah, give me a minute. I took a nap and . . . I guess I wasn't quite awake. I got up too fast. I need to sit down." I turned and walked back to my big chair and carefully lowered myself into it. I laid my head back and looked up at the ceiling, waiting for the room to stop spinning.

The Boss stood in the doorway. I knew he probably didn't

want to come into my cabin, but I couldn't have stood at the door any longer, and I wasn't sure I could get up and move now even if there was free land involved.

"Well, your being sick kind of changes things, but I don't really know how to sort it out yet. Jerry Padilla called me at home and said he wanted to talk with you. He couldn't find a phone number for you, and wanted to know how to find you, said he needs to question you. I told him you didn't have a phone, but I would have you meet him at the BLM at seventeen hundred hours. He won't tell me what it's about. Do you want me to tell him you're sick and can't come?"

I sat up straight in the chair. "No, Boss, I'll be fine. I'm not sick, just tired. I'll get changed in just a second, and I'll come."

When I got to the BLM, Deputy Sheriff Jerry Padilla was waiting in the lobby. I asked him to come to the employee break room with me and I started a pot of coffee.

"Man, you look worn out. You getting any sleep?" he asked.

"No, I haven't had much sleep this week."

"Well, drinking coffee this late in the day isn't going to help."

"You're probably right. My timing stinks. I'm trying to wake up so I can talk to you, but I need to go home right after this and go to bed. I guess I won't have any coffee after all. Do you want some?"

"Sure, I'll have a cup. Listen, there's a new twist. We have a positive I.D. on the body that went over the bridge on the cross on Wednesday. Hey, you probably ought to sit down, Jamaica; you don't look so good."

I took a chair.

"It's a priest, guy we think you might know, name is Father Ignacio Medina."

"Father Ignacio? But—no! How can he . . . "

Jerry sat quietly and didn't speak, watching me.

I grabbed the front of my shirt and wadded up a fistful of the cloth. "I can't believe . . . " I felt short of air. "My book . . . "

"This the priest that was helping you with your book?"

I nodded my head. I felt like I should cry, anything, but I was going numb inside instead.

Jerry continued to watch me. After a minute or so, he reached in his pocket and took out his notebook. He opened it on the table and thumbed to a page filled with writing in black ink. Then he looked up at me again. "The reason I wanted to talk to you is to find out why you were trying to reach him at the Indian school in Santa Fe on Thursday afternoon."

I didn't speak.

Jerry's eyes studied my face, but now he looked down at the notebook. "Woman at the school says, let's see . . . " He consulted his notes. " . . . Says you called at about one o'clock that afternoon."

My skin was tingling, as if my whole body had physically

gone to sleep, every muscle full of pins and needles and totally unresponsive. I remembered Father Ignacio's vigilance at our meeting, his warning: *There is something going on right now. I cannot speak about it. It is not safe . . . You must be very careful . . .* I swallowed hard. I wanted to feel something, but I couldn't. Instead, I spoke, almost mechanically. "I called to get a name from him. A name that he had given me before, but I had forgotten. The name was written in my book."

"The book that got stolen?"

"Yes." I went on, "It was a Spanish name—it was unusual. I'd never heard it before. I couldn't remember it."

"So this priest, he's the one you mentioned Saturday night?"

"Yes. He's the one who knew about my book, what was in it. In fact, he was the only one who had ever actually seen what I was sketching and writing. He hadn't really read the whole thing, just a few things I sent him. And he looked at the maps and the drawings in the book, just scanned it, really."

"And, let's see, what was his angle?"

"You mean, why was I consulting him?"

"Yeah. Was he some kind of expert or something?"

"Yes. He had written a book about the Penitentes. I read it and looked him up. He hadn't wanted to see me, but I persuaded him. I only met him the one time. The Catholic Church evidently did not look kindly on his research."

"Oh? Who told you that?"

"He did. And another priest that I met in Agua Azuela just this morning."

"This priest in Agua Azuela, is he working on the same stuff?"

"On the same stuff? Oh, no. No, he just held mass there. No, he said—well, actually, he told me that Father Ignacio was . . . that the Church did not approve of the work he was doing regarding the Penitentes. And then he said he thought my book was ill-advised."

"Well, that makes two of us. So, this priest—what's his name?"

"Father Ximon Rivera."

"Father Rivera. So, he knows about your book, too?"

"No. Well, he didn't. I mean he didn't until Regan announced that I was writing it."

"Regan?"

"Regan Daniels. She's a friend of mine."

"Regan Daniels," he said, as he wrote the name in his notebook. "So, let's see, she's the woman from Agua Azuela you mentioned, and the priest from Santa Fe—that'd be the late Father Medina—they were the only ones who knew what the book was about."

"Right."

"So you don't think she could have had anything to do with your book getting taken?"

"No. No, absolutely not. First of all, she is a friend of mine. And she's the only local elder who has given me direct, firsthand accounts of Penitente rituals she has observed. She's been a valuable resource. She's told me dozens of stories."

"Do you know if she knew Father Medina?"

"I don't know. I don't think so. Why?"

"Oh, I don't know, really. I'm just seeing if there's a string that ties all this stuff together, but if there is, I can't see it. So you called Father Medina to try to arrange to see him again, right?"

"Right."

"But the receptionist told you he wasn't there?"

"Yes. No. Actually what she said was that he wasn't available right then. That's what she always said when I called. The only difference . . . " I closed my eyes and replayed the conversation in my mind.

"The only difference?"

"Well, she hesitated before she said it. For more than a few seconds. And then when I told her I didn't have a phone and couldn't leave a number, but I really needed to talk with him, she covered the phone up and talked to someone else."

Jerry was taking notes on his notepad. After a few seconds, he looked up. "And then what happened?"

"She just said she would leave a note that I called, and she hung up on me."

Padilla looked up at the ceiling and he tapped his pen on his notepad repeatedly, beating out the rhythm of his thoughts. Finally he stopped tapping and said, "Okay."

"Father Ignacio, when I met with him, he said something was going on with the Penitentes. He said someone was . . .

let me think, how did he say it? He said someone was trying to 'steal their power.' And I think he was . . . I don't know, expecting something to happen. He kept watching the door. He told me it wasn't safe. He said no one trusts anyone, and no one would trust me."

"He did, huh?"

"Yes. He kept checking the door, like he was afraid he was being followed. When I asked if he was expecting somebody, he just said, 'Perhaps.' "

Padilla bit the end of his pen. "Is that right?"

"He said the Penitentes had been betrayed by traitors."

The deputy's eyes had thinned to two narrow cracks, his nose wrinkled almost in distaste. He didn't speak.

"Jerry, what do you know about this crucifixion thing and Father Ignacio?"

"Nothing." He shook his head. "I don't know nothing. Like I said, talk to Christine Salazar. I don't even want to know as much about this case as I do now. Whole idea, a priest—well, the whole thing gives me the creeps."

I gave a heavy sigh. "Hey, whatever happened with that guy from the club, Manny?"

"Not much. Guy seems clean. He's a decorated veteran, no record. Doesn't have so much as a smudge against him. I don't figure him for it. But we're still looking into it."

"But why did he say he was making sure I was all right? Did you ask him about that?"

"Yeah, we asked him. He said he didn't think you belonged there. That was all he said."

I put my hand to my forehead and closed my eyes, rubbing my temples.

"Well, I don't have anything else. I'm gonna get out of here. You try to get some rest, okay?" He tucked his pen and notebook in his pocket and got up. "And you don't know where that book of yours is now, right?"

I shook my head no.

"I think that's probably a good thing. You be careful, Jamaica. I can't prove it, but I still suspect that you were the target last night at that club. Until we figure out why they're after you, or what they want besides that book of yours, I'm afraid that you are going to continue to be the target. You ought not to be alone."

◀ 22 ▶

Bullet Hole

The next morning, I checked in at the Bullet Hole for target shooting. Armed federal agents were required to qualify on their weapons quarterly and present their targets and scores to their supervisor. I picked up ear protectors, goggles, and two boxes each of 5.56mm shells for my Ruger Mini-14 rifle and 9mm for my handgun.

I used the rifle first, my favorite, and ran the target out as far as it would go. I could only load five shells in the magazine at once, with another in the chamber, but it didn't take me long to spend both boxes of ammo, drawing the slide handle all the way to the rear each time I had loaded the magazine, then moving the safety to off and pulling the trigger until the magazine was empty. I pulled the paper target up for review: I had drilled out a hole the size of a softball in the heart of the poor stiff on the paper, and nailed each of his ears and his forehead.

I loaded the clips for my Sig Sauer P229 9mm Luger next. Technically, resource protection agents carried a sidearm for protection from animals. We weren't supposed to use them on people unless it was for self-protection. Mine usually languished in the glove box of my Jeep. I preferred the rifle for range riding, and I was good with it, even though I had only needed to fire mine twice in the line of duty—once to kill a snake, and the other time to scare off a mountain lion. I wasn't as good with the pistol, but I was getting better.

I ran out another paper target. Squaring my stance with my right foot slightly forward, the gun in both hands at shoulder height, I painted the body on the target and the area around it with holes. I reloaded and did it again, firing thirteen shots with the semiautomatic without stopping, all of these hitting the body on the target. As I did this, I wasn't thinking, just aiming and firing, as if I were part of the gun's mechanism, managing the recoil, staring down the sight. The shell casings shot out to the side and in front of me and littered the floor like peanut shells in a beer bar. I kept reloading the clip and firing until all the ammunition was gone. My hands and wrists felt a little sore from the kickback when I was done. There was a good kind of burned metal smell in the air. I liked it.

I pulled the second target off the clip and noted that I had at least got him three times as often as I'd missed, and I felt satisfied. I headed for the checkout desk to have my targets scored and initialed.

At the desk ahead of me was a man facing the other way, but I noticed a familiar brown haircut. Kerry Reed turned as I approached and gave me an engaging smile. "Well, look who's here! It's that Wild woman."

I was glad to see him. "Hi. You putting in the obligatory target time, too?"

"Me? Nah, I come here to pick up women." He winked at me.

"I would have figured you more the type to be out cruising for redwoods," I joked.

He laughed. "No redwoods in this state. But you look like you might do in a pinch." Then he reached for my targets. "Let me see how we did today." He looked them over approvingly. "Not bad. Not bad. Yeah, those guys are both definitely dead, Jamaica. You got them. You know, I think I'll try to stay on your good side, not do anything to make you mad. What do you think?" he said over his shoulder to the target master, holding up the two sheets.

The target master nodded. "Yeah, you don't want to cross a woman with a gun, let me tell you. You look like you're getting a little better with that Sig Sauer, Jamaica." He went back to shelving boxes of ammo.

"Let me see yours," I said to Kerry, and I reached for the target on the counter behind him. He moved his body to block my hand, holding the paper behind his back. This put me inches away from him, my arm around him, and I could smell his scent again, like that morning in the truck, a smell like soap and clean air and *man*. I felt heat from his chest. I looked up into his eyes. Our faces were only three or four inches apart. His breath fluttered against my forehead.

"Ah, I'm no good with a handgun," he said, as we hung there in sensual space, inanimate. "I only fired my pistol today. I am much better with a rifle." He still blocked the target with his body, still smelled good, still emanated warm signals to my flesh. He was smiling that smile again.

I moved back a step, fortified myself with a little air. "Hey, I showed you my targets, now you show me yours." I reached out again, extending my open palm between us.

"Okay." He shrugged and placed the paper in my hand. I looked at it. He had shot perfectly through the pupil of each of the target's two eyes, made a third eye in the center of the forehead, nailed one right through the midpoint of the mouth, and engraved a heart-shaped series of dots like a valentine over the target's chest. Inside the valentine was a single, perfectly centered shot through the middle of the heart.

I drew in a breath. "Wow! Where did you learn to shoot like that?"

He took the target from me and handed it to the target master to initial and score. "Army Rangers. I was point man on my squad."

"Oh." I pushed my two papers across the counter next.

"You're a pretty good shot, too," he said, "especially with that Ruger rifle. Where'd you learn to shoot?"

"I grew up on a farm." I folded my initialed targets in half, then in half again, and tucked them under my arm. "Well, I gotta go. I'll see you on the job tonight."

"Hey, wait." He followed me as I went out the door. "How come you act that way whenever I ask you something about yourself?"

I had been pushing a good stride toward my Jeep, which was parked around the side near the back of the building. I stopped and turned to face him. "What way?"

"Like I'm about to find out that you were really raised by wolves or something."

"What do you mean?" Irritation made my nostrils flare.

"Well, just like back there." He gestured toward the door of the Bullet Hole.

"I have no idea what you're talking about."

"I just wondered where you learned to shoot. You're really good."

"I told you."

"No, you didn't." He let one corner of his mouth turn up in a smile, then tilted his head and raised his eyebrows in a tiny, beckoning gesture.

I saw the grin start, and for some fool reason I grinned, too. Then I giggled. So did he. "Well, I was raised by wolves . . ."

"I knew it!" We both laughed now, and he put out a hand and grabbed hold of my shoulder as he doubled over trying to howl like a wolf but sputtering too much to get it out, clutching his holstered gun with the belt wrapped around it against his abdomen.

I tried to howl, too, with my rifle in one hand, my handgun in the other, laughing too hard to sustain a decent wail.

"I knew you would tell me eventually," he said, as his laughter began to wind down.

This felt good, really good. "My dad taught me to fire a rifle when I was seven years old," I said finally, wiping my eyes with the back of my hand. "We had a farm. He said everyone who lived in the country should know how to shoot a gun. We had a lot of rattlesnakes. I was there by myself a lot. He wanted me to know how to protect myself."

"Seven, huh? And did he take you hunting as well?"

"No. He didn't hunt. Oh, I think he did when he was a boy. By the time . . . well, when I was growing up, he . . . he didn't hunt anymore. Anyway, I've run off a few coyotes from the compost heap, but my favorite target was soup cans."

"I see. Knocking them off of logs, rocks, and fence posts, right?"

"That would be it." I pushed the toe of my boot around in the dirt, looking for something to prod.

"Well, you sure are good with the rifle. But you could use a little more work with that pistol. Hey, I have a night scope that you might like to use while we're working together on this night assignment. I'll bring it with me tonight."

"Wow. That would be fun. I never have tried one, but I'd like to."

"You know, we should come here together and work on our pistols sometime. And I'll bring a rifle along just to show you that I really can shoot."

"I can't imagine how you could top that target I saw today."

"Let's come down here some time together and I'll show you—you'll see."

"Okay, it's a deal. But I have to go now," I said, reluctantly.

"Yeah, me, too. So, I'll bring that scope and I'll see you tonight."

"You bet." I turned and went to my Jeep. I opened the door to the driver's seat and pushed the back of the seat forward, then bent down and leaned in, carefully placing the Mini-14 on the floor alongside my shotgun. When I raised up and pushed the seat back into its upright position, I saw the back of Kerry Reed's head in his ranger hat as he drove away in his truck.

I looked around the parking lot, across the road. For a moment there, I had forgotten to watch my own back.

◄ 23 ►

The Confrontation

Christine Salazar met me at the sheriff's office. Like most of New Mexico's field deputy medical investigators, she worked part-time for the Office of Medical Investigation, or OMI, and most of the time at another endeavor so that she had steady income. After several years as a private investigator, Christine's other endeavor was teaching science at the University of New Mexico.

"I understand you knew the deceased," she said as she showed me to an interview room.

"Yes, I had met him. Once."

"Well, I'm sorry for your loss," she said, closing the door and gesturing for me to take a seat at the table.

I sat down.

Christine sat down opposite me. "But when you witnessed the scene that morning, you didn't know who it was, correct?"

"That's right, I didn't know who it was."

"Okay, then. For the purposes of this interview, I think it would be best if we tried to proceed as if you didn't know who the deceased was, even now. It will keep you more detached, and you will be able to retrieve the information from your memory without emotions clouding the data. Do you think you can do that?"

"I think so," I said. "I'm still kind of in shock about it, and I don't know why, but I haven't been able to feel much of anything since I heard."

"That happens a lot. Now, tell me what you saw that morning," she said, poised to take notes on the legal pad on the table in front of her.

"I saw movement on the bridge. A big, light-colored truck or van had stopped in the middle. Two people with hooded coats or jackets were moving around. One of them may have walked to the rail and looked over. Then they went to the back of the van or the truck or whatever it was. They were there a long time—or at least it seemed like that—they were doing something at the rear of the vehicle. I thought it was either base jumpers or bungee jumpers getting out their gear."

"And what happened next?"

"They wrestled something to the rail pretty quickly, before I could tell what it was. And then I saw it happen."

She looked up from her note taking. "Yes? Saw what happen?"

"I saw the body on the cross, falling into the gorge."

"Tell me about that."

I shook my head. "I saw a man on a cross plummeting down into the void."

"Close your eyes, Jamaica," Christine said.

I did as she said.

"Now try to run the tape as if it were in slow motion. What do you see?"

I sat for a few moments trying to get myself focused. Then I saw the cross falling, only it was so fast, I almost missed it. I shuddered.

"Take a deep breath," Christine said. "Now center yourself and keep breathing big, deep breaths."

"Are you trying to hypnotize me?"

"No. I just know we all store more data in our brains than we often utilize. Let's see if we can call this memory file up and examine it a little more closely."

I tried again, and this time, when the cross started to tip over the rail, I managed to replay the scene slowly. "Okay," I said, my eyes still closed. "Okay, maybe I can do this."

"Now tell me about the man on the cross."

"He has a rope around his chest." I opened my eyes. "Wait, Christine. I don't know if I'm saying what I saw as the cross was falling or if I'm adding to that what I saw from the bridge through the field glasses when the cross was still partly on the bank of the river below me."

"Let's try again, then," she said. "Close your eyes and take three long, deep breaths."

I did as she said.

"Now, just picture the cross falling and see if you can hit the pause button in your mind."

"Okay," I said, "okay, I think I can do this."

"What about his face, his head?"

"I can't see his head. It's like he doesn't have a head. All I see is the pale body against the cross."

"What about his body?"

"It's lean. There's a white . . . wrap or something around his lower torso." I was quiet for a few moments.

"Do you see anything else?"

"His skin—it's light. But it's not white."

"Can you look at his body carefully? Do you see anything else?"

I drew in a sharp breath.

"What do you see?"

"He has a wound. In his side."

"Which side?"

"The left side."

"Where on the left side?"

"Kind of, maybe at the bottom of the rib cage, I think." I reached a hand and felt under my own rib cage, and then I started to lose concentration and I shook my head.

"Take another big, deep breath, Jamaica," Salazar said. "Look again at the scene you witnessed that morning. Can you look at the bridge and tell me who is there?"

I inhaled and exhaled, my eyes still closed. "It's too dark. I'm too far away."

"But you can see the body on the cross?"

"When I first see it, they have tipped it over the rail, so it is in front of the rail and the fence. And it's so . . . shocking to see."

"Just try to look back up at the bridge now; don't force it too much, but try. What do you see?"

I shook my head. "I don't see . . . they're gone. The truck or the van is gone, it's . . . "

"It's what?"

"It's almost dawn. There are stars in the sky and I can make out the silhouette of the mountains against the horizon because there's a faint purple glow just at the top."

"Okay," she said, "you can open your eyes now." She made more notes on the legal pad. Then she straightened and looked at me. "We know he wasn't killed by the fall from the bridge."

"I know," I said without thinking.

"You know? How do you know?"

"I . . . I can't remember." I tried to cover. "I think I heard it from someone on the task force, I'm not sure."

"The OMI hasn't said anything about that to anyone! I'm furious that it has gotten out. Somebody has a big mouth—that could possibly blow it for the investigation." She shook her head back and forth and let out a big breath of consternation.

"Christine, that wound in his side. I never saw that through the field glasses from the bridge."

"Yes, you may not have been able to see right under his

rib cage from the angle you had up on the bridge. But when you saw the cross falling, the body was more directly in front of your line of sight. Sometimes you have more data in your memory bank than comes immediately to mind, but with some work—"

"But I don't think I saw the rope around the chest that time. I think that was from looking down through the field glasses. So I sort of have the two memory files mixed up."

"Actually, that's not uncommon either. You did well, Jamaica. Really."

"So, the ropes, the cross, the black bag over his head—was this a Penitente crucifixion, Christine?"

"It certainly looked that way."

"But I've been studying the Penitentes. This can't be them."

"You've been studying the Penitentes? Are you on the team investigating the stolen icons?"

Stolen icons? Team investigation? I remembered Father Ignacio mentioning icons being stolen. "I'm working on a related matter."

"I don't have anything official about sharing information with you."

"I know," I bluffed. "I shouldn't even be talking to you about this either. It could compromise our case."

"Get the BLM to write me a memo."

"Oh, come on, Christine. This whole thing will be over before I could get the BLM to write you a memo. You know that."

She studied me carefully.

I studied back—alert, looking for signs, a predator watching for a hint of weakness in my quarry.

A hint of fatigue had begun to show in her face. She took a few moments to make up her mind. "Well, you better keep a tight lid on this, or heads will roll. And I'm going to find out where the leak is and personally put a cork in it. So if any more information gets out, it will be you I come looking for next. Do you understand me?"

I didn't want to be on the wrong side of her if I didn't have to. "I'm not even able to pry my own lips apart, Christine. I had them hermetically sealed last week." I smiled, trying to lighten things up between us.

It didn't work. Not even a little bit. "It's not funny when you have a snitch letting out the clues in an important case, Jamaica. That is not something I can laugh about."

"Okay, sorry. Look, you remember when we did the cattle mutilations cases? You know I can be trusted."

She put one hand up to her hairline and pushed her fingers into her thick hair, pulling it back and holding it off of her face, as if this helped her to focus. "Okay. The body was probably wearing a breechcloth, typically worn by a figure playing Christ in the Penitentes' rituals. There was no evidence of flagellation, no blood on the back or on the shoulders, but there were marks on the wrists, ankles, and chest from where the body had been tied to the cross. But the body had not hung on the cross—we know that from the nature of the marks the ropes made on the body. There was also a black bag tied over the head, as is done in Penitente rituals.

That rope also left marks on the victim's neck. But all these marks were made after the victim had died."

My mouth opened in surprise and confusion. "Father Ignacio was already dead, and then someone put a bag over his head and tied him to the cross?"

"Apparently so."

"How can you know that?" I was incredulous.

"Well, ordinarily after the trauma to a body from the fall to the bottom alone, we wouldn't. And the trip downriver did even more to destroy forensic evidence and deteriorate the body. But oddly enough, being tied to that cross left the torso more intact than most we see in these gorge rescue incidents. And we know the body was tied to the cross after death because of the way blood pools and congeals at the time of death. That affects the bruising and the related marks from any postdeath trauma to the body."

"So do you know what he died from?"

Christine Salazar nodded. "Again, Jamaica, I have to be absolutely certain that this is going to stay in this room until the task force is ready to release the details to the media."

"Hey, I'm the only witness. That puts me in jeopardy. I'm not even talking about what I saw to anyone. I won't say a word."

"They had to do an autopsy to confirm. He died of an incised wound of the spleen. The wound you remembered on his left side? It was really an unusual one. There was bruising *and* slicing, as if the tip of the weapon was bent but the side of the blade must have been sharp. The knife, or whatever it was, lacerated the diaphragm and incised the spleen. Death had to have been within a matter of thirty minutes after that, probably sooner."

"But why . . . why would anyone . . . I mean . . . Someone murdered him with a knife or something and then they tied him to a cross and took him to the gorge? Why not just throw his body over and hope it gets carried downriver and lost in the reeds like that guy I found?"

"Someone is trying to send a message, either to make it look like it was done by the Penitentes or maybe it *was* done by the Penitentes. I don't know. This is a tough one. It was really difficult identifying the body. Since we couldn't commence the raft rescue until the next day, the deceased was in the water for so long that the remains went decom and had begun to turn green. The outer layer of skin had separated, and the forensic pathologist down at OMI had to do a glove to get prints. That's when they use a scalpel to cut the skin off the hand or the fingers, and it just folds over on itself and drops off, like a glove turned inside out. The pathologist picks it up, turns it back inside out, and there it is.

"But this priest's fingerprints weren't in any databases. He didn't have any tattoos or identifying marks we could make out. Bloat from the water had skewed the weight, but we had his height and hair color—his hair hadn't fallen out yet, but his eyes had clouded up so we couldn't tell what color they were."

"Dark," I said, almost too quietly. "They were very dark brown, almost black."

She looked at me for a few moments. "Enough of this gruesome stuff. You don't need to know all the details. His mother finally filed a missing persons report when the school where he taught contacted her, looking for Father Medina. When questioned, Mrs. Medina told the OMI about a childhood break in her son's arm. That matched the forensic evidence, and we went from there."

"I still can't imagine why anyone would want to kill Father Ignacio. And to make such a spectacle of it!"

"They are still keeping a tight lid on the details of this case. They had to release the name to the media, once they had identified the body and the family had been notified. And it's officially a murder. But they haven't revealed any details about how he died or any other information about the case."

"Well, will you keep me posted if you learn of any new developments? I don't have a phone out where I live, but you can leave a message at the BLM, and I'll call you back."

"Sure." She stood and took her coat from the hook on the wall. "I've got to get back to work. It's Holy Week, and there are going to be a thousand claims of miraculous healing up at the Sanctuario in Chimayo. The pilgrimage has already begun. There was a story on the news today about a one-legged man who's walking there on crutches from Albuquerque and a ninety-year-old woman who's rolling down the highway from Gallup in a wheelchair. Our phones have been ringing off the hook for comments, opinions, interviews."

I stood and pulled my coat on. "It's crazy for us, too. I'm

working a temporary team assignment up in the area along the High Road."

"Hey, I heard a rumor about you being in some lingerie fashion show," Christine said, turning her head inquisitively and smiling as we walked out of the room and headed down the hall. "A fashion show with a lot of excitement."

"Oh, that." I tried to act nonchalant. "Let's just say I was working undercover." I forced a little laugh. "Maybe I'll tell you about that some other time, but I've got to get to the BLM now." I headed out of the sheriff's office at a quick pace.

Damn that Jerry Padilla. I should tell Christine who her leak is.

✠

I was almost to the BLM when I spotted Santiago Suazo's truck parked in the dirt lot in front of El Toro. I pulled in and went inside. Suazo was sitting at the counter eating a hot roast beef sandwich and flirting with the waitress. There were two empty beer bottles on the counter, and he was working on a third. I sat on the stool beside him. "Rob-bie Sua-zo," I said.

"What do you want?" His voice was loud and thick, his breath boozy. "Hey, man, why did you go talking to my old lady the other day?" He might have been stocky once; he had broad shoulders still, but his fondness for speed and crank had eaten away at his muscle base and left him looking like a puppet: a large head, long in the torso, short-legged, and listing a little, almost off balance. His face was pocked with deep holes left by acne, and his skin was sallow and grayish. His thin mustache and beard made him look dirty, unkempt, and his wavy dark hair was tied at his neck in a pathetic attempt at a ponytail. He looked like he hadn't changed his clothes in a few days.

"I want to know what you were doing on BLM land up by Boscaje."

"You can go to hell, *puta*." He pulled hard on the beer bottle, draining it. He set it down, got up, drew a twenty-dollar bill from a thick roll, and threw it on the counter. "We were all better over here before you people came and fenced off our land." He spoke so loud, he was nearly shouting. "I don't need a *coño* like you coming in here when I'm trying to eat! And I don't like you coming to my house, talking to my old lady, man! You got no business with my old lady, you hear me? Someday, somebody's going to do something about you sticking your pretty little *cola blanca* in other people's business. Your *pucha* stinks so bad, I have to get out of here. It's making me sick." He turned and swaggered away, one shoulder tilted slightly backward, the arm and hand dragging just a little.

I sat there a moment. The waitress grabbed the twenty and began clearing up the counter, avoiding looking at me. I got up. I was livid. I felt a clear bolt of energy move through me, and as it surged into my center, I felt invincible. I hurried after Suazo, caught up with him in the parking lot just as he was about to get in his truck. I tapped him on the shoulder from behind. He was only about five-nine, not much bigger than me, really, and certainly not in good shape, though possibly tough in a wiry sort of way. Suazo whirled on me and took a swipe with his better arm. I ducked. That swipe was all I needed. I threw my body into his solar plexus, and I heard the wind rush out of his lungs with a grunt as my shoulder lodged deep. I grabbed his scrotum with one hand and his windpipe with another, and I rammed him against the side of his truck, squeezing the lower hand hard. His arms didn't have time to reach for me before his face contorted with pain. He raised both hands in the air in defeat. I loosened my grip a little, but held him there. "I want you to apologize for the insulting things you just said about my anatomy and my profession, Mr. Suazo." The words barely escaped my gritted teeth. I was a reservoir of seething rage.

"*Lo si-en-to, señ-or-i-ta.*" His voice wheezed from the blow, but his voice was still bitter. He wouldn't look at me. His eyes were slits, one lid lazy, almost closing on his fierce stare past my shoulder.

"Now, tell me. What were you doing up by Boscaje?"

"*Nada.*"

I squeezed hard, and he tried to double over, but I pressed against his windpipe.

"Just looking for fun, man." He half choked. "Looking for a good time with *la rubia*—some gringa like you."

"I'm in no mood, Suazo. You may like to beat on your poor little wife, but this is one woman you better not screw around with. I'd just as soon rip these little jewels right off you as stand here and smell your foul stench."

"*Sí, pero,* you're not going to do that," he puffed. "You got no jurisdiction here. You got nothing on me, man! You can't do a fucking thing to me!" His raspy voice attempted bravado, but his eyes protruded from fear and pain. He looked like a big lizard.

"You took a swing at me, Suazo. That's all I need. I can have you arrested right now for attempted assault on a federal agent. Or you can talk to me about what you were doing up by Boscaje." We stood there a moment, my forehead almost touching the side of his pitted face, both of us panting, neither one of us moving. I could taste the stink of his beer breath, his fear. His crotch felt damp in my hand. I heard a car door slam behind me and footsteps coming toward us, but I didn't take my hands away or even dare to turn my head around and look.

"Can I be of any help?" a baritone voice asked. I knew that voice. Where did I know that voice from? I released Suazo, whose eyes were wide with fright. He scrambled into his truck as I turned around and saw Andy Vincent, and behind him Regan.

"Jamaica?" she said, her face full of worry. "Are you all right?"

Suazo's truck roared to life, jumped the curb, and squealed away.

◄ 24 ►

Uncivilized

My blood still coursed with unspent adrenaline when I walked into the BLM office a few minutes later. I felt like sopapilla dough when it hits the hot grease. I knew I shouldn't have let Suazo get to me like that—I should have called the sheriff when he took a swing at me instead of taking him on myself. But if I hadn't pinned him against his truck, Suazo would have been long gone before a deputy could have gotten there, and it would turn out like all the rest of the times we'd tried to press charges and he'd gone free. Either way, nothing stuck to Suazo, so what had I accomplished?

Rosa Aragon was at the desk again, a telephone receiver pressed to one ear, her head bobbing up and down in agreement with the caller. *Roy here?* I mouthed. She nodded more emphatically and pointed a thumb toward the hall.

Roy was in his office, rubbing his head with consternation as he stared at a pile of papers in front of him. I tapped my knuckles against the door frame. "Having fun, Roy?"

"Hell, no, I'm not having fun. I hate this stuff. What are you doing in here now—come to give me an excuse to give up on this blasted paperwork for a while?"

"Actually, I brought you some more paperwork." I put my targets on the desk. "But if you need a break I'll buy you a cup of coffee."

"No, no. Sorry, I can't. But sit down a minute, I want to talk to you about something. I was just thinking about you this morning."

"Uh-oh." I sat in the gray-green metal and vinyl chair in front of his desk.

"No, no, it's nothing bad. In fact, I talked with the wife a little about this, too. No, I was just thinking maybe we ought to look for a different assignment for you here when this team effort with the Forest Service is done."

"What do you mean?" My chest tightened.

"I mean, something where you get around people a little more. Not so much of that remote-area stuff. I think you got too much talent to be a range rider."

I stood up. "I don't want a change of assignment, Roy."

He got up, went around me, and closed his office door. "Sit down, Jamaica. This is just you and me here. Just relax, you're not in any trouble."

I sat, but right on the edge of the seat, ready to break with it, if need be.

Roy saw it. He sat back in his chair, picked up a pencil. He twirled the pencil like a baton—over his knuckles and under his hand, again, then again. "Will you just settle down? You're like an unbroken filly!"

I released my grip on the arms of the chair, tried to find a place for my hands in my lap.

"Jamaica, you don't have to make the switch today. I'm just saying I think it's time we found something better for you, something where you got to be around civilization once in a while."

I laughed. "You think I'm uncivilized, huh?"

He smirked. "I wasn't saying that. I just want you to have a chance to be around people a little more. I had an idea maybe we'd put in for—"

I cut in, "I'm okay, Roy. Why are you doing this? Do you think I can't handle my job?"

He threw the pencil down on the papers in front of him, but it rolled across the desk toward me, then fell onto the floor. Neither of us moved to get it.

He broke the silence. "I used to do your job. I did it for years. It's hard, mean, low-paying, lonely-assed work. Nine out of ten resource protection agents don't last three years at range riding. You been doing it six. I see all the signs in you: you're burned out. If I don't move you, I'm going to lose you. That's all I know. Besides, I don't know how much longer that will even be a job classification with the BLM. Things are changing."

"You used to be a range rider?"

"Hell, yes, I was, for almost seven years. It damned near cost me my marriage. I got so used to being alone, out by myself, I got to be like you said—uncivilized. I couldn't open up and talk anymore. I didn't have any patience with people. But I was lonely, too, and down. I was real down. I just didn't know how to reach out to anybody."

"I never knew that about you."

"Yeah, well, take it from me. You want a change of assignment. And I'm not talking about a desk job, either, so don't worry about that." He surveyed his piles of paperwork. "I wouldn't wish this stuff on a dog I didn't like! No, I'm talking about one of the other resource protection agent posts, maybe with the Rio Grande Use and Management Division, or liaison with the Ski Valley or the pueblo. Something where you aren't out by yourself in the backcountry all the time."

"Those are all a grade higher rank than me."

"I know that. But let's don't get the cart before the horse here. I'm just thinking out loud, wanted to see what your reaction would be."

"I don't think so. I see a lot of politics in all those things you mentioned. I'm no good at sucking up."

"Well, ain't that the truth!" He twisted his mouth up at one side and gave a little snort. "I didn't think I could do the job of field manager either when my boss offered it to me. Hell, I still don't like the paperwork. But when I get sick of people and these four walls, there's plenty of stuff to do out there." He jerked his thumb toward some unknown point behind him. "I'm only here a few hours a day. It's good to have a healthy balance between the two."

"Roy, I just don't know. This job is pretty much why I came here. It's what I've always wanted to do."

"You know anyone at Tanoah Pueblo?"

I thought of Momma Anna—and immediately about the assignment she had given me. "I know a few people with the tribe."

"The Santa Fe office wants us to appoint someone to work as a liaison to the Tanoah and manage the public lands that abut theirs."

"Liaison? You can sure bet I wouldn't be any good at that."

"Yeah, I remember that first day you come in here with your paperwork to be a range rider. There was a lot of money lost on bets then that you wouldn't last a month."

"Oh, yeah? Who won?"

"I did. Now get on out of here and let me do my work. You need to rest before you go out tonight."

I got up and started for the door. "Roy, can I just say something and you won't say anything back?"

He eyed me suspiciously and didn't answer.

"If I've ever done anything to hurt you or offend you, I'd like for you to forgive me."

Roy screwed up his face, as if he'd encountered a bad smell. "What in the hell are you talking about?"

"Nothing." I started to close the door.

"Is this about you showing your ass all over the county on Saturday night?"

I took a deep breath and blew it out. "Never mind."

"It's none of my business what you do in your time off," Roy said. "But you could have had your lights put out instead of that other gal. That's the part that worries me."

As I was heading back out the front of the building, Rosa hung up the phone. She motioned me over to the front counter and asked, "I didn't get a chance to talk to you when you came in before. How was your reunion with your brother?"

"My brother?"

"Oh, no, I hope I didn't spoil it."

"Rosa, I don't know what you're talking about. I don't have a brother."

"You mean you . . . you mean, you don't—? Tell me the truth now, Jamaica. You don't have a brother?"

"I don't have a brother. I'm an only child."

"Ay-ay-ay!" she squealed. "This man called on Friday and said he was your brother. He wanted me to tell him where you live. I told him I don't know where you live. He said he was just back from overseas in the service."

"What did he sound like?"

"I don't know. He sounded like an Anglo, like you. I didn't tell him anything, Jamaica. I promise. I don't know where you live, and Roy wasn't here. You know, all you got for an address is a rural carrier box."

"What did he say when you told him you didn't know?"

"He just said, 'Thank you very much, I'll find her,' and then he hung up. He sounded like a nice man. But, ay! That don't sound so good, a man trying to find out where you live and saying he's your brother, when you don't have a brother!"

◄ 25 ►

Just a Kiss

That night, after I'd ridden the fence line in my section, I returned to the base camp that I had established a few days before. I gathered some wood and kindling and put them near the circle of stones I had set up for a fire. I took my saddlebags off of Redhead and then removed her saddle and blanket. I got a curry comb out of my kit and started brushing her down. Not only did this give me a chance to clean the horse so chafing didn't occur under her tack, but it helped create a bond between Redhead and me that carried over into handling and riding. Without this, I might not have been able to manage a stubborn mare like her. Redhead did not communicate with me as she sometimes did by nibbling at my arms or hat, flipping her head or tail, or even nodding her head and whinnying and blustering. Instead she made funny snorting sounds as she kept busy pulling at some dry grass. These little appreciative snuffles kept rhythm as I brushed the bits of duff and dirt from her coat, telling me that Redhead was enjoying this attention immensely. An occasional quivering at the withers gave me clues as to when I was working a particularly good-feeling spot.

In the quiet night, my mind began to worry over the puzzling set of circumstances that had occurred over the past five or six days. Someone stabbed Father Ignacio, crucified him, and threw him over the gorge bridge. What a gruesome and horrific deed! Three men I had never seen before stole my book. Why? How did they know about it? Who was the driver who came to get Father Ignacio when we met, and could he be involved in all this? What about the Lexus that followed me from Santa Fe after I'd been to the library? The library! The librarian knew I was researching the Penitentes. What was that problem she said she'd had with my library card? Could that have had something to do with the car following me? Or was that whole thing with the car tailing me just a coincidence? Should I have told Jerry Padilla about the Lexus? Did someone really try to kill me and injure Nora instead? Somehow, all of this had to tie together. In the pit of my belly, I could feel an ooze of fear begin rising. I bit my lip and held back the anxiety, brushing Redhead's rump and running the curry comb through the tail as best I could.

The air was sharply cold. I pulled up the collar on my coat and buttoned the top button. There was little wind, only a faint breeze. Coyotes whined and yipped occasionally, and the cottonwoods down in the draw made a sound like sheets of rough paper being rubbed together when the breeze picked up.

I stood at Redhead's side, facing her tail, then ran my hand down her leg to the fetlock. She was well trained and responded to this by picking up her foot so that I could examine it and pick out any rocks that might cause stone bruises. As I checked the mare's feet, I mulled over the only thing that my book, the icons, and Father Ignacio had in common—the Penitentes. The brotherhood was a group of lay brothers—peace loving, humble, and charitable—whose only violent acts were against themselves in penance as they emulated the suffering of their Savior. Although they had been known to throw rocks at uninvited observers during their ceremonies, tales about their "stoning" others to death, as Regan had feared might happen to her and her friend when they were children, or the *reata* that Jerry Padilla had mentioned, had never been substantiated. The Penitentes' most earnest wish was to be left alone.

What if they wanted me to leave them alone? I had tried to talk to some villagers who lived near shrines and moradas I had mapped and sketched. Maybe I had unknowingly approached *hermanos vigilantes*. My questions, taking notes, and drawing their shrines might have been seen as an intrusion. Even so, surely they would not have resorted to murder to deter me.

And what about Father Ignacio? Los Hermanos would never kill a priest. They were staunch Catholics and members of their local parishes as well as the local morada. Imagine the penance for murder, especially murder of a priest! No, I couldn't believe the Penitentes were responsible for Father Ignacio's death.

Then, who?

Father Ignacio and I were both studying, writing about the Penitentes. That's all we had in common. He knew much more than I did. He had more resources . . . Resources! Could there be a clue in the two resources he told me to bring together for my book? Could that be why my book was stolen? Or why someone had tried to kill me, as they had killed Father Medina? What did the tract by Padre Martínez have to do with any of this? And what was that other name, the man's name I had written down? I tried to fathom this, and the information that Christine Salazar had inadvertently given me—that there was an investigation into stolen icons. Could Santiago Suazo have been involved in the theft of those icons? Was that where he was getting all that money? I had heard that religious icons sold for huge sums on the black art market.

A high, shrill whistle sliced through the quiet night. It made an eerie shrieking sound that seemed to find my spinal column and travel right down the stem from neck to tailbone, jangling every nerve. I started, felt a jolt of fear surge through me. Redhead drew up from the grass and flared her nostrils. Then I recognized the sound. It was the *pito*! It was a *pitero* playing his flute! I grabbed my rifle with the night scope that Kerry had loaned me, threw the mare's reins over her neck, jumped up and mounted her bareback, and kicked my heels gently into her sides. We tore off in the direction of the whistle.

I guided Redhead back through the woods, aiming for the Boscaje morada, certain that the procession had originated there. Just short of the thickest growth, I stopped the horse and dismounted. I tied her reins to a branch and made my way forward again on foot, carrying my rifle. I heard the raspy metallic whir of the *matraca* in the distance—a wooden instrument similar to an old-fashioned party noisemaker. I approached the edge of the meadow where I had hidden last week. The pito whistled shrilly again, to my right. I followed the sound through the trees; I did not have to go far. Above me, higher up the slope, a small procession was in progress.

I looked through the night scope on the rifle. A body was being dragged by two men, each holding one of his arms over a shoulder. I drew back in alarm, then looked again through the scope. As I studied the scene, I saw that it was not a body, but an Hermano who had been doing penance and was now unconscious from the self-inflicted torture. His lolling head was covered with a black cloth bag. His feet were bare. His back was torn and bleeding, and a cold cloud of steam rose from his wounds. The seat of his white cotton pants was black with the blood draining from his back.

Behind this trio came three more Hermanos. One carried a large crucifix in one hand as he steadily plodded, head down. Another whirled the matraca with one hand as he dragged the blood-soaked whip that had probably been used by the unconscious Penitente in the other. The third, farthest behind, was the pitero. He was an old man, thin and bony in his long black robelike coat and black pants. His blue-white hair stuck out like thick thatch over a black bandanna he had tied across his forehead.

The moon, nearly full and directly overhead, illuminated the cavalcade like a spotlight as they marched up the slope and across the meadow, leaving a wide silver trail in the frost-covered grass. They approached the morada, where, once again, two men armed with rifles stood outside. One of the sentries opened the door and leaned out of the way as they dragged the unconscious Penitente through. The door slamming after them sounded like a muffled shot echoing across the meadow grass, breaking like waves on the silent shore of the cold, still night.

I watched for ten or fifteen minutes, but nothing else happened. The two *hermanos vigilantes* pulled blankets around their shoulders and hunkered against the adobe walls on either side of the morada door. They looked to be settling in for the night. I headed back to my camp to do the same.

When I got back to my campsite, the tiny, downlike hairs on my forearms seemed to be standing up and reaching out like sensors to detect any danger. I slid off Redhead's back, still holding my rifle in one hand. I looped her reins over a branch and stood stock-still as I scanned the area. A tingling sensation ran down my shoulders and gave me gooseflesh on my arms. Had my gear been moved? Was that where I left my backpack? The saddlebags? Or was I just unnerved by the grim scene I had just witnessed?

The moon had climbed higher and I could see all the way down the slope to the draw, where the crevice in the earth made a black shadow. If someone had been in my camp, they could be hiding in there, or behind those cottonwoods, or even farther up the slope from me, in the denser thicket of junipers and piñons. I heard a noise behind me, raised my rifle to my shoulder, and whirled around, wondering at the same time where I should go for cover.

"Jamaica? It's me!" He was coming through the low growth of some sage scrub on his way down from the forested land above my camp—the same way I had just come.

"Kerry! What are you doing? You're lucky I didn't shoot!"

He took long steps down the slope and reached my camp before I finished speaking. "Easy there. Hold on. I just came over to check on you and found you gone and your horse's saddle and your gear still here. I was worried. I thought you might have headed up toward that morada by Boscaje, so I went back through there looking for you." I noticed he was carrying a rifle, too.

"We must have barely missed one another. I just came back from there. I saw a small procession. That's why I left camp—I heard the pito."

"Yeah. I heard it, too. Eerie sounding, isn't it? I've heard that before. It really travels across the mountains, and sometimes it echoes. The first time I heard it was over in the Mora

Valley, and I thought it was a wild animal cry or a woman shrieking. It nearly drove me crazy. I tried to follow the sound, but it seemed to move all over, and the way it echoed, I couldn't tell if I was after the sound or its twin. I finally gave it up. So, you're okay?" He dusted off his jeans.

"I'm okay. I just had the strangest feeling." I looked around my camp area again. "I thought we weren't going to meet up until morning."

"Yeah, well, I don't know. I just thought I ought to see how you were doing over here." He fidgeted with a tiny nest of cedar needles that had attached themselves to the cuff of his coat. "I keep forgetting to ask—how's your . . . where you fell off your horse? You seem like you're all better." He looked at me and grinned, his hat brim casting a moon shadow across his eyes.

"Oh, that." I blushed. "Yes, all better, thanks. And I forgot to ask you: how was your trip to Santa Fe?"

"It was good. There's a gallery there that carries some of my photographs. I sold two last month. So I dropped off two more and picked up a nice little check. Helps pay for my equipment, printing and framing, stuff like that. Hey, that reminds me." He reached into his coat pocket and held up something. "This should work for that memory card you found." He moved in closer and turned slightly so the moonlight would shine on the item in his hand. "You plug that card in this slot here, see?"

I nodded my head.

"Then you plug this end into the port on a computer. It

should open up on your computer's desktop like another drive. If there are any photos on that memory card, you'll be able to open that drive and see them."

"Thanks," I said, taking the device from him and holding it up to examine it more closely. "I'll have to try that the next time I'm in the office. I don't have a computer myself, but maybe I can use the one there that I do my reports on."

"Good. Now, come on and let's get a fire built, what do you say? It's cold tonight."

We worked together and quickly built a fire. While Kerry nurtured the first flames, I once again unrolled my extra horse blanket and spread it on the ground. I brought my bedroll over to use as a back cushion, sat down on the horse blanket, and offered him a seat beside me. He sat down beside me and then stretched out his legs and leaned back, one elbow on the bedroll, his arm so near it was touching my side. I could smell that scent of his. I leaned back, turned onto my side to face him, and put my elbow right beside his on the bedroll. "Did you move any of my stuff?" I asked.

"No, I didn't move anything. Why?"

"You didn't move my backpack, or those saddlebags over there?"

"No. I didn't touch anything. I just saw you had left your things. I worried, especially when I saw the saddle. I went right off in the direction I thought you'd gone. I was concerned about you." His face was twisting, as if he were lying about something.

"Why are you all of a sudden so worried about me?" I asked. Our eyes met.

He broke into a wide smile and shook his head slightly. "You know, he asked me not to let you know this, but being right here next to you and looking into your face, I can't lie to you . . . "

I interrupted. "Roy. The Boss asked you to check on me."

He closed his lips, but there was still a boyish grin that couldn't be reined in. "He did. And I said I would. And here I am."

I didn't say anything. Part of me felt annoyed that these two men didn't think I could take care of myself. And another part was grateful right now that I wasn't alone.

Kerry reached across his chest and took my chin in his hand. He turned my face toward him. His hand felt warm. His eyes reflected the fledgling firelight. "I wanted to come. I would have found some excuse to check on you anyway. I wanted to see you as soon as I could. This just gave me a reason to see you before we exchanged reports in the morning." He released his hold on my chin, but did not take his hand away. Instead, he began gently stroking my cheek with the backs of his bent fingers.

It had a strangely calming effect. I closed my eyes for a moment and felt his tender touch. I exhaled and let tension slip out on my breath. I opened my eyes and looked into his. "I'm glad you came. But I can take care of myself. This is my job. This is what I do, and I do it all the time. Nobody has to check on me."

He continued touching my cheek, brushing wisps of my hair back from my face. He didn't say anything, and his eyes never left mine.

"I have something I want to say."

He grinned. Now he was making small strokes with his thumb on my jawline and in front of my ear. "I'm listening."

"If I have ever done anything to hurt you or offend you, I hope you will forgive me."

His grin broadened into a big smile. "I forgive you for being so perfect and for making my heart beat wildly." He reached for my hand and pressed it to his chest.

I held my palm against his coat, and Kerry pressed his hand on top of mine, as if to gather me into his heart. But it was my own heart that I felt beating wildly—it felt like a large bird fluttering its wings in my chest.

Kerry's hand moved to my shoulder and pulled me toward him. I could feel the warmth of his face moving toward mine. I turned my head slightly and touched my lips to his. His hand traced my shoulder to the nape of my neck and he pulled my face closer to his, his other arm opening as he pulled me into the warm cave of his chest and shoulder.

It was just a kiss. Nothing more. But when our lips met, I felt a current of euphoria move through me and my mind became a void through which only pleasure passed, everything else forgotten except for those lips, his hand, his chest and shoulder, his arm, the smell of him, the warmth of his skin, the taste of his lips. One kiss.

I gently pulled away. "We shouldn't be doing this now," I said.

He sat up straight and then quickly got to his feet. "Maybe not now," he said. "But we should definitely be doing this." He took a long look at me, his eyes brimming with excitement. "I'll see you in the morning."

After Kerry left camp, I got up and stroked Redhead's face and gave her a cold piece of carrot that was in my coat pocket. I picked up my rifle and took it back to my seat by the fire.

◄ 26 ►

The Bruja

The next morning, before I went home, I drove to Agua Azuela. I hoped Regan could help me figure out what the Penitentes had to do with all the other strange events that had been occurring. But, once again, Regan was not at home. When I got to her house, I saw that her Toyota was not in the garage, so I backed down the drive, turned around, and drove back across the bridge over the rio. At the intersection between the bridge and the road, I stopped to check for traffic. Ahead and to the left of me, several cars were parked in the wide dirt turnout in front of the ancient church. Regan's Toyota was among them. The local villagers were probably conducting their lay services in place of mass. I pulled my Jeep across the road and drove to the back of the lot near the arroyo, thinking I might snooze in my car until the service was over and then see if I could talk with Regan. But as I started to settle back in my seat, I remembered the old woman who had approached me in the churchyard after mass, insisting I come for tea.

"Why not?" I said aloud. I would go visit her and have a cup of tea while I waited for my friend.

The old woman's strange instructions proved to be precise. After I rounded the boulder with the hand on it, I climbed up the goat path on the south slope of the mountain, and above me a few hundred yards I could see a brush arbor and an adobe casita. As she had predicted, the crone who had demanded an audience two days ago after mass was waiting for me on the *portal*. We had not set a date, nor had I agreed even to come, but nonetheless, she seemed to be expecting me. She waved a dish towel in her hand, motioning for me to approach. The path was steep and the morning sun was just rising over the other side of the canyon. Frost on the sage scrub sparkled like thousands of stars.

"Come! Come! I made you tea," she said, again waving the dish towel as I stepped onto the *portal*. She trundled through the doorway of the adobe, and I followed. The opening was small and I had to stoop to enter her one-room dwelling. A table, crudely made from a slab of wood, with deep scars and four crooked limbs for legs stood in the center of the room, and two similar slab-and-stick chairs were placed on opposite sides of it. There was no other furniture.

In one corner, a large, deep *nicho* was carved into the

adobe, and this housed at least a dozen santos, before which at least as many votive candles were lit. Braids of dried sweet-grass, fat cigar-shaped smudge sticks, ancient-looking green glass jars of herbs and twigs, and several dried skink pelts, which the natives used to store a baby's umbilical cord after birth, lined an inset shelf in the earthen wall.

A shepherd's bed grew out of the long wall, over the fire-place. These old-fashioned sleeping berths were found in many old rural adobes: a massive fireplace, used for both cooking and heating the home, was built with an adobe slab over the top, and a bed was made on this slab to keep the occupant warm at night. The bedding looked to be crude cotton bags of straw, but there was a thick, woven wool blanket folded neatly at the foot of the rumpled bags. There were no pillows or sheets.

Flanking the fireplace on the low adobe hearth stood cast-iron pots, pottery cups and bowls, and an olla—a pottery water jar—filled with water, to which a waxed dipper gourd had been tied on a thin hemp rope circling the jar's neck. In the fireplace itself, a metal grate supported a small pot of simmering liquid, and a huge cast-iron teakettle hung from a hook, emitting contrails of steam.

"Sit! Sit! I made you tea," she squeaked. Again I was re-minded of bats when I heard her shrill, high-pitched voice. Her plain sackcloth dress and worn, curled-up-at-the-toes men's wing tips without laces were the same as the day I had first seen her at the church.

"How did you know I was coming?" I pulled out one of the chairs and sat down so that I faced the fireplace, where she was ladling liquid from the simmer pot into a cup.

"What is your name?" she asked as she brought the cup to the table.

"My name is Jamaica Wild. But how did you know I was coming?" I could smell a lovely lemon fragrance from the tea as she pushed the cup across the table and directly under my face.

"It is not important. You are here. That is what is important. Drink! Drink! It is hot now, but it will not be if you talk until your tongue is tired." She turned back to the hearth and poured dark liquid from the teakettle into a second cup.

"What is your name?" I asked.

She turned and looked at me with a mischievous grin that made her look as if she were just a child, an effect considerably contrary to the deeply lined face, bushy white brows, and fewer teeth present than missing. She turned her chin up and her ear down, so that her face lay sideways on the hump that extended from her neck to her shoulder on one side. She ambled over to the table with her own cup and sat down. "My name is Esperanza," she said, "but the people over here call me Tecolote."

I took a drink of the lemony tea. It had a slightly bitter taste but was not unpleasant. "This is good tea. What kind is it?"

"Hush! Do not insult me! Do I ask you what you serve when I come for a little meal with you? This is what you need, that's what kind it is. If I told everyone what I was giving them, they would not need a *curandera* at all, and I would be out of business. Now drink!"

"So you are a curandera? I guess I should have known. I'm not sick, though. I don't need—"

She stood up with astonishing speed, given her twisted frame, and the chair made a loud scraping noise across the adobe floor. "You don't think you need help? What about *la carreta de la muerte*? I have seen you on it!"

"The cart of death?"

"You do not see that the Black Spirit hovers behind you? You stuck your bare bottom out for men to look at and the Black Thing almost devoured you! And you don't think you need help!" She slapped one twisted hand on the tabletop and shook her head back and forth in disbelief. "You better drink up, little Mirasol. You better drink up while you can." She stared at me, then pointed a bony finger at the cup and raised it up as if to will it to my lips.

I picked up the cup. "I'm sorry, I didn't mean to offend you. How did you know about—"

"You are always wagging your tongue, asking foolish questions, while your *taza* sits waiting for you to empty it."

I drank from the cup. It tasted good now, the bitterness having the effect of cleansing my palate. The warm liquid felt good in my stomach.

She watched me intently, her face moving up and down each time I lifted the cup to my lips, drank, and then set it back on the table. Her eyes were two black pin lights. "Lucky

for you there is a *bruja* like me, and also an *ángel* to help you.
You are going to need a lot of help, Mirasol. You are not finished with the thing that tries to devour you!"

I felt drowsy, very tranquil, and slightly drunk. "I don't
understand. I don't understand anything you are saying.
What is '*mirasol*'?"

"The flower with yellow petals that grows so tall, as tall
as a man, with all the seed for the birds in the center. The
flower that grows where you grew."

"Sunflower? Sunflower? How did you know—"

"No more of your questions!" she snapped. "This is not
a social visit here. I did not tell you to come in order to ask
me foolish things, Mirasol. I told you to come because you
need help!"

My eyes were wide with a combination of anxiety and
disbelief. *How did this old woman know about the fashion
show, and about the attack on Nora?*

"Tomorrow, you will need to go to the *velorio*—the wake,
you know? You will need to be in Truchas early in the morning to honor your friend the father. So we must work quickly
so this *cura* has time to work and also time to leave you
before morning. You will not be riding on *la yegua* tonight,
Mirasol. You will not be strong enough."

"I didn't know that Father Ignacio's funeral is tomorrow.
I'll go, but I have to ride tonight."

"You will not ride tonight, I assure you. You will need to
go to the corral in a minute. We will talk until you do, and
then when you go to the corral, you will need to leave after.

Wild Penance

I will put something for you on the stump by the horno, and you will take that with you when you go. Now you must listen to me. There is an old sad story here that is not finished. There have been very bad feelings about something that happened a long time before, and no healing has been done, even though many winters have passed. You must look into the past, look at *los niños*. Any answers you want will be there. It is the only weapon you have to defend yourself against this Black Thing. You cannot stop now, or go back. You can only go to the next place. The people over here do not like it when their secrets are unfolded, but your heart is clean, so you have been given protection. It is the Black Thing—the one that hunts for you—that the people over here fear. That is the thing that will end it all. The people know this, but they are in the time of La Cuaresma—you know, Lent?—they cannot raise their hands at this time. This is a very tender time for the people, and they are convinced that you mean them no harm. That is why you have been given protection. You have an *ángel*, and that is who has brought you the gift that I will leave for you by the horno. Do you have to go to the corral now?"

All the while she had been talking, my gut had been growling, and now intense cramps threatened to make me lose control of my bowels. I felt dizzy and weak. I was sweating and cold at the same time. I stood up and felt the world shift. The room was sitting at an odd angle, and all the lines were distorted. The table was undulating. I moved for the door and felt as if I were wading in chest-high water.

"Down beyond the willow there." She pointed as she followed me out on the *portal*. "Watch out for the *macho cabrío*—he doesn't like strangers! And don't come back to *la casa*. I have another *cura* to do now."

I made for the willow, saw the corral with the goat and the privy just beside it. The door of the outhouse had a cutout shaped like an owl. I sat on the splintered seat until my insides were empty. The goat pawed at the side of the privy time after time, his sharp hooves making a thunderous sound on the old, dry wood. Finally, I stopped sweating and felt my belly relax.

I left the privy and went to the horno. At first I didn't see the stump Esperanza had spoken of, or any gift I could recognize as such. The world still seemed to be wavering and sitting at strange angles, the tea having had a hallucinatory effect on me. A large yucca behind the horno moved as if it had been stirred. I heard the rustling of its razor-sharp leaves, but I saw nothing that might have brushed it. I looked at it again, and the sword-shaped leaves of the plant seemed to rise up, as if to open its arms to welcome me. *Oh, boy, Jamaica! You've tied one on with a teacup!*

Again the yucca shifted its leaves, and then I saw the low stump behind it, and on the stump . . . my book!

I approached with a strange mixture of awe and trepidation. What if the yucca is feeling territorial about the book?

I could feel the plant as an intelligent presence. There was a strange but exciting heaviness to the air between us, thick, sweet, like a celestial stew—a heath of infinite life possibilities ready to pop into form—the plant palpably breathing and emitting an energy field into which I was about to intrude. I held my breath and moved my palm, open and extended as if in friendship . . . slowly . . . slowly . . . toward the yucca.

Again, the leaves rose slightly, almost so slightly that I might have imagined it, except for the rustling sound and the faint trace of purple tails of light trailing the leaves like the sheer wisps of Salome's veils in ultraslow motion. I kept moving my hand, my pace crawling, the plant still breathing, its scimitar fingers rising . . . and falling . . . rising . . . and falling . . . I could hear it breathing now: low, erogenous, carnal, quivering, and reverberating a message beyond the comprehension of a mere two-legged being, something about life: sweet-loss-sacred-death-gift-fear-pleasure-pain . . . not this, more than this . . . something about harmony: love-joy-holy-all . . . not this, more than this . . . something about presence: Now, Only now. Only. One. Not this, more than this . . . none of this.

May I have my book?

The leaves relaxed. I picked up the book, its cool deerskin cover a living thing in my hand, the eyes of the deer in my mind, deer looking through my eyes, then one with my eyes, the buds of my antlers sprouting in sweet spurts of pain from my head. As I willed the book toward my chest, I kept my pace snail-like, solar, tidal, seasonal, millennial, my arm having swung out into the yucca's world like a pendulum and now coming back as evenly and as languorously, as calculated and measured as Moon's slow cycle of death and resurrection as she plods across the night skies from one month to the next.

The yucca was finished with me.

I took the book into my arm and held it next to my chest. No deer there. I felt a sweeping sadness that our interlude—mine and the yucca's—was over, that I didn't fully understand what it was relating, that I could never understand.

I turned and went down the slope toward my Jeep, which waited near the arroyo, light-years from where I had just been.

◄ 27 ►

All That Remains

By the time I got back down the mountain to the turnout area in front of the church, my Jeep was the only car there. I was feeling too odd to talk with Regan, so I headed toward home. But on the way through Taos, I had another attack of cramping and queasiness, so I stopped by the BLM offices to use the facilities.

There were two notes in my message box. One indicated that Christine Salazar wanted to talk with me. I phoned her from the cubicle in the back where I normally made out my reports.

"You asked me to keep you informed," Salazar said. "So I wanted to let you know that the body of Father Ignacio Medina, or to be more precise—all that remains of him after the autopsy—has been released to his family."

"Actually, I just learned that the services are tomorrow in Truchas," I said, my gut still growling. "Have you heard anything else?"

"No. I'm afraid that I'm pretty well out of the loop now because the OMI has released the remains. I'm not going to be a good resource from here on out. Sorry."

The other note was a pink slip with the name "Mrs. Suazo" and a phone number. I tried calling the number, but a message said the line had been disconnected or was no longer in service. I felt churning in my stomach that may not have derived from Tecolote's *cura*. Had Santiago Suazo gone home after our confrontation and taken out his ire over what I had done to him on his poor wife? I hoped not. I tried the number again. Again, I got the "out of service" message.

I walked out to the lobby where Rosa was doodling on her calendar/desk blotter. Even though I thought it was probably a futile effort, I held the pink slip up and asked Rosa, "Did you take this call?"

Rosa looked at the slip skeptically, then said, "Am I in trouble if I did?"

"No, I just wondered if you remembered anything about the caller, Mrs. Suazo."

"What about her?"

"How did she sound when she called?"

"What do you mean?"

"Did she seem afraid or worried?"

Rosa took the slip from my hand and studied it, as if

the answer were there on the paper. "I don't think so." She handed it back to me.

"Did she sound like the matter could be urgent?"

"Oh, wait a minute. I remember her now," Rosa replied. "No, she didn't sound like anything was wrong at all. As a matter of fact, she sounded very happy."

"Really?"

"Yes, really. Eeeee! Did I forget to write down that she said she wanted to tell you some good news?" Rosa grabbed the pink message slip from me again and studied it. "I guess I didn't put it on there. I'm sorry."

On the way to my cabin, a gnawing pain started to work in my stomach. It felt like a dull meat grinder was working its way through my midsection. By the time I was halfway home, I knew Tecolote's prediction about not being able to ride that night was already true. I stopped at the café on the highway a few miles from my place and used the pay phone to call Roy. I asked him to relay the message to the ranger station in Peñasco so Kerry would know.

When I finally got home, I was doubled over from the pain. I hobbled into my cabin, propped a chair against the door under the doorknob, laid my rifle and pistol on the bed, and collapsed beside them, without removing clothes or boots.

◄ 28 ►

The Funeral Day

As I drove to Father Ignacio's funeral the next morning, I was more keenly aware than ever of the abundance of small crosses along the roadside that spoke of mortal tragedies. The highways of northern New Mexico are trimmed with ornamental remembrances of death. These memorials are usually composed of a crude wooden crux held upright by a cairn of small stones, and any of several sorts of brilliantly colored adornments: artificial flowers in electric hues, neon fake-flora funeral wreaths, ribbon banners emblazoned with *Beloved Son* or *Love Forever* in gold glitter. I have seen rosaries dangle from many of the crosses, sometimes gold chains, and Purple Hearts, Silver Stars, or other military insignia. These shrines are carefully tended. For Nuevo Mexicanos, these places are sacred, full of grief. Unlike other parts of the country, the Land of Enchantment cannot contain its sorrows and losses in neat, tidy parcels of land. Loss is everywhere. La Muerte grins from the shoulders of highways, the intersections of dirt lanes, the cattle guards across county roads.

Driving around a curve where a cluster of crosses marked multiple calamities, I wondered if all this carnage might not be due to the wild landscape that loomed in the darkness, ready to steal back its power from those who would conquer it—on the very roads they'd made to do so. Or perhaps it was due to one of the highest per capita incidences of alcoholism in the fifty United States.

Although I was driving more than eight thousand feet above sea level, I was less than two-thirds as high as the tallest crests of the Sangre de Cristo Mountains that scaled onward to the east when I entered the wide alpine mountain valley cradled between the High Road and Trampas Peak. On the western ridge of the basin, the High Road passed through the village of Las Truchas, which means "trout," so named because of the wealth of these fish in the mountain streams.

Just before arriving at the village, I went by a cemetery overlooking a breathtaking vista of piñon and pine forests as far as the horizon. The graves in this *campo santo* were embellished with the symbols of the culture. A shiny helmet and the front half of a Harley Davidson Sportster rose, half buried, over a grave, angled toward the sky, ready for the departed to don headgear and gun it hard into the next life, popping a wheelie as he took off. Intricately carved granite crosses were draped with chains, dripping with fuchsia fabric flowers. Statuary of saints and the Blessed Virgin had artificial bouquets of impossible colors at their feet—turquoise, lime green, neon pink, and red, red, red. White picket fences, scrupulously painted and repainted—and others made of chain and poles—staked out turf for the deceased. Hand-carved cottonwood crosses, some of them nameless, others with etched appellations worn smooth by sandblasting winds, tilted blanched and weathered in tenacious weeds.

The death of Father Ignacio created more loss, more sorrow, than the tiny community of Las Truchas could contain. The outpouring of affection from so many mourners meant that the tiny sanctuario could not hold all those who wished to attend the funeral mass, and more than a hundred people waited outside the church in the raw, frozen air, slapping the arms of their thick coats and breathing cold vapor clouds until the mass was finished. Even the large churchyard, surrounded by high adobe walls, could not accommodate the throng. Clumps of people huddled together all along the narrow dirt road through the village.

Since I'm used to being out in the cold, it wasn't the chill that was making me uncomfortable. It was standing for more than an hour in a pair of dress boots that looked good with my long black skirt but did my feet a disservice. That, and the wailing of Las Dolientes.

From the thick adobe walls of the chapel the sound of

their cries rose to the rim of the nave and then crept like a fog out the cracks in the mortar, around the seals of the windows and doors, bringing with it the weight of a thousand hearts suffering the ultimate sorrow.

After the mass, Father Ximon Rivera pulled on a long, dark coat as he stepped outside with an elderly woman I presumed to be Father Ignacio's mother. Two priests dressed in splendid vestments came out. These two waited with the mujer and watched the mourners file out, while Father Rivera followed the pallbearers with their charge to the old wooden horse-drawn wagon that served as a hearse. A group of Carmelitas brought an exquisitely embroidered white cloth and draped it over the coffin. Then the Hermanos came from the church, each carrying a rosary, and they took up positions before the cart.

I stood just inside the dilapidated wooden gates, which sagged open from their hinges in the adobe wall. The arch above them supported the old iron church bell and was crowned with a simple white cross. The morning sun, just cresting the high mountains to the east, cast a long, blue shadow of the rood across the front of the church. As everyone filed forward on their way to the cemetery, the procession came right past me. A group of more than thirty men— mostly elders—dressed in long, black coats from another era, walked together in silence toward the road, the first three of them carrying crosses high above their heads—one a large crucifix, the polychrome figure of Christ distinctively New Mexican. Eight younger men came behind them, also dressed in antiquated dark clothes. Two led the horses, and the six pallbearers remained in formation as they had while carrying the coffin, each with one hand on the cart, the other holding a rosary. Some of them looked like they were having trouble walking. They all wore pained expressions, as if their clothes were hurting their backs. I felt the heaviness of despair in my neck and shoulders as these Hermanos trudged past me.

Behind them came Las Carmelitas. At the front of their group, five Verónicas carried a platform bearing a bulto of Our Lady of Sorrows. In two disciplined rows behind them, Las Hermanas followed, with seven women in a cluster taking up the rear—Las Dolientes.

Los Penitentes led the procession to the *campo santo*. The long, slow walk through the village seemed to take hours, the *cánticos*, or chants, of Los Hermanos drawing time out like molten lead, blue-gray with the heavy weight of this gruesome, incomprehensible tragedy. Periodically, the brothers halted the procession and the elderly were directed to sit in the folding chairs that had been set up along the road at each of these *descansos*, or resting places. Members of the family or friends of the deceased placed small crosses at each of these spots, piling up rocks to support them. Las Carmelitas decorated each of these with white roses that had been dipped in wax, and each time flowers were laid before a crux, it raised a new rash of wailing from Las Dolientes.

At the *campo santo*, the *hermano mayor*, the elder or leader of the brotherhood, waited respectfully until the group of priests completed their graveside ceremonies. When they were finished, he began singing in a clear, deep baritone that seemed to well up in his round chest and come out in tones the color of dark beer. He sang an alabado that repeated the phrase *adiós al mundo*: good-bye to this world.

While the *hermano mayor* sang, Las Carmelitas came forward with three long, purple satin sashes and handed them to the younger Hermanos, who eased the coffin from the wagon, placing the sashes beneath it as they did so. They held the embroidered ends of the sashes and lowered the coffin into the ground as the banshee voices of Las Dolientes rose in an insufferable wail.

As the *hermano mayor* sang the final stanza, I tried to translate in my mind from the rich, beautiful Spanish: something about being made from the earth, then about being the earth at last again. Members of the family, Los Hermanos, and Las Carmelitas came forward one at a time and sprinkled a handful of red dirt onto the coffin, the sound like rain splattering on a big drum.

The elderly woman I had identified as Father Ignacio's mother stayed near the grave to receive condolences, along with the rest of the family. I stood well off to the side, out of the flow of traffic, as the mourners left the *campo santo*. I watched the river of black coats, capes, and woolen shawls, called *tápalos*, until it slowed; then I looked back at the grave. The rest of the family had moved on to follow the procession, but the bereaved mother remained before the burial pit, alone but for one companion. A bent old woman was speaking to her, gesturing animatedly. Father Ignacio's mother made a measurement with her hands, holding them shoulder-width apart. Then she put one hand five or six inches above the other, palms facing, presumably describing the size of an object. They focused intently on one another, talking back and forth, apparently working something out between them. They turned in concert and looked at me, and I saw the bent one gesture, pointing a bony finger at me. *Esperanza!* She saw the recognition in my face and shook her head, raising a finger to her lips, signaling me not to call out. Then she made like she was pushing me away. She repeated the motion several times, indicating I should stay back. She reached for the shoulder of the other woman and turned her away from me, directing attention back to their conversation, still gesturing with her other arm as she talked. I watched them. Were they talking about me? Why did Esperanza point at me?

They talked for several minutes, each one taking turns listening, then talking. Every once in a while, the bruja would look up at me and make another pushing-away gesture, reminding me to stay back.

Father Rivera's voice interrupted my confused speculations. "Miss Wild, I see you've managed to brave the cold." He tugged his long wool coat together at the collar, his breath like smoke in the chill.

I was about to answer when the two mujeres approached.

Father Rivera seized the opportunity. "Doña Medina, I'd like you to meet Miss Wild. She was something of an *asociada* of your son's. Miss Wild is also writing about Los Hermanos, señora." He was acting the perfect diplomat, as if we had not had the terse discussion at the end of our last meeting. I noticed that he had chosen to ignore the bruja.

"*Con mucho gusto, Señora Medina.*" I extended my hand. "*Lo siento* for your loss. Even though I did not know your son well, I considered him a friend."

She was a tiny woman, as her son had been small. She was very thin and her brown skin hung from her cheekbones, her scant white hair barely visible under her black mantilla. She looked up at me and clutched my hand. "Do you know why he was killed?" Her face was full of pain.

Startled, I opened my mouth but couldn't speak for a moment. Then I said, "No. But I, too, want to find out. And if I do, Doña Medina, I will tell you what I learn."

She looked at Tecolote, then at me again. "*Señorita, por favor, venga a la casa,*" she said, pressing my hand with hers.

"Oh, I couldn't come to your house now, Doña Medina. It wouldn't be right. I only met your son once, and we talked on the phone a few times. This is a time for you to be with your family and close friends." I looked at Father Rivera.

He nodded approval.

Mrs. Medina also looked at Father Rivera. "Do you think we could have a moment together, we three women?"

Father Rivera looked at me with consternation, then menacingly at the curandera. He gave an exasperated exhale. "Certainly. I'll go see about the car."

After the father had left us, Esperanza spoke up, her eyes telegraphing in quick, black strobes. "Mirasol, you must do as the señora says. She has something for you."

I looked from the bruja to Mrs. Medina. "For me? But . . . "

"*Sí*, it is something important," Mrs. Medina said, making a loose fist and waving it between us to emphasize her point. "It is something he told me to keep safe for him. He told me . . . " She looked at the priest, who was only a few yards away, and stopped. She turned back to me and whispered, "Maybe you can help. At any rate, it is meant for someone else now . . . now that Ignacio is in heaven." Her eyes filled with water. "Maybe it will help you find out why he was killed." She released my hand and fumbled in the sleeve of her coat for the lace-edged handkerchief she had stuffed there.

Father Rivera approached. "We had better go now, Señora Medina. I think they're ready." He led her away. As he was helping Mrs. Medina into a black car at the road, he looked back at me across the cemetery. His blue eyes transmitted either concern or disapproval, I couldn't tell which. And his lips were pressed together so hard they looked blue, too.

I turned around to see what Tecolote thought of this, but she was gone.

◄ 29 ►

La Arca

A large man stood like a sentry in front of the door of the Medina home. I recognized him as the driver who had come for Father Ignacio at the end of our meeting at the coffeehouse. "Señorita, you are expected," he said as he reached for the door.

"Wait," I said. "You were the one who came for Father Ignacio—"

"*Sí, señorita.* I have been close to you several times. You see, when Father Medina did not arrive at the school to teach his classes last week, I knew something was wrong. I tried to call you at your work, but I could not get in touch with you there, and the woman who answered said you did not have a phone. My friend Ignacio told me that he had given you some things to look for in your research, so I notified one of our Hermanas at the library to watch for anyone asking for them."

"So you were the one following me that day in the Lexus."

"*Sí, señorita.* I was the one. Because you had questioned Ignacio about Los Penitentes, we arranged for a group of Hermanos to examine your book—"

"You arranged to steal my book?"

"I am sorry. I—"

"One of your thugs hit me hard with something and . . . "

"We are so sorry for that unfortunate incident. I assure you, we did not—"

"Why didn't you just approach me? You knew Father Ignacio had come to trust me."

"When Ignacio did not come to the school to teach his classes, and no one could find him, we could not trust you or anyone else until we knew what had happened to our beloved *hermano.* We had to know what you were writing in that book, if you were involved—"

"Involved! You thought I—"

"Señorita, once we saw the book, we were satisfied that you meant the brotherhood no harm, and so we arranged to have your book returned. But we still do not know who has done this terrible thing."

"So, did you call the BLM a second time, pretending to be my brother?"

"No. But we are concerned for your safety now, too. We have provided you with an *ángel* for your protection. He has been near you much of the time."

"Was the angel the one pretending to be my brother?"

"No, señorita."

Just then, the door opened. An immaculately dressed, darkly beautiful woman in her late forties or early fifties stood in the doorway of the Medina home. "Miss Wild?" she asked, before I could say why I had come. "I am Theresa Mendoza. I understand you knew my brother, Ignacio. My mother has something for you. Please come in."

People packed the main room and both of the passages leading away from it, most of them eating from foam plates filled with beans, *calabacitas*, posole, and *torta de huevo*—a deep-fried omelet with red chili—the traditional Penitente feast foods for Lent. Theresa Mendoza led me through the narrow maze of add-on adobe rooms, past the woodstove, through a mudroom off the kitchen where brown-skinned women fussed with huge pans of food, through a bedroom with two beds on which several children were sleeping, and finally to a meager space at the back of the house.

Theresa Mendoza drew the thick, nubby Chimayo blanket across its wooden rod above the doorway. Inside the room it was cool, dark, and quiet—the space not much bigger than a closet and furnished only with a narrow, frameless bed, a rustic chest, and a crucifix on the wall. One small window faced west. We had to choreograph our movements so Theresa could get past me to the chest. She opened it and delicately extracted a large bundle, taking great care not to bump it against anything. The outside of this bundle was woven tan cloth embroidered with skulls. It was tied with ancient *mecates*, a painstakingly crafted horsehair rope that I had read about. Ms. Mendoza closed the chest, sat on the bed, the bundle on her lap, and nodded her head toward the place on the bed beside her.

I sat.

Father Ignacio's sister wore a tiny gold cross in each ear, and her blue-black hair was pulled into a glossy, perfect bun at the nape of her long, slender neck. Like her mother and brother, she was small in stature, but not in demeanor. "I will show you what this is." She lifted the bundle from her lap and looked for a place to set it. I scooted to the end of the bed, opening up space between us. She laid the parcel down like a baby. She closed her eyes, drew breath, and crossed herself. Her deft fingers began to work at the horsehair knots as she spoke. "This is something very old. Ignacio was given the great honor of caring for this only a few years ago."

When the knots were untied, she pulled the rope away from the package and smoothed the fabric across the top several times with the palms of her hands, making it just so. Then she drew back the cloth. The box was the size of the object Mrs. Medina had been describing to Tecolote outside the church. It was made of hand-hewn cedar—large, perhaps eighteen inches by twelve, and six inches deep. The lid was like a three-dimensional retablo, with a beautifully detailed relief carving of the Last Supper, the multicolored hues of the wood creating the effect of shadows and light on the scene. At the center, the face of Jesus was disproportionately large, the carving deep—so that he seemed to be rising out of the box, emerging from the mortal plane, transcendent. His disciples on either side were caricatures of Hispanic villagers like the ones I'd seen all morning. Cracked, brittle-looking leather hinges held the top and bottom together, and a clever clasp had been made using two leather straps with slits that an antler tip passed through, securing the box shut.

Theresa Mendoza did not touch it. "This is what my mother wanted you to have," she said, looking directly at me.

I gasped, wonderstruck. "I can't take this!"

She pulled her head back, offended. Her nostrils flared. Her eyes were the same as those I had looked into that night in the coffeehouse in Santa Fe. She also carried herself with the same nobility and poise that her late brother did. "I have been instructed to give this to you, Miss Wild. I do not think you can refuse."

"But what am I supposed to do with it? What's in it?"

"I don't know."

"You don't know what's in it? Open it!" I fanned my hand at her, urging her to do this.

She placed her palm over her chest and leaned back. "I am not permitted."

"What do you mean, you are not permitted?"

"I am not permitted to touch La Arca."

"Well, then, what am I supposed to do with it?"

"La Arca was carved by a very famous santero from Las Truchas a long, long time ago, before even my grandfather was born. It was commissioned by Los Hermanos de la Luz for the morada in the nearby village of Boscaje. They say that when the santero finished La Arca, at noon on Miércoles de Ceniza—Ash Wednesday—the women in our village, here in Las Truchas, all began weeping uncontrollably at the same time. They cried all day. That night, the Holy Virgin came to them in the moonlight, at the well in the village plaza, and gave them comfort. And after that, she appeared to the santero and told him what would transpire. The santero gathered the people of Las Truchas the next day and told of the prophecy.

"The following Navidad, just as the santero had predicted, twelve sons were born in the village of Las Truchas within a period of seven days. The village *partera*—the midwife—had to go without sleep all that time just to get them all birthed. Since those days, it has been the tradition that we share our sons with the morada in Boscaje, as they do not have many men, it is a small village. La Arca belongs to the morada in Boscaje, for which it was made. It has always been kept there. But La Arca is a shared treasure, and there are many legends about it in Las Truchas. We only get to see it once a year, in our sanctuario on Good Friday, Viernes Santo. And no one is permitted to touch it except for El Guardián. That was Ignacio. Now it is you. You are La Guardiána."

"Me? I don't understand. I know nothing about this. Why give it to me? What am I supposed to do with it?"

"Someone else will have to provide you with the answers to your questions, Miss Wild. I do not know. I only know that Ignacio was chosen to care for it, and he left my mother with instructions in case the time came when he could not. She has consulted with someone, according to Ignacio's wishes, and you have been designated La Guardiána. At least for now."

"But why not keep it at the morada? You said it belonged there."

"Someone has been stealing the sacred objects from the moradas in several of the villages. Ignacio felt that someone was stalking La Arca. He did not feel it was safe in the morada. Now Los Hermanos believe he was right . . . now that he died. In fact, since the news of his death, the Hermanos from Boscaje have decided to perform the remainder of their ceremonies this week together with their brothers at the morada here in Truchas. They do not feel safe in their little morada any longer because it is so isolated. Among the things that have been stolen are the cuadernos—these are handwritten prayer books, but they are also often ledgers with the names of the members of the moradas, together with their family records. So, you see, La Arca is not safe with anyone whose family name is on one of those lists. It has to be entrusted to someone outside of the brotherhood, outside of their families. My brother named you."

"Am I allowed to look inside?"

She did not answer me directly. Instead, as she drew the cloth back around the box, she said, "Of course I do not know, but I think that La Arca contains important documents, records of things that have happened, maybe papers regarding Los Penitentes. One of the legends about La Arca tells that it contains a directive from Saint Francis himself. But no one who knows for sure will say. Whatever lies within

La Arca, it must be important because Los Hermanos kneel before it in the sanctuario on Easter and shed tears. They say it is what keeps the brotherhood alive."

We were both quiet. I stared at her fingers as she retied the horsehair rope. I felt certain this was all just a strange dream. I hoped I would wake up any moment now.

Theresa Mendoza interrupted my thoughts. "I also wonder if perhaps La Arca contains something that may explain why my brother was killed. My mother and I dearly hope you can shed some light on what has happened to our beloved Ignacio. Please do what you can with this, and may God be with you, Miss Wild. Do not argue with my mother's wishes, please. If you cannot keep La Arca safe, please find someone who can. But do not let my brother's sacred obligation fall into the wrong hands, I ask you."

I swallowed. *Why me?* "I'll do what I can, Señora Mendoza."

She tenderly transferred the package to my arms. "Wait here a moment." She moved the blanket aside and slipped out of the room. She returned with a purple-and-white-striped Mexican blanket, the kind you can buy for a few dollars just across the border. "Put this around it." She held the thin blanket up and we draped the bundle. She pulled the ends of the blanket over the top. "Do you mind if I ask you to leave through the mudroom door? There are many people here who do not need to be made curious about what you have in this blanket . . . This is not the time for us to have to be explaining things, wouldn't you agree?"

"Oh, yes, I agree. Yes, I'd be glad to spare you any inconvenience." We walked back to the mudroom, and she held the door for me. I looked down at her. "I'm very sorry for your loss, Señora Mendoza."

"Miss Wild, a great honor has been bestowed upon you today. And a great responsibility. I beg you, keep La Arca safe!" I wanted to respond, but I didn't know what to say. I stepped out onto the flagstone path, where another man stood guard over the house. He looked at me and nodded, then looked out into the backyard, alert. Theresa Mendoza moved to close the door after me, then opened it again and looked at me with moist eyes. "Miss Wild, I have faith in you."

I looked at her in surprise. "I'm not sure why you said that, but I'll try to earn your faith."

"I'm not exactly sure why I said it either." She gave a small smile. "But there is something about you; I see it. I think you have a good soul."

◄ 30 ►

Pursued

I had a hard time getting out of Truchas. The narrow road was so packed with parked cars that I had to take at least a dozen detours down rutted dirt alleys no more than a few inches wider than my Jeep. Once, I had to get out and threaten a stubborn goat to move so I could get by. I finally eased onto the paved, high mountain road leading northeast through Carson National Forest on the western edge of the mountains.

I made good speed on the straight leg of the High Road toward Trampas. As I came down into a deep bowl of a valley to the low point near the Trampas church, the only traffic was a white Ford Ranger closing in behind me. It only took me a couple of minutes to drive through the sleepy, deserted-looking village, and then I was on my way up the side of the next mountain, heading for a series of crest-line S-curves and high-elevation switchbacks.

My mind was full of my new responsibility. I looked down at the blanket-wrapped bundle in the passenger seat, wondering what to do with it, then quickly shifted my eyes back to the winding, roller-coaster road. Lost in my thoughts, I didn't notice the pickup moving to pass me until it was right beside me. We were headed around a hairpin curve—what a time to pass! Startled, I flinched and pulled the wheel slightly to the right and the Ford moved right also, into my lane, as I dipped two wheels onto the narrow shoulder. As we made this lateral move around the turn, I saw a propane tanker barreling toward us in the oncoming lane. Instinctively, I hit the brakes. The driver of the Ranger hit the gas and burst ahead, swerving around me, just barely in time to avoid a head-on crash with the tanker. The sound of the big horn on the propane rig blasted as it sped by, the wind drag from the enormous truck rocking the Jeep with its velocity.

I was so rattled I wanted to pull over and stop, but there wasn't a safe spot to do so for several miles. Instead, I slowed my speed and stayed on the road, taking deep breaths and feeling my pulse race under my skin. *Idiot driver! We could've all been killed!*

I lowered the window a little in spite of the cold. I could smell the clean sap of ponderosa pine, feel the bite of the crisp, rare air on my lungs as I inhaled. As I started to recover a little, I brought my Jeep up to speed again—but my adrenaline had leaped into overdrive just minutes ago, and it would be some time before I felt truly at ease. I drove through the heart of the forest past several gated Forest Service roads. When I passed the turnout for one of the trailheads, I saw a white vehicle emerge from the cover of the trees alongside the track and nose onto the highway behind me. It was the Ford Ranger again.

This time the driver didn't waste any time letting me know that the previous incident was not just a random act of reckless driving. The truck closed on my tail, the shape of the driver little more than a silhouette in my rearview mirror, wearing a hooded jacket or sweatshirt and sunglasses, and likely a man from what I could tell. As he moved to pass me again, I put all 195 horses in my engine to work. Around two dangerous curves, my tires singing like Las Dolientes, we fought for the lead. I knew the pursuer would again try to edge me over the side if I let him flank me. Going up a steep rise, I gained markedly on the pickup, wishing I had enough line of sight to a repeater so I could radio ahead to the Forest Service ranger station for help. But in this steep, curving terrain, it was hopeless unless you were atop one of the peaks or on one of the high stretches.

Coming downhill again, we were nearing the turnoff to Llano, a dirt road that culminated in a cattle guard at the paved highway. The pickup edged out into the oncoming lane, his front bumper just even with my rear quarter panel. I kept the pedal down hard, not wanting to give away my plan. My adversary followed suit, his engine roaring in my left ear as he gradually gained an inch at a time, clearly looking to get far enough to force me over. When the sign for the cattle guard appeared on the right shoulder, I slammed on the brakes and veered onto the dirt turnout, spinning counterclockwise into a red dust cloud as the white Ranger zoomed on by. I looked quickly for its tag number. The plate was packed with mud, unreadable.

I lurched to a stop and immediately stretched over and popped open the glove box. I pulled out my pistol, yanked it from the holster, and clicked off the safety. I opened the door of the Jeep, which was now perpendicular to the highway, its front bumper just at the edge of the cattle guard. I stood on my left leg, my right on the running board, and propped my forearms on the roof, squaring my gun sights at the highway ahead, my body in the cover of my Jeep.

The Ford Ranger came veering back in reverse at high speed. I sighted in on it, hoping to hit a tire, cause a blowout. I squeezed the trigger when I thought he was in range, but I heard a *ck-zzzzzngggg* and knew I'd hit the tailgate just above it instead. The pickup squealed to a stop, then slammed into drive, and the tires screamed. I took another shot before it could peel away. This one made a metallic *kunnnkkk* as the bullet penetrated the side of the truck bed just over the rear tire. The Ford Ranger sped off.

◄ 31 ►

No Place to Go

I stopped at the ranger station outside of Peñasco and used the phone. The Taos County sheriff's dispatcher told me she would radio Deputy Jerry Padilla and have him call me right back. While I waited for his call, I went out to my Jeep. I looked around the grounds, the parking lot, and down the road in each direction. I opened the rear hatch, unzipped my backpack, and pulled out my book for the first time since I'd gotten it back at Tecolote's place the previous morning. I turned to the page where I'd written down the two things Father Ignacio had told me, and I copied the name I'd been struggling to remember onto the back of one of my business cards: Pedro Antonio Fresquíz of Las Truchas. Then, closing the hatch and again scoping the area, I took the book and set it in the passenger seat on top of the bundle I'd been entrusted to guard. Theresa Mendoza was right—someone was stalking me, but was it me or La Arca he was after? I tucked my book under a fold of the blanket, making it a part of the bundle. "I know someplace you'll be safe," I told my charge. "For now anyway."

"A white Ford Ranger?" Padilla said.

"Yes, a fairly late model, but not new. There was mud packed over the plate; I couldn't read it. The driver was probably a man, but I couldn't guarantee that. The truck had tinted windows. But I could tell he was wearing some kind of garment with a hood. And dark glasses."

"Listen, I can send an officer up there to investigate, but this is getting pretty weird, don't you think? Have you got someplace you can go for a while? Maybe stay with some family?"

I swallowed hard. "No."

"A girlfriend, anything like that? Anyplace you can stay for a few days until we figure out what the hell's going on?"

"I don't know. I need to think."

Padilla was quiet for a few moments. "Roy said you live almost to Tres Piedras, all by yourself, no phone. I don't think it's so good for you to be all the way out there by yourself. And what about work? Are you working alone?"

"No. Not right now. I'm doing a team assignment with the Forest Service. I have a partner in my section—a forest ranger."

"Well, let's see . . . I got a meeting in a little bit; I couldn't come for another hour and a half. How 'bout I send a deputy up there to cruise around the area, see if he sees that Ford Ranger anyplace nearby?"

"There will be a ding in the tailgate and a bullet hole in the rear of the bed on the passenger side."

"Good to know that." I could hear him rustling his notepad. "I'll put it out on the wire and have everyone keep a lookout for a vehicle like that, countywide. Do you want the deputy to stop by the ranger station there and talk to you when he gets up there?"

"No, thanks, Jerry. I'm going to head on out after I get off the phone. Let me know if—"

"Don't worry, I'll let you know. Now, this is twice this bad guy has tried, Jamaica. Three, if you count when he took your book."

"No, he's not the one who stole my book."

"How do you know?"

I couldn't tell him about La Arca, or about the driver. I couldn't even tell him that I'd gotten my book back without revealing too much. "I just know."

"You just know, huh? I wouldn't be too sure. Doesn't seem like we know much of anything yet. Now, before I let you go, I'm going to try this one more time: I think it might be better if you took some time off, maybe got out of town. Take a vacation. Go see family or friends."

I felt my chest tighten. I drew in a breath, my lips pulling into a hard, tight line. "I hear you, Jerry. But I have no place to go."

Tecolote was not home. The turquoise-colored door was pulled fast to the frame, and there was no answer when I knocked. I had been counting on her to bring clarity to my muddled mind. An army of questions trampled my thought processes into mire. Esperanza would know what to do.

I decided to kill some time and try the bruja again in a little while, so I stopped by Regan's place. It was the middle of the day now, and the sun was lifting over the rim of the canyon and warming the red dirt of her rutted drive. An old, rusted beater truck was backed up to the corral, blocking the way so that I had to park in the entrance to the drive. Two men in the corral were laboring hard at digging in the hard caliche. I walked around the truck's listing tailgate and saw Regan above on the path leading to the barn. She wore the same huge, unlaced, muddy work boots as the day I first met her. She caught sight of me and made her way rapidly down the path, as if to intercept me. Her expression was frantic.

"Jamaica, I'm having a frightful day. I'm afraid I can't receive any visitors." She held one gloved hand over her left eye.

"Sure, Regan. I'm sorry. I should have called. I was just in Truchas and I thought I'd stop by on my way back to Taos."

"Yes, I see." She grabbed my elbow with her free hand and

edged me around, urging me back toward my Jeep. "I am so sorry I can't visit right now. This is just a hectic time; you know it's Holy Week, and there have been people trespassing across my land to that place up there, and my horse has gone lame, and now—for whatever reason—I have lost the sight in my left eye! I am having to put my horse down, poor old dear; I knew it was coming, but just the same . . . " Her voice, which had been rapid and full of vibrato, seemed to run out of gas, and she gently shook her head very slightly back and forth, her forehead supported by the fingers of her glove over her left eye. "The men are here digging, I can't leave. We had to move all the cars around so they could get in with their truck. And I can't even get the doctor on the phone about this eye."

"I am so sorry to hear about your horse, Regan. And about your eye. Is there anything I can do? Can I take you to the clinic down in Embudo?"

"No, no. I should be apologizing to you. But you know how I get, I just can't have any visitors right now. I am just so overwhelmed, I wouldn't be good company. And with the horse . . . " As she was saying this last, a green Land Rover pulled up behind my Jeep. The driver gave a short blast on the horn, and then Andy Vincent emerged from the driver's side. The workmen looked up from their digging. Andy Vincent pulled off his sunglasses. There was a look of agitation on his face.

"Oh, there's Andy," Regan said.

Andy marched toward us. He looked into my Jeep as he

went past, as if he were going to accost anyone inside. He was clearly annoyed.

"I guess I better get my Jeep out of the drive so Andy can get his car off the road," I said.

"Andy, Jamaica was just leaving," Regan called, her voice pushed, squeaking.

"Yeah, if you'll just back up there, I'll get out of your way," I called, as I turned from Regan's side and started for my Jeep.

Andy continued toward us.

"Jamaica just stopped by on her way back from Truchas," Regan explained. "I told her I just couldn't entertain any visitors right now."

"Truchas? What's going on up there?" Andy asked. "I just came from the High Road, and Truchas looks like it's hosting a rock concert. There are at least a hundred cars parked along the road through there." By now, he had reached me and was looking down into my face. The brilliant sun behind him kept his expression in dark shadow.

I squinted, but the sun was too bright; I had to look away. "A funeral for a friend of mine," I said to Andy, then to Regan, "Father Ignacio Medina. Remember our conversation about him on Sunday?"

Regan's face was directly lit by the sun. She looked pale, drained. Her jaw dropped and her mouth fell open, but she didn't speak. Her hand came away from her eye, and there was a large blue bruise on the brow above it.

"Regan! Did your horse kick you?"

She didn't seem to hear me. Her face muscles remained limp, her normally tan skin now ashen.

Andy Vincent went to Regan's side and put his arm around her. He gave her a little shake. "She's had an awful time with the horse." He tipped his head in the direction of the men digging. "I'm glad I've been here and can offer a little help and comfort."

Regan still didn't speak.

There was something I had wanted to ask her a moment ago, but suddenly, I couldn't remember it. I was puzzling over this when Andy spoke again. "You say this father—he was your friend?"

It had been something important. *What was it?* "Huh? Oh, yes. Yes. He was my friend."

Regan had recovered now, and she spoke kindly to me. "Oh, Jamaica, my dear, I'm so sorry. I have been so selfish, telling you all my troubles. I didn't know you were having a hard day, too. That's the man Father Rivera was talking about, isn't it? I didn't realize he was your friend. I'm so sorry." Her eyes grew moist, her bruised face still strained, but compassionate.

"Well, he wasn't really a close friend." I felt a twinge in my gut. I was uncomfortable, embarrassed by her outpouring of sympathy. But there was something else: I felt unfaithful, like I'd just betrayed Father Ignacio. My mind skirmished, one part trying to justify, the other trying to know the truth. We had only one meeting. But there was so much intensity. And now he had bestowed such trust in me.

We were all three standing quiet. But my brain went around and around like a gerbil on a wheel. In the span of a few seconds I flashed from the thought of La Arca to the chase down the High Road to wondering if Tecolote was home and whether she would have some answers about what to do with the sacred ark, and on from there to realizing that I would have to get some sleep before I went to work tonight, to wondering where I would be safe. All this, all at once.

I sighed. I looked at Regan and Andy. They seemed to be waiting for a cue from me. "Well, I had better get going." I turned once more toward my Jeep.

Andy Vincent stayed behind to talk quietly with Regan for a few seconds, and then he followed me down the path to our vehicles.

I opened the door of my Jeep, and Andy took the handle and held it while I got in. "You must have the day off," he said, his lips flattening, as if he'd tried a pleasant smile and failed, still not over his irritation. There was a terrible weight in his countenance, like that of the Penitentes at the funeral. And an urgency, not unlike Regan's demeanor. It made me tired just to look at him.

"No, I took last night off so I could go to the funeral today. I have to work tonight. I need to go home and take a nap. I am all turned around."

He closed the door without speaking and walked back to his car. I watched him in the rearview mirror as he got in the Land Rover and backed down the dirt road. I felt tense and fatigued, as if I had soaked up some of his and Regan's anxiety and added it to my own.

I backed out of the drive and crossed the bridge over the rio. At the junction where the bridge met the road, I looked left—no oncoming traffic, then right—none coming, and when I turned to look left again, Esperanza's face was pressed against the driver's-side window. My heart stopped, then pounded. I heard a high ringing sound as the sudden escalation in my blood pressure looked for a way to escape the constricting confines of my arteries. I rolled the window down, my eyes dilated from the jolt.

"Don't come to *la casa*, Mirasol! It is not safe. I will let you know when it is all right to come again." She was wearing her thick lavender shawl wrapped around her head and shoulders. She stood beside the car and peered at me. Her eyes were at the same level as mine.

"Esperanza, I need to talk to you."

"You must wait."

"No, I need to talk to you now." As I said this, I looked for a place to pull over, in case a car needed to come past.

"No! *¡Deje de hablar! ¡Escuche!* Stop talking, you must listen!"

She had my attention.

"You must wait and watch out now. You are in danger."

"I know. I have so many questions—"

She shook her head in exasperation. "I have already told you everything that you need to know. But you do not hear me, Mirasol."

"What about La Arca?"

"Hush! Do not wag your tongue at me! Your mind is like a dog with fleas, always scratching, digging at itself." She plunged her arms in the window and seized my head in a viselike grip. Then she pressed her thumbs over my eyes, holding them tightly shut. Her voice gained that high-pitched bat-cry quality. "Wait. And watch out! That is what I am telling you. Keep yourself safe. You will be all right to go home today and sleep. You must sleep to be strong. You will be protected at your house by the *ángel* today so that you can get the rest you need." I felt her grip relax, then release completely. I opened my eyes. She was gone.

I sat unmoving for several minutes, then turned my Jeep toward the highway and drove at an idle down the graded dirt road through the village. Soon the acequias would be full of the snowmelt and running with sparkling water down the slopes to the rio, their banks swelling with poleo, wild asparagus, and new, tiny shoots of red willow. The rio would run full and fast, rapids would foam over jutting rocks into the low places beneath them, and the wildflowers would bloom again. Centuries-old orchards of apples, plums, and pears would swell with buds and flowers, the ground beneath them full of wild watercress from the flood of water through the acequias, and this little crack in the earth would be lush with new life. The people of this valley would be planting their kitchen gardens with corn and squash and chiles and taking their cows to pasture on land leased by permit from the BLM. And some would gather straight saplings for coyote and *latilla* fences to keep the animals out of their gardens. And some would fly-fish in the river. Most would live on their land just as their families had lived since the Spanish conquistadors came, harvesting and putting up their fruits, drying the chiles in beautiful ristras and perhaps selling some of them along the roadside or in town, trading eggs for flour, milk for sugar, bartering their skills among themselves until all their needs were satisfied. A few would take jobs with the government in Los Alamos or find work during the tourist season as hotel or wait staff in Taos or Santa Fe. Some would grow up, some would leave home, some would get married, some would have children, and some would die.

Like Father Medina.

In a little while, nobody would much remember what it was like before, when he was here, what his days were like, how he looked, his wonderful melodious voice, his dark eyes, the white streak in his hair, his love for his work, his passion, what he lived for.

And they sure as hell wouldn't remember what he died for. Not, especially, if they never knew.

◄ 32 ►

Disappeared

At dawn the next morning, Holy Thursday, I completed an uneventful shift. Roy had assigned Art, the BLM ranger from the Taos Field Office, to team with me in my section. We had spent the entire night in sight of one another, and I was grateful for the company and the extra protection. After we had put the horses in the stalls and dropped the truck and trailer at the ranger station in Peñasco, Art left to go home and get some rest. I was getting ready to load my gear into my Jeep and do the same when Kerry drove up.

"I missed you the other night," he said. "Are you feeling better?"

"Yes, I am, thanks. Sorry to let you down. It must have been something I . . . imbibed."

He smiled. "That's an interesting way to put it. But don't

worry, you didn't let me down. It has been quiet up here for a few days now. No more fence cutting, no more signs of trespassing. Want to go and get some breakfast after I check in my gear?"

"Sure."

In less than a minute, Kerry came back out the door of the station and strode toward me in a hurry. "Jump in my truck. We're going down to Suazo's place."

"Why, what's up?" I closed the Jeep's hatch and locked it.

"The dispatcher said Suazo's wife called the sheriff's office to report him missing. They said she asked for you and 'that forest ranger' to come talk with her." He handed me a message slip. "And that's from your office in Taos. I guess she tried to reach you there, too. They relayed the message up here for you."

"Well, that's interesting. I was just wondering about Santiago Suazo myself." I got in the truck and we lumbered down the slope in low gear.

"It can't be such a big deal that he's missing," Kerry said. "She said he always goes off when he has money, and she told us he had money."

"Yeah, I hear you. And what is this—Thursday morning? I saw him Monday in town, and he was definitely loaded, in more ways than one. We had a little altercation." I reached for the radio.

His hand caught mine before I could turn it on. "An altercation? Why didn't you tell me about that?"

"I saw his truck at El Toro. I went in to ask him what he had been doing up around Boscaje, where you had seen his truck those two times. I was just going to talk to him, but he blew up and started hurling insults, and even made an implied threat. I went after him, and he took a swing at me."

"You went after him?"

"Well, at first I just tapped his shoulder to get him to turn around and talk to me after he had hurled a string of particularly unsavory insults at me at the top of his voice in the restaurant. But after he tried to slug me, I pinned him up against his truck. I tried to get him to say what he's been doing up here in this area. But he wouldn't say. Just kept threatening me and insulting me for being a woman. It sounds weird, but even though he was acting like the same little banty rooster we know, it was almost like he was scared of something."

Kerry looked at me, incredulous. "Hey, whether they're scared or not, if you plan to wrestle with the bad guys and don't want backup, will you at least give me a shout so I can sell tickets?" His tone was angry.

"It wasn't like I planned it. You weren't around. I was on my way in to the BLM and I saw his truck. We haven't been able to catch him sitting still, so I took advantage of the opportunity. Luckily, it played out better than it might have. A couple people I know pulled up and it ended peacefully. Suazo saw his moment and bailed. Unfortunately, though, I never got any information from him."

"All right, but can I just ask you something?"

"Sure. What is it?"

"Is something going on with you that I ought to know about?"

I didn't look at him. Suddenly, my face felt hot and I noticed I was clenching my jaw.

He didn't wait for me to answer. "The other night, Roy asked me to go check on you. Then last night, he doubled you up with the BLM ranger. It's almost like he thinks you need protection."

I thought about denying that anything was wrong, but I couldn't do that. It would have been lying, and I didn't want to lie to him. "I can't talk about it," I said.

He kept his eyes on the road, but he raised his eyebrows. "You can't talk about it?"

"No, I'm sorry. I really wish I could tell you, but I can't."

He drove a minute or so in silence. "Well, can you at least answer my question? Do you need protection?"

I took a deep breath in and slowly let it out. "I don't know."

Kerry shook his head. "What kind of answer is that?"

"It's . . . it's about a case I'm involved in. I really can't talk about it."

He gave an exasperated sigh. "Listen, you said the thing with Suazo happened on Monday. We worked together that night. Why didn't you tell me about it?"

So much had happened, I had to think back. "Monday night was when you checked on me at my base camp. As I recall, we didn't talk much while you were there." I looked across the cab at him, studying his profile, remembering the warmth of that kiss.

He turned and caught me staring at him and smiled. "No, I guess we didn't."

⧧

Mrs. Suazo was feeding two little kittens when we drove up. She looked a lot better than the last time we had seen her. Her hair was clean and loose around her face. She was wearing a navy dress with flowers on it, a cardigan sweater, and white cotton socks folded over the tops of some new-looking boots. The porch had been swept and the cat litter raked away. She looked up at us expectantly, and then, seeing the Forest Service truck, her look moved rapidly through disappointment and into an expression of hurried anxiety. She moved quickly to put the lid on the tin container of cat food, brushed her hands on her skirt, and then, catching herself, rubbed them back and forth on each other. She hurried off the porch and almost made it to the truck before we could open our doors. Something was missing . . . *Right! Where were the dogs?*

"I thought you might have been him," she said, taking hold of the handle and yanking the passenger door back as if to hasten me out. "I ain't seen him in two days. Something has happened to him." Her brow was like a plowed field. "I can't get the sheriff to listen to me."

Kerry and I got out of the truck. I looked around the place, then spoke. "Well, Mrs. Suazo, when we talked to you

before, you did say he is sometimes gone for days at a time."
I didn't know how to put it any more kindly.

She stopped the frenzied pressure of her approach when
I said this—it seemed to affect her like a red light does traffic. "Well, you're right. I did say that. And he does do that. I
reckon you're right." She twisted at the ends of her sweater.
Then she looked into my face. The bruise under her right eye
had turned yellow and was fading. "Would you just believe
me when I tell you that this time it's different?" Her tone was
flat, but her look was pleading.

By this time, Kerry had come around the truck and was
behind her. He moved to the side so she could see him when
he spoke. "Mrs. Suazo, why don't you tell us what you know,
and we'll see if there is anything we can do to help."

She turned toward him. "He came home Monday in the
middle of the day and said we needed to leave town."

I glanced at Kerry. Our eyes met, but neither of us spoke.

"He promised to take me back home to Texas. He said
he would take the dogs to his cousin and sell or give away
whatever we didn't want to take with us. We started right
then going through stuff. I knew he really meant it, because
that evening, he took the dogs and told me to keep packing
things. He kept saying we were going to make a brand-new
start, and we were going to be happy again. When he came
back, three of his cousins followed him in their trucks and
they went through our stuff and took a lot of it and gave us
some money for some of the things, like the TV and such.

Listen, I know the sheriff don't believe me, but this time it's different. Santiago never went through giving stuff away or selling it off like that before. And he wouldn't never have gave those dogs up if he didn't mean to do what he said."

"What happened after his cousins came?" Kerry said.

"He said he wanted to get out of here the next day, if we could get our packing done. We worked right on up until late that night. The next morning we got up and started in packing again. By a little after noon, we were done. Santiago went to get gas in the truck, and we was going to load it up when he got back and then get on down the road. But he never come back."

"He was just going to go get gas in the truck?" I asked.

"That and pick up the rest of the money he was owed for something. He said it was all set up and it wouldn't take long."

"Do you know who he was meeting for the money, or what it was for?" Kerry said.

"I don't know nothing about that. Santiago never tells me nothing about his business. But he said it was all set, and he just needed to go get it. And then he was going to get some gas, like I said."

"And that was Tuesday?" I asked.

"Yes. Two days ago. I know I told you he goes off for days sometimes, but he don't never give away his dogs and sell the TV and tell me he's taking me back to Texas. This time, it's different." She was quiet for a few seconds, as if she was thinking over the events of the past few days. Then she said, "I don't know if it's got anything to do with it, but I think I better show you what I found out here in the shed."

Kerry and I pulled up to my vehicle. He looked at me. "I'm worried about you. Why not come to my place? I can roll out a bedroll on the floor. You can have the bed. Just until we know that you are safe again."

"I can't. But I need your help."

"Just name it."

"I left something here at the ranger station. It's in the lockbox where I keep my tack. I put it there yesterday and it was still all right this morning, but it is very important that no one gets to it. I need you to make sure it stays safe."

"It will be safe there. No one is going to mess with your tack box. The ranger station is staffed all day, and we'll be back tonight for the next operational period. I'm more concerned about you. Nothing is more important than that."

"I will be all right. I have a full day, I'll hardly have a moment alone. I really need you to help me with this. I need what's in the lockbox to be safe."

"You put your own lock on it, right? No one else has a key?"

"I locked it, and I put the key in an envelope and put it in your message box. I don't want you to use the key unless you have to, though. I need you to make sure no one gets in that lockbox."

"Why? What's in there?"

"I can't tell you."

He slumped. "You don't trust me."

"No, I do. That's why I gave you the key. I do trust you. And I will tell you, when I can. Just—please, can you do what I'm asking? Don't open the lockbox. And don't let anyone else open it either."

"Okay. I'll stay here today. I'll guard it with my life. But what about you?"

"No, you can't be obvious about it. I don't want anyone to even think there's anything in there worth guarding. Just watch out for . . . I don't know, just check on it every once in a while. Maybe you could take some apples to Redhead late this afternoon, you know, and check on it. Try to watch when things quiet down, when there aren't so many people around. If anyone knows that it's there, that's when they would try to steal it."

"Well, it's busy up here all day, but I'll stay here, too. I can even sleep in the stables right there by the tack boxes. But what about tonight? We have a big night ahead of us."

"I've been thinking about that. They close some of the Forest Service roads, post checkpoints on Holy Thursday, don't they? Because of the Penitentes?"

He nodded.

"Well, it might be all right then."

"So you're not worried that someone from the Forest Service would steal this . . . this . . . whatever it is. You're thinking it would be someone else."

"Yes, if that someone figures out that it's there. I would have bet money that person would have been Santiago Suazo. But after what his wife told us, I don't know. It could be someone he was in cahoots with. It could be anyone."

"So I'm starting to put a few things together now."

"I wish I could tell you more, I really do. Now, I've got to go. There's a meeting I have to go to at the BLM. I'm not going to get much sleep before tonight. And tonight, I'll stay in short range of my base camp if I can. Come get me if anything happens, okay?"

"Sure. I'll check in on you anyway."

"Okay, I better go now." I started to open the door of the truck.

Kerry took hold of my arm. "Wait. I meant to ask you: did you ever look at that photo memory card to see what was on it?"

I felt in my coat pocket. The device Kerry had given me was still there. "No, I forgot about it. I'll try to take a look at it when I'm at the BLM today. I gotta go."

His eyes beckoned me. I hesitated. He leaned over and touched his lips to mine. "Please be careful, Jamaica."

◄ 33 ►

Picture This

I stopped by the library in Taos and asked the reference librarian to help me out with some information. I handed her the business card on which I had written the name I had copied from my book. She was able to get me what I needed in a matter of minutes. After that, I reported in for the meeting at the BLM.

"We're going to work closely with the sheriff's office and the Forest Service these next few days," Roy said, "to try to manage the influx of people wanting to see the Penitente processions. There will be folks trying to camp and drive where they shouldn't up in the areas around the High Road and out in Arroyo Seco. We're going to put extra night details in both areas." The Boss used a laser pointer and a map to flesh out the assignments for everyone. "Jamaica, I'm going to have to put Art out in Seco. You'll have Reed working with you up in your area, though, so I want you to stay in close range of him, and vice versa. The weather forecast says we've got a big system coming in that could produce a lot of snow. And you all know how these early spring snows in high country can be—they're usually the heaviest ones we get. Everyone gear up for that, and that means chains for your rigs, parkas, whatever you need to survive in case you get stranded."

After the meeting, I headed for my cubicle to use the phone. As I listened to the ring on the other end of the line, I took the memory card that I had found a week ago in the illegal camp where Redhead had thrown me and inserted it into the reader device. I plugged the reader into the port on the computer.

"Deputy Padilla." He fired it off fast.

"Jerry. This is Jamaica Wild."

"Well, hello there. No more car chases, I hope. How you doing? You all right?"

"Yeah, I'm fine, thanks. Hey, I have a favor I want to ask of you."

"You do? Well, now, tell me this: am I going to want to do it?"

I was opening the images from the file on the memory card reader drive. The pictures had been taken at night, and several of them were almost completely black.

Padilla continued, "What I mean is: is this something I need to brace myself for? Seems like whenever you're involved, things gets pretty complicated."

"What? Oh, no. No, I—sorry—I was looking at something else and lost concentration. No, I need you to do something for me, Jerry. It's not complicated. And I'm going to give you a little information in return."

"Well, that sounds a little better. What do you need?"

"I want you to try to find Santiago Suazo."

"Hah!" he snorted. "You and half of all Taoseños! What's he done to you?"

"Nothing, really. At least I don't think so. It's his wife. She believes some harm has come to him. I guess she tried calling your office to file a missing persons report, and then she phoned here to the BLM and asked to see me."

"Yeah, I saw that she had called in, but, see, we have to play by the rules. We can't file an MEP until someone has been missing three days, unless it's a child or someone in need of medical attention or infirm in some way. Besides, you know it's only a matter of time before something bad is gonna happen to that little bastard, anyway. You can bet he's got a bull's-eye on his butt no matter what he's wearing."

"Yeah, I know. I know. But Mrs. Suazo told me some interesting things. I think he might have gotten in way over his head this time."

"Well, let's see," he said, "what sort of things would that be? Maybe I might get concerned about all this if I knew what we were even talking about, Jamaica. But I don't know why we're even talking about Santiago Suazo. Instead, I'm more concerned about you. Did you find someplace else to stay?"

"Suazo told his wife he was going to take her home to her people in east Texas. He found homes for their dogs and gave them away, sold or gave away everything they could, and helped her pack up the rest of their things. He had been flashing around a lot of money lately, like maybe he had just scored at something major, Jerry. Mrs. Suazo said she saw two big rolls of bills. Anyway, he left Tuesday at midday to run into town to get gas in the truck so they would be ready to leave—and to meet someone to pick up some money he was still owed. And he never came back."

"Way I hear it, Jamaica, that guy disappears for days like that a lot."

"I guess this time it sounds like it's different, Jerry. It did to Mrs. Suazo, and it did to me, too. She thinks someone has done him in."

"Well, see, there's just about a five-mile-long line of people who'd be suspects for that. You hear what I'm saying?"

"Yeah, Jerry, I hear you. But there's more. Suazo was involved in the theft of those Penitente icons. That had to be where he was getting all the money from. His wife showed me a shed on their property. It's full of bultos and retablos."

Padilla whistled into the phone. "Well, that might be, but I don't have any authority to go look through Suazo's shed without—"

"Do you have the reports on those stolen icons? Couldn't you have someone go out and compare the descriptions of the stolen property with—"

"But that's just it, Jamaica. There are no reports. You

know the Penitentes. They aren't going to talk about what's going on with them to the law."

"But isn't there some kind of team investigation or something?"

"Team investigation? Who told you that? Salazar? It's just another one of those concurrent jurisdiction things where we got a phone call from the sheriff of Rio Arriba County and a fax from the sheriff's office in Santa Fe County, and everyone's hearing the same rumors, but nobody's got nothing. That's your team investigation."

"Well, if you send someone out to Suazo's place, I know his wife will show you what's there; you won't need to get a warrant. I told her I was going to call you and talk to you about it. I'm pretty sure some of the stuff in those rumors is in his shed."

"Okay, I'll go out there myself."

"And, would you just keep a lookout for Suazo? Like I said, his wife said he was going into town to collect some money and then to get gas in the truck. Maybe you could ask around at the gas stations—"

"Speaking of trucks, I haven't had any luck looking for your shot-up Ford Ranger. You don't think that could have been Suazo driving it, do you?"

"It wasn't his truck. And it doesn't jibe with his wife's story. She said Suazo disappeared midday on Tuesday, the day before the Ranger tried to run me off the cliff."

"Well, let's see then . . . do you think Suazo is tied in to the incident at the gorge bridge?"

"I don't know."

"That's the thing, see? We're over a week out from that, and we still don't have any idea who did it or why. The trail is getting cold, and we don't have a single lead. Nine times out of ten when I have a murder, I know who did it within a day or two. This one has us all stumped."

"Well, Suazo could be a lead of some kind if you can find him."

"Okay, Jamaica. I'll get on it. I'll let you know if I find anything. In the meantime, you keep yourself safe."

I turned my attention to the photo files on the computer's desktop. Twelve images had been dark or blurred and were impossible to make out. But six more showed the same scene over and over again, each with a different icon centered in the picture. Someone had photographed Los Hermanos as they performed some important ceremony in front of the Boscaje morada, their large crucifix at the head of the procession, then the *carreta de la muerte*—the large wooden cart with its life-size carved wooden skeleton figure of death holding an ax nailed to its seat—and *el hermano mayor* holding La Arca! I scanned the images carefully, looking at the men's faces. One of them I recognized immediately. I was sure it was him, the big man standing there behind the elder with the ark. He looked the same, even in that old-fashioned long, black coat. The dark hair, the dark eyes . . . it was him. There was my angel.

◄ 34 ►

Looking for Something

After I left the BLM, I drove to my cabin to try to get a few hours' sleep before I had to go on duty again. When I pulled up, I saw at once that the front door was open. I took my pistol from the glove box, turned off the engine and pocketed the keys, then quietly opened the Jeep door, stepped out, and scanned the area. This was starting to be my homecoming routine.

There was no other vehicle, no sign that any other cars had been there. But the frozen ground wouldn't have taken a track impression from tires anyway. This time, I wasn't going to screw around. I holstered my pistol on my belt and reached in the back and got out my pump-action shotgun. I walked quickly to the *portal*, then eased myself to the side of the doorway and raised the shotgun barrel, holding it with both hands. I pointed the gun into the cabin and swept a semicircular pattern from one side of the room to the other, my eyes following the barrel, my finger on the trigger, ready. I pulled my left hand away, still holding the gun in my right, and pressed the door back until it hit the wall, assuring me there was no one behind it.

Someone had ransacked my cabin, leaving it in total disarray. But my spartan living quarters didn't offer much place for a person to hide. The log bed made of thick aspen limbs sat high off the ground, its covers torn from the mattress and thrown to the side. Beneath it, I could see the floor all the way to the wall. On the other side of the room was the kitchen, with its stove, fridge, sink, and cupboard, the contents of which had been emptied onto the counter and the floor. The one big chair had been shoved all the way into the corner, and the only other furnishings, besides a small table with two chairs, were my dresser, the open shelves of books, a portable stereo, and my nightstand—all of which had been emptied, their contents rearranged or knocked to the floor. I moved cautiously across the room toward the pass-through closet that led to the bathroom, still holding the shotgun at the ready.

The bathroom door was open. The shower curtain had been pulled aside, revealing the empty tub. The cantilevered doors to the closet, too, were open, and everything had been pulled off the shelves, the clothing pushed aside on the hangers, the shoes strewn apart, and all the boxes that had been stacked on the top shelf had been dumped out onto the middle of the closet floor.

Nobody there. I lowered the shotgun barrel.

I looked down, still in the habit of following my gun with my eyes. Among the scattered items at my feet I saw a yellowed sheet of lined notebook paper with the familiar blue lacy script. I stooped and picked it up, squatting over my boots, and read again what I had read before many times:

A woman
with her head down
gone underground
trying to hide herself
in the tying of a toddler's shoelaces
the washing of a family's dinner plates
the gathering of the eggs.

A woman
with her dreams gone
barely holding on
having lost herself
somewhere in all the sunsets
forgetting why she
ever wanted to see the sunrise.

A woman
hollowed out from the wind
burned out by lightning

scorched by dry sun
forgetting who she was
knowing not who she is
blows away like dust.

I felt like I was going to cry. *Come on, Jamaica, you better keep it together,* I told myself, as I laid the shotgun on the floor next to me and picked up the rest of the poems my mother had written, placing them in the box with the few other things of hers I had kept. I knew that whoever had trashed my cabin was looking for La Arca and knew that I was its guardian now. I grabbed the shotgun and walked back into the main room where the door had swung back to a halfway position, drew back my left leg, and kicked the door as hard as I could. It shook the whole room when it slammed shut.

◄ 35 ►

Holy Night

Clouds as dark as flint began to pile up over the Jemez Mountains as I went on duty that night, and the temperature sank with the sun. It looked like snow. It looked like a lot of snow. Roy had briefed us at the meeting that morning that the Forest Service road would have a checkpoint at each end, and the gate to the four-wheel track would be locked because it was Holy Thursday.

Any curious Anglos hoping to see a Penitente crucifixion in this area would have to take the High Road through Trampas and Truchas, where they would be met by menacing-looking villagers, some with rifles slung on their shoulders. The cars of these prying intruders, if they dared park them and set out on foot, would be stripped and looted. Villagers would conveniently have chickens or goats escape from pens and fill the streets so traffic would be stalled. And then the windows of out-of-town cars would be pelted with eggs or fresh animal dung as the occupants sat helplessly within. Law enforcement officers at remote locations would be suspiciously delayed from responding to distress calls from cell phones in Mercedes, if they were in cell range at all. The inhabitants of these vanity rides would be fearful and complaining, waiting hostage with windows rolled up tight, their expensive parkas and fur-lined après-ski boots too much for spending the evening trapped in their car.

I sat astride Redhead at the top of a knoll overlooking the four-wheel track. A thin line of fiery orange still edged the top of the Jemez range as the sun tried to paint blazing colors in a sky heavy and dark with impending snow. Behind me, the full moon would rise unseen, behind rumpled blankets of black and blue vapor held back by the tips of the Sangre de Cristo Mountains.

To the east, up the slope and through the trees, the Boscaje morada would be empty tonight, according to what Theresa Mendoza had told me. Its members would have gone to Truchas for the rituals, in fear for their safety. Beyond the deserted morada—somewhere higher up—the Calvario would also be abandoned. This was the place where the Boscaje Hermanos would have directed their procession, following the fourteen stations of the cross—and perhaps even raised a cross on which one of their own was hung.

In the old days, this ritual would have been done at noon on Good Friday, after the procession to the church. There, the stand-in for Christ would have his last earthly meeting with his mother, portrayed by a bulto of the Virgin Mary carried by the women of the village. All would then proceed to the graveyard for the crucifixion. But, as Father Ignacio had said, the intrusion of outsiders had forced many moradas to hold clandestine midnight rituals in remote places carefully guarded by villagers.

All over the Rio Grande Valley, in villages, towns, and pueblos, the faithful were going to mass at this hour for the consecration of the Eucharist, representing Christ's flesh and blood, reenacting the Last Supper in the ritual of communion—the last time this would be done until Easter Sunday. Tonight, their world would enter a figurative darkness, symbolizing the betrayal and crucifixion of their Savior. The threatening weather seemed perfect for this.

In the past, my book, my job, even the spartan comfort of my little cabin, were all things that shielded me from the feeling that I was utterly alone. Now even this country—this beautiful corner of northern New Mexico that was the only place that felt like home to me—offered me no protection. Its wild beauty made me feel helpless, assailable. I had been unable to sleep in my cabin, afraid of another attack, robbery, or violation. In my heightened vulnerability, even my budding relationship with Kerry—which had both thrilled and terrified me—seemed bound up with this string of mysteries now.

I wasn't even tired anymore. A vague, unnamed fear had taken hold deep within me and begun to expand. Some hidden accelerator inside me had been pressed hard to the floor, causing my breathing to grow short and my skin to tingle in a random pattern of synapses.

I rode the fence line south, climbing in elevation. The air felt heavy, wet, and cold. It was going to be a hell of a snow. There had been a sickly cast to the last remaining light, like the slick, blue-gray underbelly of a snake, so that I was glad to see it ending. I was only planning to ride a short way. On a night like this, in this rough terrain, a person could get trapped in a blizzard and die just going out to check the mail.

Redhead was skittish, as horses are before storms. She jibbed and volted, feeling the wildness in the weather as her mustang ancestors did, wanting to outrun the storm. She bridled and we halted.

"*Shhhhh*. Are you going to calm down, or are you going to wear your bit through your gums?"

She whistled, shaking her head, fussing with her bit.

"Well, all right then. Getup!" I gave her a tiny press with my heels.

She balked. Then she whinnied loud and snorted, her nostrils flaring back in fear.

"What is it?"

I waited, senses alert.

I smelled smoke—not unusual in a land heated by wood-stoves and fireplaces. Then, as I scanned the horizon, I saw the red glow. Fire! There was fire in the forest land above me. I gouged Redhead with my heels. She was ready and took off like a bullet. As we bounded up the slope, I knew in my heart what was burning. I made straight for the Boscaje morada. Small limbs smacked into me as I tried to guide the horse at top speed through the dense thicket. The foliage switched my face, stinging it with sticky juniper sap. It was getting so dark I couldn't see where I was going. Redhead slowed, nervously pulling her head back to avoid vicious swipes from low limbs. Reluctantly, I dismounted and led her, picking my way along through the forest with one hand outstretched. Finally, as I neared the meadow, I could see the golden flames coming from the morada's roof and slapping the low sky, hissing at the cold moisture. The perfect black silhouette of a cross stood at the center of this high hat of yellow fire.

The inhabitants being away at the morada in Truchas, a lone man was hurrying into the morada. I let go of Redhead and raced to the door, just as he came out again. He was carrying a large carved figure, nearly half his height. "Here!" I yelled, beckoning him to hand it to me. Our eyes met, and in the glow of the fire, I recognized him. I had seen his picture only a few hours before, and here he was. "Manny! Are there any people inside?"

"No people. Save this!" he snapped. "There are more!" He shoved the bulto into my arms and went back in the door of the morada. In spite of its size, the cottonwood bulto was light. I looked around for a safe place to set it and saw the cart that had been parked a few yards away in front of the morada. I went to it, put the figure on the ground beside it, and was returning to get the next one when I heard the high whine of a rupturing viga, one of the wooden beams that spanned and supported the earthen roof. There was a terrible sharp squeal, the vicious dogfight sound of dense wood tearing, and then a heavy thud. Sparks flew up in the doorway, and a great cloud of thick smoke caromed out.

"Manny?" I screamed, trying to see in. Fierce heat boiled out of the opening, and I held one arm over my face and forced myself to step inside. The light of the flames inside the morada made the whole shrine seem like a flickering candle, the walls glowing yellow gold, the micaceous flecks in the adobe sparkling. The huge black and red ember of what was once a viga had severed in two, its stems like wicks in the ground at the center. The roof was torn open above this, and flames rose toward the night. Dust of broken adobe and earthen roof danced in the scorching hot air. "Manny!" I screamed, trying to make my voice louder than the roar of the fire.

I couldn't see him. The blaze seemed to be centered at the rear of the room, away from the door, and so I edged my way along a wall, the air making my lungs feel like they were roasting in a furnace each time I breathed. The smoldering viga was starting to gush smoke now. I pulled my muffler over my face and tied it behind my head to screen the air. I moved in front of a long bench that had been set against the wall. "Manny, where are you?"

"Here!" he grunted. The sound was ahead and to my left, just beyond the downed viga.

I saw him then, in its shadow. He was sitting on the floor

before the altar, which was covered with a woven cloth embroidered with small black skulls, like the one covering La Arca. On the altar stood a bulto of Saint Francis, another of the Holy Virgin, and a human skull. Manny was still, his expression pained. He was holding a huge crucifix, its face against his chest, the top of the cross extending at an angle over his head, the arms stretching as if to embrace and comfort him. The splintered base of the cross passed like a stake through his right leg and pinned him to the floor.

"Oh, no!" I screamed, and ran to him. I straddled his legs with my feet, bent my knees into a deep squat for leverage, and pulled up on the crucifix, extracting it from his flesh. Blood pooled in the hole left by the cross, and the shards of Manny's broken femur poked through the leg of his pants. He looked up at me with fear in his face.

I loosened the knot in my muffler and pulled it off. It took some maneuvering, but I got it to pass under Manny's thigh, and found it soaked with blood as I pulled the end through. I tied it off above the break, and the pool of blood stopped growing.

"We gotta get you out of here!" I urged, trying to figure out how I would lift a man twice my weight.

"I'm not going without the crucifix." He coughed, and then gasped as he inhaled smoke.

I winced from the heat. There was no way I could lift that big cross and help him, too. "Manny, we have to get out of here!"

"Not without the crucifix!" he shouted. He pulled at the altar cloth behind him and dragged the bultos on it toward him. Again, he started coughing.

I looked around, frantic. Then I spotted a square table in the corner. I rushed to it, turned it upside down, and slid it across the floor. "Let's get you on this." I reached down to turn him around.

"I can get on it myself! You get the crucifix!" He gathered the two bultos and the skull into a bundle and tied the ends of the cloth around them. He pushed down with both his hands and raised himself slightly off the floor, turning himself as he did so. He repeated this movement, edging himself over the lip of the table's framework and cried out in pain as his broken thigh met resistance. I moved to help again, and he barked at me, "Get the crucifix, or I swear to God I will get up and get it myself!" He pulled the bundle onto his lap.

I hoisted the great cross again and carefully placed it beside him, then moved to the other side of the table. I leaned forward and—using the power of my legs—pushed on the upturned frame, sliding Manny, one thrust at a time, across the floor toward the door. This worked surprisingly well. The smooth adobe floor offered only a little friction, and Manny was reaching out with his hands on the floor to help, pushing each time I pushed. We developed a wrenching rhythm, each of us throwing our pain-filled voices into it as we *ahhed* and *ughed* our way across the shrine. Each time I inhaled—heat searing my airways—I blew out hard, using the same force to contract my abdomen and give everything I had to the push.

Halfway across the floor, I had to stop. "Wait, wait!" I said, holding my sleeve over my face. My eyeballs felt like they were broiling. The room was an inferno; there was no air. A flaming torch of splintered wood rocketed out of nowhere, barely missing me, and I used this as impetus to move on. We pushed . . . breathed . . . pushed . . . and just as we reached the doorway, another viga began to cry out in pain.

I was dizzy from the smoke, hacking and gasping for air as we finally thrust outside. Heavy, wet snow had begun to fall and had already whitened the ground. I shoved one more time, and the table slid like a hockey puck on the snow. "The cart!" I yelled above the snap and roar of the flames. "Let's get you on the cart!" I pushed him to it.

"*¡No, señorita!* No, that is the *carreta de la muerte*!"

I ignored him, picking up the crucifix and throwing it onto the cart. "Come on!" I yelled. "You're getting on the cart!"

"Oh, *Dios mío*," he cried, "please forgive me!" He crossed himself, then he twisted himself to one side and rolled onto his one good knee and his two hands. The bundle fell from his lap and unfurled, the skull rolling away from him like a ball. I moved in close beside the useless leg and pulled beneath his arm. He was up. He hopped once and cried out as he did so. He eased himself backward onto the cart, which wobbled precariously as he put his weight down on it. I checked the tourniquet I had made, loosening it slightly. The blood began to pour. I tightened it up again and went off to catch Redhead.

I was panting. "Come on, girl." I held out my hand to pick up her reins.

She volted to one side. She did not want to come, spooked by the fire.

I kept after her, whistling and talking as softly as I could and still be heard above the blaze. "Come here, baby!" I made a little clicking sound with my tongue.

She kept a pace or two ahead of me, torn between loyalty and fear. "Redhead, come on, girl." The snow was accumulating so fast, soon none of us would be able to get out to the road. "Redhead. I need you."

She stopped, fascinated with an expanse of drifting snow at her feet. I caught hold of her reins. She balked, but I led her back to the cart, soothing her as I went. "You're such a good girl, yes, you are. I need you to help me, Redhead. I can't do this without you. Don't be afraid."

The fire had stopped growing, and instead popped and spit like a huge crackling woodstove, the flames contained within the adobe shell. The vigas and wood furniture would have been all there was to consume in the earthen structure. A worse threat now was the relentless, pelting snow.

The horsehair harness attached to the front of the cart had been designed for a man to lash around himself at the chest and then over his shoulders several times, to feel its biting discomfort as he pulled the great weight in penance. I tugged frantically at these *cuerdas*, untwining them so that they would reach the length of a horse. Finally, I had a makeshift system, which I tied around the saddle horn.

Manny had been moaning as I fought to untangle the cords, but now was silent. The tongue of the two-wheeled cart had been wedged between the arms of a short, F-shaped post. I turned the post to the side, freeing the tongue, and the cart immediately tipped backward, the tongue rising up in the air, Manny's weight pulling the back of the cart down. Redhead complained loudly and began to stamp and try to free herself.

I went to her. Her eyes were gleaming black saucers. Her neck rippled with tremors. "Calm down, girl." I patted her, pacified her. "Calm down. We're going to make it out of here. Just calm down." Then I went back to see if Manny could be moved forward. He lay on his back in the teetering cart, holding the crucifix again across his chest. The figure of Christ on the cross had slipped sideways and was dangling from just one wooden hand. Manny's feet were hanging close to the ground. Blood dripped into the snow beneath them. He was unconscious.

I managed to use my weight on the tongue, and the begrudging cooperation of Redhead, to gradually turn the cart so that it could proceed away from the post. Then there was nothing to do but climb onto the front of the cart behind its driver to balance the weight. The carved wooden skeleton nailed to the seat of the cart grinned hideously from under the hood of her black cloth robe, her ribs protruding through its open front. She had long black human hair, garishly oversized human teeth, and eyes made from mother-of-pearl, which gleamed in the firelight. She held an ax in one hand, and her two long, bony legs dangled over the front of the cart. I stood behind her, my arms around her, and flapped the horsehair braids across Redhead's rump to get her going. "Come on, baby! It's just us two big, strong women now! Let's do it."

We rode out of there encrusted with a thick coat of snow. The brim of my hat collapsed under the weight, and a landslide of white fell down my face, cooling my scorched skin. I had pointed us toward the Forest Service road above and to the north of the morada. I knew the snow would be heavier in the higher elevation, but I didn't think Manny had much time. There would be a ranger posted somewhere up there, and we might be able to get help.

Redhead amazed me. A horse trained for trail riding, she was sensitive to the slightest pressure of my knees, hardly needed a bridle. But she was certainly not trained to pull a cart, and especially not from a drag on her saddle horn. In spite of that, she lowered her head and bulled into the storm, pulling us behind her as I yelled encouragement. "That's it! Come on, girl. Good girl. Come on, Redhead!" The snow accumulated on her backside, on the cart, even on the horsehair ropes between us, and it piled into high drifts around us. Redhead plodded on, barely visible in front of me. Between my extended arms, La Muerte smiled and kept her silence.

As we neared the road, a streak of blue heat raced past my face at the speed of light. Behind it, a moment later, came a far-off crack, like a chair leg breaking. *Gunshot! Oh, God! Someone is shooting at me! My rifle!* I sent out a desperate searching look through the curtain of white ahead of me, as if my eyes could close the gap between me and what lay impossibly out of reach. I'd left my rifle in the holster attached to Redhead's saddle!

Another shot whizzed past me. The horse lurched to a stop. I jumped out of the cart as the front tipped up again, and ran behind it for cover. *Redhead!* There was a loud *choomfff,* and shards of wood flew as a shot hit the skeleton. La Muerte slumped backward and slid down the bed of the tilted cart, her wooden spine severed at the waist by the bullet, her outstretched bony arm tractioned back and toward the ground by the weight of the heavy steel ax. I heard another shot crack and Redhead reared up and screamed at the danger. I looked out again, afraid of what I would see. I could barely make her out. She was standing amazingly still. She looked like she had her head down, but I couldn't be sure. I could see nothing but snow. From far off came the sound of an engine grinding in low gear on the Forest Service road farther to the right of me, and beyond.

I waited. The shooter had stopped firing. I listened for the engine; it was still in the distance, but moving closer. I heard the whine of the wheels slipping, spinning, the sound of the driver trying to rock it out of the mire by alternating between drive and reverse. I looked at Manny, the ribs of the skeleton wedged against his head, the skull against his shoulder, La Muerte's macabre eyes looking past me. Manny's eyes were open now, too—and peering at me. I put a finger in front of my lips and mouthed a silent *Shhhhh.* I could see blood from his leg dripping off the back of the tilted cart again, in spite of my makeshift tourniquet. I heard a dull thud, felt the earth shake. I bolted around the edge of the cart, screaming, "Redhead!"

She was down, but before I could get to her, a figure came running toward me, covered in snow, a rifle pointed at my chest. The fur rim on the hood of the parka was coated with white, and the face within the hood was in darkness. Instinctively I backed up, my hands in the air, until I was standing behind the cart again. The shooter followed. "Get down on the ground," he grunted.

I knew that voice!

He pushed me hard, shoving me face-first into the snow. He placed the tip of the rifle barrel on the bare skin at the back of my neck, under my hat. "Where is La Arca?" he demanded.

"I don't have it," I choked, my mouth filling with snow as he pressed me down into a drift with the rifle.

"You have it!" he yelled, pushing the barrel so violently into my neck that it snapped forward and my face hit hard against the ground, buried in the mound of white crystals beneath me. I felt a rent open on the inside of my mouth, and blood pooled behind my lower lip. He let up pressure with the rifle barrel and I raised my head and gasped for air.

"Where is it?"

I took another breath. "I'm telling the truth. I don't have it."

I felt his hand seize me by the back of my coat and pull me up fast, turning me toward him, like a puppet. The rifle barrel found the ledge of my chin and pushed hard against my jawbone, forcing my head back. His hood had fallen away from his face a little. His brows were tipped with ice crystals, and his eyes were like gleaming black glass. "You're not going to tell me, are you?"

"No." I spat, tasting blood.

He laughed, threw his head back. "I should have known!" He shook his head back and forth, still laughing.

I strained to keep my chin above the rifle barrel, edging almost imperceptibly to one side. He pulled the nose of the gun away. I slumped a little in relief and used this motion to block my left hand with my body, wishing it could have been my right. The shooter tilted his head to one side, his face suddenly sober again. "I'll find it. And when I find it, I'll destroy it, just like I destroyed that morada back there! You're going to die now!" he screamed.

I grabbed the ax with my left hand just as he released my coat. He shoved my chest hard, pushing me backward to the ground. He raised the rifle and readied to shoot.

As I fell, I drew back the ax and flung it as hard as I could. But La Muerte had not surrendered her hatchet to me. Instead, she flew with it—the upper half of her anyway. In the split second between the time I hurled the weapon and the moment it struck, I saw my assailant's startled look of incredulous fear as the hideous face of Death came speeding toward him, with her irregular, oversized human teeth and shining, milky white eyes, her stream of long, black hair sailing behind her splintered ribs like a veil. The blow knocked him off balance and caused him to turn and then lurch into a sidestep. The ax had hit hard, but it had barely penetrated his parka. He fought to regain his balance and raised the rifle again, backing up to take aim.

Behind him, in the still-tilted cart, silent as the snow, Manny rose like an angel onto his one good leg, his arms extended to the sides, like wings, balancing him. He was covered completely in white and looked like a great, hovering bird. Having gained his balance, he raised up the huge crucifix, which he held in his right hand, moved the left hand to grasp it also, and drove the splintered end of it down into the back of Andy Vincent.

The two then tumbled forward toward me in a kind of slow-motion swoop. I scrambled to the left to avoid being crushed, and their fall to the earth made a soft *whoomp*. I hurried to Manny, who had slid to one side as he fell. I rolled him onto his back and put my hands on either side of his face. His eyes looked at me with a kind of strange joy. "I was supposed to watch over you," he said. "I was your *ángel*."

"I know. Don't talk!" I begged him. I moved to tighten his tourniquet, the muffler now completely saturated with blood and stiff with ice crystals.

"Señorita," he said, "you cannot keep something alive that is meant to die."

I looked at him. "There's help coming," I pleaded. "Just hold on! I heard an engine on the road! Someone's coming!"

His face collapsed in my hands.

"Manny." I patted his cheek fervently, as if to revive him.

"Manny!" I screamed. I felt his neck for a pulse, but his heart was silent.

"Jamaica!" a voice yelled from somewhere behind me. "Jamaica, are you all right?" It was coming closer.

I stood up. A Forest Service truck sat humming less than a hundred feet away, its yellow headlights like beacons of gold through which snow was driving into the clean white field ahead. The truck's wipers beat a dull rhythm as they struggled under the weight of thick globs of ice. A familiar hat, with patches of white already beginning to accumulate on its brown brim, tilted into the driving blizzard as its wearer hurried toward me, the face beneath the hat obscured.

I turned back to Manny, who was disappearing into the snow. The figure of Christ had fallen from the crucifix and landed facedown on his chest. Beside him, a white covered mound that had once been Andy Vincent was topped with a tilted cross.

I ran to Redhead, who was lying on her side on the ground, blood draining from a hole in the front of her chest. Her eye was looking at me—a polished black globe full of fear and love. Her breathing was fast and rasped with the sound of fluid. She tried to lift her head as I came to her and threw myself onto her shoulder, my arms over her neck and head. Her neck quivered, and she tried to paw once. I lay there sobbing into her cheek as she drew her last warm, watery breath and exhaled with a deep, releasing sigh.

"Redhead!" I screamed. "No, no, *nooooo!*"

Hands clutched my arms and tried to pull me from her. I

turned and saw Kerry's face beneath a hat brim covered with snow. "Come on, Jamaica. We've got to get out of here while we can."

I turned back to Redhead and buried my face in her mane. "I can't leave her! I can't leave her here!"

"Come on, Jamaica," he said, pulling me upright. "She's gone."

◀ 36 ▶

The Secret

There was almost no traffic on the roads of Taos on the morning of Good Friday. Snow covered the tops of buildings and cars and turned shrubs into white balls of soft cotton. The trees were heavy and silent in their thick, white coats and stood like sentient pillars, supporting the close ceiling of clouds. It was as if the whole world had fallen asleep under a blanket of white and lay there still as a child.

Kerry and I had retrieved La Arca from the lockbox at the ranger station. I held it to me and looked around before we went inside his apartment. There was not another soul in sight.

I set the bundle on the table, and Kerry helped me off with my coat. My face hurt from being roasted by fire, then frostbitten in the blizzard. A swollen knot inside my mouth just beneath my lower lip throbbed painfully. And my throat was bruised where Andy had shoved the rifle barrel against my jawbone. I was dehydrated, my lips were cracked from chapping, my back ached from pushing Manny across the morada. My whole body hurt.

"I'll make us some coffee," Kerry said, dropping my coat on his bed.

I waited for it slumped in a chair, my emotions dulled by deluge. While the coffee brewed, he brought me a glass of water. As I sipped, I looked around the room again at the photographs he had made. "These are so beautiful," I said and took another drink of water.

"You like my work, then?"

I tried to smile. *Ouch.* "You know I do."

"Your mouth hurts?"

I nodded.

He picked up a dish towel, walked to the door, and opened it. He stepped outside, disappeared for a moment, then came back in, wiped his feet, and came over to me. He gently lifted my chin.

"Ow! Don't touch under there!"

"Which hurts more? Your mouth or your chin?"

"My mouth. No, my chin. I don't know . . . "

He put the cloth, packed with a handful of snow, against my mouth. It hurt. Then it felt better. "Here, take this. I'll go get our coffee."

I drank in the calm, the quiet. After we had made our way down the treacherous Forest Service road from the conflagration and carnage, Kerry and I had spent the night at the ranger station giving statements and filling out paperwork. The blizzard had delayed everything, and a snowplow was supposed to make its way up the mountain today to create access so officials could even get to the Forest Service road. It might be another day or two before the bodies could be carried out. "Poor Manny," I said. "Poor Redhead." I began to cry.

"Yeah." He brought steaming coffee, set it on the table, examined my swollen, tear-streaked face. "Poor Jamaica."

I tried to smile. "Do you have any sage?"

"You mean for smudging?"

"Yes, you know—a smudge stick, anything."

"I have some local, from the pueblo." He went to his dresser and brought a fat thread-bound sage bundle to me. "I'll get some matches."

We smudged La Arca, the room, ourselves. Then we sat down together at the table and I began to untie the horsehair rope. I told Kerry the story that Theresa Mendoza had told me, and also what I had learned from my trip to the Taos library.

"Am I allowed to see it?" he asked, respectfully.

"I don't know why you couldn't see it. They display it in the church on Easter Sunday in Truchas. But I would rather you didn't touch it."

"I won't. I understand."

When the mecates were undone, I stopped to compose myself. Just as Theresa Mendoza had done, I closed my eyes and drew within. I said a silent prayer to anyone who might be listening that I would be guided to do whatever was best. Then I drew back the embroidered cloth.

Kerry inhaled deeply, his chest rising, his eyes like moons. "It's beautiful! Wait! Let me get my camera!" He moved to get up.

I shot out my hand to stop him. "No, don't."

"But . . . for your book? Wouldn't you like a picture of it for your book? You said it's all right for people to see it."

"No. I don't want a picture of it. Then people will come in droves to see it, maybe even try to steal it. I don't want you to photograph it."

"Okay." He sat back in his chair. "Now what?"

"Now you go take a shower or something. Let me know before you plan to come back into this room."

"Yes ma'am," he said, saluting as he got up.

La Arca unfolded her secrets to me that morning in the cool, gray light of Kerry's apartment. The smoke from the sage we had burned floated in a heavy haze in the soft hues of a snowy dawn. The sound of Kerry's shower was like a distant, constant drumroll accompanying this ceremony honoring the victory of Passionate Faith over Evil.

Within, La Arca was lined with old black velvet, crinkled and shiny with age. Antique photos showed above the lip of a velvet pocket in the lid. Some of these were quite large and made from old silver or copper plates. As I removed them, I read the dates the photographers had etched right on the plates in scrawling white handwriting: 1895, 1898, 1902. There were also several stacks of small zigzag-edged photos that had been made sometime later than the larger ones, their corners just peeking out above the pocket top. I pulled them from their nests and placed them in three piles on the table.

In the body of La Arca, a small, ancient-looking brown book rested on top. I picked it up carefully and examined it. It was a cuaderno—a compact book written entirely by hand, including the words to the alabados—the hymns, written text of the teachings of the brotherhood, their prayers, chants, plays, sayings, rules. I thumbed through the yellowed, brittle pages, examining the elegant handwriting, the hand-sewn binding of woven cloth. It was written entirely in Spanish. I looked through page after page. I found the expression Father Ignacio had quoted at our meeting in Santa Fe, heard his melodious accented voice in my mind: *¡Ayuda a otros y Dios te ayudará! Help others and God will help you. It is an old Penitente saying.*

This cuaderno reminded me of my own handwritten, hand-drawn book. Cuadernos like the one I was holding were the means by which Los Penitentes had conveyed their culture and faith from generation to generation. Many Hispanos learned to read and write using their cuadernos. The old books were so rare now that only one was known to exist from before the turn of the century—because when they became worn, new ones were made and the old ones destroyed. This was probably a priceless artifact. But I put the book beside the photographs. It was not what I was looking for.

La Arca held seven rosaries made with hand-carved wooden beads; each one had an ornate crucifix. And there was one large, silver cross with three transoms, the shortest one nearest the top, each of the next two successively longer. At the crux of the second transom was a large ruby. I set these things on the table also.

Beneath that lay a sheaf of yellowed papers. I handled them carefully. Several of them were folded and sealed with wax, and they were so old and brittle that tiny bits of them chipped off the edges and fell into the box as I moved them. They would have snapped apart if anyone tried to open them.

One item interested me, though, and I took great pains not to damage it. It was a small, handwritten ledger, its cover crudely hand-stitched from plain tan cloth, with only a few sheets of thick yellow paper inside. It appeared to be a kind of log, with over a hundred Hispanic names, each one with a year following. A few of them had the word *muerto* written after the year.

More papers, all in Spanish, many of which looked to be official documents that bore an impressed seal, sworn to in both elegant and crude handwriting, some witnessed with simple X marks, others with flamboyant signatures. A name among the signatures on one document caught my eye: *A. Vigil. Where had I seen that name?* There were hundreds of Vigils in northern New Mexico. I could have seen it on an election billboard or a mailbox, anything. Still, it haunted me. I looked through more of the pages. There it was again: *Antonio Vigil.* This time, it was not a signature, but a document that contained the name over and over again—something about *crimen colérico*—an angry crime. And another name, *Arturo Vigil.*

I heard the bathroom door open and Kerry's voice called to me: "I'm just letting the steam out. Find anything important?"

"Still looking. I wish I knew more Spanish." I shook my head. I could smell Kerry's shampoo, hear him brushing his teeth. I carefully set all the papers on the table.

At the bottom of the box, I found what I was searching for. It was wrapped in a piece of crimson silk. I carefully unfolded the cloth and regarded the precious treasure within. In large, ornate black script, the title read, *El Instituto Religioso de la Santa Hermandad.* There were exquisite, block-cut, embellished letters at the beginning of each paragraph, and the printing on the yellow-gold parchment pages was antiquated and irregular. A hand-colored illustration of a man on his knees whipping himself bore the title *Imitación de Cristo. The tract by Padre Martínez! It does exist! Here it is!* I scanned it, handling it with the utmost delicacy, shaking my head back and forth in disbelief. Then I carefully returned the priceless prize to its protective silk wrapping and set it on the table.

La Arca was now empty. I closed the lid and stood up. Then I gently turned the box over. On the bottom, carved into the wooden base, was the signature of its maker and the date it was made: *Pedro Antonio Fresquíz—1831.*

At the library, I had learned about the santero from Las

Truchas, probably the first native-born santero in Nuevo Mexico. As Father Ignacio had promised, this man—the one from the legend Theresa Mendoza had told me—and the sacred tract by Padre Antonio José Martínez, who was the first New Mexico Penitente to become a priest, had come together at last. Padre Martínez had virtually risked his life to defend Los Hermanos against the decrees the Church issued condemning the brotherhood when he printed this sacred document. This tract was his opus, and that source of power Father Ignacio had mentioned that someone had been trying to steal from Los Penitentes. It was their credo. And this sacred ark was probably the last work of art Pedro Antonio Fresquíz had made before he died. Its value alone—without the tract by Padre Martínez—was inestimable. Only a few pieces of his work remained in existence, and their distinctive style was prized by collectors of religious iconography the world over.

I rotated La Arca back to an upright position and studied the beautiful, passionate carving, the deep, stainlike colors of the cedar wood's variegations on the lid of this portable shrine. I began to replace the contents, one by one—beginning with the Martínez tract in its silk cover. Then the aging documents and the cloth binder with its ledger of names. Then the silver cross with the ruby, and the carved-bead rosaries with their crucifixes. And the priceless cuaderno.

I turned then to the piles of photographs. I had seen photos like these in some of the books I had looked to for research into the brotherhood. Sadly, most of them were overexposed,

not very clear, taken from a distance—showing Penitente rituals and processions. And even a few of crucifixions.

The figures in the older pictures seemed unreal. The stark
light of New Mexico's midday sun shone on the harsh faces
of rocks, making the black-clad figures in coats appear to be
shadows, and the black-hooded, white-trousered Penitentes
hard to make out against the strata and the bare ground.

The newer photographs, those with the rickrack edges,
were clearer. There were several of the ritual reunion of
Christ with his mother. There was a series showing the stations of the cross. Many of processions. And eight pictures
in sequence of the same crucifixion. They looked like they
were hastily shot, the frames not well composed, some of
them askew. They were taken from a considerable distance—
probably in secret, from behind a rock—and then seized later.
A few onlookers, also dressed in black, appeared in several of
this series, tiny and hard to make out. I scanned these. Then
I saw the face.

It was a face I had seen in countless photographs, a face
that, surprisingly, had remained very similar over the years.

I quickly began to unpack La Arca again. I removed the
cuaderno—and the rosaries and silver cross—looking for
what was beneath them. There! I picked up the cloth-bound
ledger and scanned the most recent dates. I found what I was
looking for: *Arturo Vigil, 1954—muerto*.

"Kerry, get ready, okay? I have to go." I carefully restored
to La Arca all her treasures. All but one.

◄ 37 ►

The Shrine

I asked Kerry and Jerry Padilla to wait at the bottom of the drive. "Promise me you'll wait here for my signal."

"I don't feel right about it, Jamaica," Padilla said. "How do I know you'll be safe?"

I pulled my Sig Sauer pistol from its holster. I held it up to the deputy and raised my eyebrows at him. Then I tucked the pistol into one big pocket of my jacket, the photo into another. I patted my gun pocket. "I don't think I'll need this, but just to reassure you ... "

I walked up Regan's drive. The Toyota was in the garage. I went to the house and looked in the windows. No sign of life. I peered up the path to the casita. The Land Rover was not there, of course. There were big boot prints in the drifts leading from the rear *portal* up the slope toward the shrine. I followed them, crunching softly in the snow as I walked.

I could hear her voice as I approached. She was crying and groaning and singing under her breath, all at the same time. I came up the high side of the rocks and looked down at her back, her head draped in a black lace mantilla, which settled in folds onto her thick sweater. She was wearing some kind of soft pants and the same unlaced boots she always wore around the place. "Regan," I said, my voice firm.

She turned around slowly. Before her, on the shrine, lay the rosary I had found by the corral—the one with the crucifix with the name *A. Vigil* engraved on the back. A dozen or so lit candles in red and green glass jars surrounded the wooden piece and a carved santo—Saint Anthony.

"He's dead, isn't he?" she asked.

"Andy? Yes. He tried to kill me."

At this, she broke into a full-throated cry, "Ah-h-h-hhhh! My little Antonio! My baby brother! Look what they've done! Look what they've done!"

"Regan, I want you to come with me," I said. I stepped aside, motioning her toward the path that passed by the rocks. She didn't move.

"First they killed my father," she said, shaking her head, the mantilla edging back off the crown of her head and sliding down her hair. "Now, little Antonio!" She began whining, as a nervous dog might.

"Your father was Arturo Vigil. Is that right?"

"Yes."

"You saw him crucified, didn't you? That wasn't just some daring adventure you and your friend took, like that story you told me."

"Yes!" she screamed. "Yes, I saw it happen! I was there! They tried to keep us at a distance. I didn't know for sure that it was my father, but I found out the next day. They killed him! They killed him, and they killed my mother, too! She died of a broken heart within the year. No one would do anything about it. No one would even investigate it. I tried to talk to everyone, but no one would listen to me—I was a child!" As Regan's facade—her tightly controlled persona—ruptured, and the terrible truth she had been concealing spilled out, it seemed to be taking her substance with it. Her large, bony frame and lean, sinewy flesh seemed more pronounced, as if she were slowly desiccating, becoming a skeleton. Her face was skull-like, with the thin tissue of her amber skin stretching over a pronounced forehead and jaw. She tore each word off with her teeth. "Then, Antonio decided to get revenge. It made him crazy, you see. It made him crazy! He was just a little boy, but the next year, he put the poison on the whips and two men died. It served them right—they killed our father!" Her voice was hysterical, breaking from low to high pitch, shaking. Her whole body was trembling.

"They held a council. They agreed to suppress the crime from the authorities, but made Andy go away; that was his punishment. He was supposed to go away and never come back. Our *tía abuela* in Los Angeles took us both in. We had to live on her charity. When she died, we had no one. We had no home. We had no family. We had nothing." Her voice had calmed a little now, the poison spilled. Her chest heaved with a deep sigh.

"I want you to come with me now, Regan," I said again, and I stepped back to offer her room to move onto the path.

She looked at me with pleading eyes. "It wasn't supposed to happen like this, Jamaica. It wasn't supposed to start all over again. Andy said he was just coming back to buy the icons. He said he could sell them and make a lot of money. It was a way of making them pay—you see? For what they did to him, to us. But once he was here, he said he had to find out where they buried him," she said, looking back at the shrine. "He said he just wanted to know where our father was buried. I always knew it was here, at this shrine. But Andy said we had to find out for sure, to be absolutely certain it was here. He said the answer would be in La Arca. But that's not really why he wanted it. Antonio still wanted revenge."

Again, Regan looked at me. Her face looked like that of the girl child in the photograph I had brought in my pocket—a face full of horror and bewilderment and helpless vulnerability. Her eyes seemed to be looking to me for the answer to some unspoken question.

I had a question of my own. "Father Ignacio came here, didn't he?"

"Yes." She looked away and began to cry. "I had been cleaning my horse's hooves," she said softly. "I noticed there was a car parked down by the bridge. I knew I had another trespasser, so I came up to run him off. He was kneeling right there." She pointed a long finger at the altar and looked as if she were watching the scene play out before her eyes. "He told me that he saw some sketch of yours or something and knew the shrine was being tended. He brought our father's rosary." Regan picked up the rosary and held it up to show me. "When I saw this, I was so furious, I took the farrier's knife, and I stabbed him!"

"But why? What did Father Ignacio ever do to you?"

Regan's voice trembled. "I thought I had put it all behind me, Jamaica. I thought I had closed the book on all that. But when Andy came back here, it reminded me of it again—of what they did to us, to our father, our mother. And Ignacio Medina, he used to be Andy's playmate at school when we were children. How could he dare to show his face here at our father's grave? He was trying to keep Los Penitentes alive! He even became one himself!" She shrieked, "I want them all gone, history!" She waved one arm wildly out to the side, as if to erase their memory. "That is why I was telling you all the terrible things they did. I thought you would tell the truth about them in your book. I thought, 'Here is someone who will write about the foolishness, the horror, the brutality of their ways. Someone who is not bewitched by their archaic superstitions.'"

"But why did you crucify Father Ignacio?"

"That was Andy. Antonio went wild. He wanted to get the police to think it was the Penitentes that killed him. He wanted justice for our father!" She started sobbing.

"So he took the body somewhere and tied it on a cross?" I asked.

"He didn't have to take it anywhere," she said. "This place was the morada where our father was killed. But after Antonio's . . ." Her voice trailed off.

"*Crimen colérico?*" I said. "His crime of anger?"

"Yes, soon after that, they closed this morada. They said it was stained by what he had done and couldn't be made pure again. Most of the Hermanos went to Boscaje. That's where they took all the icons from here, and they left this place untended, forgotten, like junk they could throw away!" She gnashed her teeth as she spoke. "Andy wanted them to have to leave Boscaje, too, to drive them out of existence. He wanted to destroy La Arca like they destroyed our family." Her face reddened, and tears began to stream down her face. She looked right into my eyes. "Andy wanted to kill you from the beginning, Jamaica! But I wouldn't let him. I protected you. He was afraid when you found our father's rosary, with all your research, that somehow you would find out."

"You mean the day I first met him here? The day after you threw Father Ignacio over the bridge?" I asked.

She didn't even blink at my mention of the incident at the bridge. She seemed caught up in her own replay of events. "Yes. He was sure you knew something." The long strand of carved beads dangled back and forth in front of her body like a pendulum. "He even tried to find you after that, to find out what you knew. But when you came here after mass, it was obvious you didn't know anything or you would have . . ."

She stopped talking for a moment and watched the beads swing back and forth. Then she began speaking again, forcing the words through tightly clenched teeth. "But that little thief Suazo! He was making plenty of money on those icons! But then he told us you almost caught him when he was photographing the Boscaje processions. And he said he lost the pictures he took, and maybe you found them. And then we saw Suazo with you . . . " She looked at me now, and her eyes looked clear and bright, as if what she were about to say was simple and obvious. "Well, we had to kill him. It never would have ended. You know how Suazo was." There was a strange, mad certainty in her expression.

"Regan, I want you to come down the hill with me now." This time I stepped forward, reaching for her arm.

"All right, Jamaica, I'll come." Her voice was suddenly childlike. "I know it's over. I'm glad it's over, I really am. I'll come. Just let me pay my last respects to my father, would you, dear?"

I stood for a moment pondering all the possibilities. She wasn't armed. She couldn't get far in those floppy boots. I couldn't see what it would hurt. "Okay." I stepped back. "I'll let you have a few minutes. I'll meet you down at the house." I turned to walk down the slope.

I had just begun picking my way over some snow-covered rocks when I felt the movement behind me. I whirled around to see Regan poised in midair like a hawk about to light on its prey. My eye caught the glimmer of a slender sliver of silver, and then I recognized the farrier's blade she held raised in one hand as she made to plunge it into my back. The crucifix dangled from her other hand, the wooden beads swinging wildly. I lunged to the side to avoid her stab, and she wobbled briefly, then regained her balance and raised the knife again. This time, I caught her arm on the way down and felt the knife blade rip the shoulder of my coat as it went past. We struggled. Regan's face was molded into tight ropes of corded flesh and muscle, so that it seemed a drape of skin had been pulled over her skull when wet and then dried into hard ridges. She was surprisingly strong, and her stance above me gave me a disadvantage. Her knife arm began to tremble violently, but I was losing my grip and my balance. The thick cotton strands of her sweater were all I could hold on to, and I dug my fingers into the woven spaces. The fibers began to stretch, I was still tottering, off balance, and then a hole opened up in the sleeve of her garment and Regan's powerful shaking arm flew up, free of my grip. She curved her weapon down again toward me just as her hand reached the top of its flight.

I felt myself falling, so I grabbed for her, seizing her sweater with both hands—this time about the chest—and I pulled her over with me, on top of me, as I fell back and down the slope. In a kind of terrifying slow-motion pas de deux, we tumbled over and over, first me above Regan, then her above me, her mouth open in a perfect oval of surprise, the knife still clutched firmly in her hand, the tight cords in her neck giving way to slack skin and her expression moving from madness and anger to shock and fear. All this as we tumbled, still wrestling, my hands moving from her sweater to the ground to her arms above me to the ground again, my chest crashing into hers, then hers into mine, the two of us like a lopsided wheel bumping and collapsing down the incline, when finally we slid into a shallow level place and Regan was on top of me scrambling to gain her balance and strike again with the knife. I scrambled, too, and, failing to wiggle free as she sat on my hips, I could only roll to the side as the knife came down. "Regan, stop! Why are you doing this?"

She didn't answer but drew back again, her weight still pinning me to the ground. My head was out over the edge, unsupported—and my neck strained to keep it from falling back. I reached for Regan's arms but gravity gave her the advantage and the knife came down again, this time catching the top of my shoulder as it plunged into the ground beneath my left ear. I felt a searing pang shoot through my trapezius and up the side of my neck. Regan's weight was full on me, and I shoved against her as she drew the knife back again and struggled upright. A stab of pain went down my left arm and I felt it weaken, felt the muscle tearing and the warm, wet blood pooling under my upper back. Once again, she raised the knife, but this time she pushed my right shoulder down with her free hand, to prevent me from rolling out of the blade's path. Her face was a white mask with hollow eyes—nothing human, nothing of Regan there.

As the gleam of silver began to arc toward me, I could see in my peripheral vision the wooden beads from the rosary that she held against my right shoulder, and the carved form of the crucified body on the cross in the snow beside my neck. I closed my eyes for an instant, then opened them and did what I had to do.

I felt a rush of grief as I thrust my hand into the pocket of my jacket and pulled the trigger. I heard the bullet make a dull, wet connection just a split second after the muffled blast, felt a spray of moisture hit my face. In the center of Regan's forehead, where a smudge of ashes had marked her just weeks before, a dark circle marked where the bullet had entered. On her face, a frozen look of disbelief. And then, lifeless as a rag doll, in what seemed like slow motion, she toppled forward and rolled past me down the hill, the tongues of her boots flapping at the snow as she went.

I turned over, my shoulder throbbing, and raised myself up. I looked at the pocket of my coat, singed with smoke and eaten through by the shot. I looked down the hill. At the bottom of the slope, Kerry and Jerry Padilla were already rushing toward me, their guns at the ready.

◄ 38 ►

The Wolf

Before coming home to my cabin, after the paramedics had dressed my wound, I delivered La Arca to Tecolote for safe return to the Penitentes. Once I had seen the old cuaderno and the other treasures inside the ark, I realized that I didn't need to preserve the fading history of the Penitentes—they had done so themselves, reverently, but privately. And some things were meant to remain private, even held in secret. Esperanza smiled with approval when I placed my book inside the box, its deerskin cover looking strangely new by comparison with the other treasures, in spite of all that my book had been through. I felt a small pang of sadness as I took my hand away.

Oddly enough, I had more difficulty returning the photograph I had put in my pocket before going to see Regan than I did giving La Arca my book. I studied the snapshot carefully before giving it back, something drawing me to look at it again and again. In faded black and white, it had captured Regan as a youth, dressed in black, clutching the hand of a small boy, their faces wide with horror as they watched five men in the distance struggle to raise the cross on which their father hung. The image troubled me in the way that something does when I'm about to receive an important life lesson. I told Tecolote as much, but she only smiled and nodded her head.

It was certain from what Regan had told me, and from the evidence in the shed at the Suazo place, that Santiago Suazo had been stealing icons for Andy Vincent. Investigators at the scene uncovered Santiago Suazo's body, along with the nag Regan had put down, in the pit grave dug by her unsuspecting neighbors. And they found the bullet-scarred white Ford Ranger and an old beat-up cargo van locked in Regan's barn, both registered to Regan and bearing New Mexico plates. I had to assume that Andy was almost certainly the one who had tried to wipe me out at Bennie's, too, but hit Nora instead.

The next day, I was nursing the wound in my shoulder and the confusion in my mind by sitting in my big chair in my cabin with a cup of tea, trying to figure out how to occupy myself for the next month while I was on medical leave. I was surprised when I heard the sound of a vehicle coming up the drive. Eyeing the nightstand where I had placed my revolver, I moved to the window to look out. I saw a pale green Forest Service truck pulling up to the house. Kerry Reed got out, then spent some time easing a big, flat parcel wrapped in brown paper out from behind the seat.

I opened the door and waited for him.

"How's your shoulder?" he said.

"It hurts, but it's getting better."

He stepped inside with the parcel. "I brought you something."

While he took off his hat and coat, I set the package on the table and opened it. It was a photograph of Redhead, grazing in a meadow behind the stables at the ranger station, her red and white coat gleaming in the high mountain sunlight, a backdrop of kelly green forest and turquoise sky behind her. There was a small inscription in the corner:

To Jamaica, my favorite Wild woman—All my love, Kerry

Tears filled my eyes as I looked at it. "This is beautiful," I said, kissing him. "Thank you."

"I have some good news, too." He grinned. "I'm moving to your neighborhood. I just got my new assignment. I'll be bunking from now on at the ranger housing in Tres Piedras."

Before sunrise on Easter morning, I sat on a rock outcropping outside my cabin, wrapped in a blanket. I held the Old One, the smooth stone that had been with me these past twelve days. I had never thought of it before, but right then it occurred to me that the stone had come to me on the same day that I witnessed the body of Father Ignacio, tied to a cross, falling from the bridge. And then I thought about Regan and her painful life of grief over the death of her father. I remembered the image in the photo. She had been just a child, just a child when it all started.

And then I thought of my own father, now gone.

Suddenly I understood the lesson of forgiveness the Old One held for me. I stood and cast off my blanket. I spoke aloud. "Daddy, please forgive me for not being there when you were injured. I was just a child, being a child, having a little fun after school."

I waited quietly, as if my father might answer me from beyond the grave, but the woods surrounding my cabin were silent. And I did not feel any relief from what I had just done. I opened my hand and looked at the stone. Then I did as Momma Anna had demonstrated—I closed my fingers around the Old One and placed it against my chest. I drew in a big breath and waited. The sun's face peeked over the top of the mountains in the distance and golden light began to flood across the sky. I let out the breath and felt a release of anxiety and tension, a lifting of emotional pain that had been with me so long I had forgotten I was carrying it. I had finally forgiven myself. *I had finally forgiven myself!* I said out loud, "I was just a child!"

But despite my having learned such an important lesson from the Old One, it was my friend Bennie who brought the most change into my life that Easter Sunday. In the afternoon, I traveled to the Wildlife Center in Española, where Bennie and a wildlife ranger had arranged for me to temporarily adopt a wolf cub in dire need of saving. The cub's mother had been shot by a rancher outside of Yellowstone, and after several unsuccessful attempts to get another pack to adopt the pup, the little one had been taken in, starving, by the rehab center. Hopes for an unmothered cub were not high. Since I was on leave for a month and could be with the babe constantly, I was a temporary stopgap until they could find a sanctuary that would take the wolf in.

"Come on, kiddo," Bennie said. "I'll show you how to bottle-feed this guy, so that you two will bond." She gave me instructions and left me sitting cross-legged on the floor, alone in a room with my new companion.

A whimpering ball of yellow and brown fur with short legs and a distended belly soon waddled up and took a seat out of my reach. His eyes were yellow gold, and his face was marked with a distinct brown and black mask and tufted ears—one of which failed to stand up. He couldn't have been much over six weeks old. He studied me warily, drool dripping from his lips, the hunger making him bold. He edged toward me. I didn't move. Finally, unable to control his desire to feed, he came forward and took the nipple extending from the bottle I held in my hand. He rolled onto his side, pushing gently at my leg with his paws, a look of ecstasy on his little wolf face. I looked down at my new living companion, careful not to threaten him with too direct a stare. Two yellow eyes looked back at me—wild eyes, a kindred spirit. He looked up at me like an infant does his mother—with adoration.

A half hour later, Bennie came into the room as I nuzzled the little ball of fur tucked sleeping in my arms like a baby, where I held him after he'd had his fill. "He's so cute," I said.

"Yeah, he's cute now, kiddo," Bennie said, "but he'll weigh around a hundred, maybe as much as a hundred thirty pounds when he's grown, and he won't look cute to anyone then. Right now, you are our answer to whether he lives or dies, but it gets harder every day he grows toward maturity to find him a permanent place that will take him in. A lone wolf is not sought after, and I don't want him to have to go to a zoo. We'll just have to keep trying. In the meantime, you two look like you're developing a good bond. What do you want to call him?"

"Mountain," I said. "I'll call him Mountain."

Later, I drove home with the little ball of fur tucked inside a sling next to me so that he could feel my warmth as he snoozed in his little cocoon. I made up a silly little song and sang it as I drove, a soothing little lullaby for my new companion, and for me:

> *Stars shine on us,*
> *Wind sings to us,*
> *Moon smiles on us,*
> *You and me.*
> *No more lonely,*
> *We are family.*

About the Author

Sandi Ault celebrates her love for the wild west in this series. She loves to write, to explore, to adventure, to research, and to discover. She spends her free time hiking mountains, deserts, and canyons, searching out new sources of wonder and amazement, new places of magic and enchantment. She is at home in wild places, in the ruins of the ancient ones, in the canyons, on the rivers, on cliff ledges and high mesas. She loves to visit her friends and adopted family at the pueblos. She lives in the Rocky Mountains of Colorado with loving companions: a husband, a wolf, and a cat. Visit her on the Web at: www.SandiAult.com.